PAINT CHIPS

SUSIE FINKBEINER

Micah 6:8

WhiteFire
Publishing

This is a work of fiction. All characters and events portrayed in this novel are either fictitious or used fictitiously.

PAINT CHIIPS

WhiteFire Publishing
13607 Bedford Rd NE
Cumberland, MD 21502

ISBN: 978-0-983455-69-1

To Alisha Renee:
You were created to do beautiful things for Jesus.

Save me, O God,
for the waters have come up to my neck.
I sink in the miry depths,
where there is no foothold.
I have come into the deep waters;
the floods engulf me.

Psalm 69: 1-2 (NIV)

South of the city, past all the tall mirror windowed buildings and the long twisting highways. Past the billboards and stores. In an out-of-the-way, behind-the-trees sort of place. That's where I lived out the punishment for my sins. Separate from the schools and churches and parks and neighborhoods. An off-to-the-side, overlooked place is best for hiding hell. That's where I lived.

A winding and curling driveway unfurled itself through the dense woods. The deep gray path ended at a coarse fence, barbed wire pointing in. Within stood a large, tan building.

Up the flights of stairs, through secured doors, down an empty hallway, the third room on the left. My room. And in that space, dreams haunted. Each dream a variation of the same thing.

Five gunshots. His dark eyes. The blood. Her screams.

"Cora." The voice of an orderly jolted me awake. "Breakfast."

"I'm not hungry," I replied. "Leave me alone."

"All right."

I sat up, the hard, plastic-lined mattress made a cracking sound, stiff under my movement. Standing, I flipped on the light. The bulb buzzed and let off a sickening green-blue hue. I pulled my bathrobe on and turned the knob, opening the door.

"Good morning, Cora," the nurse at the desk said.

I ignored her and made my way to a seat in the dayroom. Ugly, burnt-orange chairs lined one of the walls. A brown couch sat under the large window. I slid my fingers across the smooth green Ping-Pong table, trying to remember the last time someone played. The net hung limp.

A box, placed on the table, distracted me. I put my hand on the cardboard lid, wondering what it contained. Had it been there the day before? Had I not noticed?

An orderly pushed Edith into the room. She sat, silent. Her wheelchair squeaking. The orderly stopped her, leaving her near the window. A ray of sunlight touched her face. She didn't acknowledge it.

"What is this?" I asked the orderly as he walked past me.

"Just some books somebody brought over," he answered. "Go ahead. Look through them. Maybe you could read to Edith."

He removed the lid. Books, spine up, filled the box. Musty, dust-covered titles. I touched them. Each one. Until my finger rested on a blue book. Gold letters, without flourish, joined together, spelling a title that I recognized. I pulled it from the box, rubbing the cover on my sleeve.

"What did you find?" the orderly asked.

I jumped, holding the book against my chest. Hiding it.

"I'm sorry," he said. "I didn't mean to scare you."

"I forgot you were here," I whispered, my breath choppy. "I'm okay."

Still, clinging to the book, I took slow steps to the chair furthest from the table and the box and the orderly. Sitting, I peeked at the book.

"*Sense and Sensibility*," I read the cover, my voice sounded wispy. "Why this book?"

I opened it, letting the book rest on my lap. Turned the yellow pages. So gently, slowly, afraid they might crumble. Closing my eyes, I tilted my head back. Trying to recall. Images swirled through my mind. So rapidly, I couldn't catch one.

"Cora." A voice broke through the spinning of my thoughts. "Cora."

Opening my eyes, the lights above me too bright, I winced. Exhaled. One of the nurses leaned over my face.

"Time for your morning meds." She put a tiny cup full of pills into my hand. "In they go."

I swallowed numbness, forgetfulness, apathy. Chased them down with tepid water.

"That's good," the nurse said, walking away. "You'll be feeling just fine soon."

Feeling. All anyone ever seemed to care about around that place. How I felt. What my feelings told me. They couldn't understand. Or I couldn't articulate. I felt nothing.

Nothing but the poverty of silent emotions. A memory that hid from me. And guilt for destroying everyone.

2

The grit of the sidewalk made a grinding sound under my feet as I walked home from the store. The eggs and milk and bread in my bag grew heavy, hanging from my hand. I wanted to get into the kitchen, put the groceries away, and start on my homework. And to be inside before dark.

"Hey, Dorothea," a neighbor called out to me from his porch. He drew on a cigarette and squinted as he exhaled. "You makin' some of them cookies?"

"Hi, Lee. I guess I could bake a batch," I said, turning toward him. "What kind?"

"Snickerdoodle. Extra cinnamon." Lee smiled at me. "You know how I like 'em."

"No problem. I'll have Lola bring them over later."

"You're my favorite."

"I know it." I waved at him and continued walking.

He watched me as I went past him and up the street. But he wasn't a threat to me. None of the men who lived on our street were. They might have been drug dealers or gangsters. But they watched out for me. For all the girls who lived in Lola's house.

Passing by the old, broken-down buildings, I kept my eyes on the bright pink house at the end of the street. It stuck out among the dingy, condemned structures around it. The paint had been donated. The leftovers of some hardware shop's mistake.

"You should have seen the look on the neighbors' faces when we started painting," I remembered Lola saying shortly after I moved in.

"It was like we were Noah building a boat in the desert."

When I reached the porch of my house, I turned and waved at Lee. Letting him know I was safe. He gave me a thumbs up before he went inside. I opened the door and slipped into the safety of Lola's House.

I unloaded the groceries when I got into the kitchen. The setting sun glimmered through the windows, turning the room orange. I'd lived in that house for five years. Most every evening, I made sure to watch the sunset from the kitchen.

Five years of sunsets. Not all of them left an impression on me. The ones I remembered connected me to important days or changes I'd made.

"Sunset time?" Lola asked, joining me in the kitchen. "I always know where to find you at this hour of day."

I nodded, not knowing how to say what weighed on my mind. How to thank her. I could only smile at the changing colors.

"You know what day it is, don't you?" I asked after a quiet minute.

"Of course I do." She put an arm around my shoulder.

Ten years ago, on that day, was the last time I saw my dad.

"The time has flown by since you came here."

"I've changed a lot, right?"

"I should say so." Lola opened a drawer. Pulled out a camera. "I think we need to take a new picture of you for our wall."

She had me sit at the table, my favorite spot in the house. She snapped a picture.

"Let me see," I said.

"That's a very nice picture." She smiled and handed the camera to me. "Your brown eyes really stand out."

I squinted to see the small picture. My brown hair fell limp against my face. I frowned at the photo.

"You should have let me do my hair. It looks stringy."

"The word is 'smooth.' Your hair looks smooth." She took the camera from my hands. "I'm going to print this up."

After she left the kitchen, I crossed the room to look at the picture wall. Portraits of the girls who had lived in Lola's house over the past twenty years hung so close together, I could barely see the paint. I touched the frames as my eyes glanced at the pictures.

Each girl was different. From different places. With different stories. One thing they all had in common; they'd all been sold. Used by other people who just wanted to make fast money or find easy pleasure. And every girl had come to Lola's house to get help. To change.

My fingers moved along until they rested on my picture. Lola took it a few weeks after I moved in. Thirteen years old and suffering so much. That's what I saw in that old picture. I tried to push down my emotions.

Lola hummed as she came back into the room. I cleared my throat.

"How'd it turn out?" I asked.

"Absolutely beautiful," she answered, joining me by the old photo. "Ah, yes. This picture certainly brings back the memories."

"I'd rather not think about that." I turned, headed for my chair.

"You know, dear, I realize that you don't enjoy dwelling on the past. However, you may find that dealing with your memories will help you continue to grow."

"I know." I sat, pulling myself close under the table. "But that doesn't mean I want to."

"That is understandable." She handed the newly printed picture to me. "Your story is important, Dorothea. That scared little girl is part of you. You wouldn't be the same without her."

"Why do you always have to be right?" I shook my head. "You never let me take the easy way, do you?"

"That I cannot." Lola winked at me.

"You want to help me make some cookies?" I asked.

"Are you changing the subject?"

"Yes, I am." I stood. "Lee asked me to make him some Snickerdoodles."

"With extra cinnamon."

"Just the way he likes them."

"I would love to help you," Lola said.

The two of us stood at the counter, mixing together cookie dough. Rolling it in the sugar and cinnamon. And the whole time, I thought about my past. And wished that I didn't have one to remember.

"Everyone in the dayroom, please," a nurse called, walking through the hallway. "Thursday. Visitor day."

I wandered in, sat in a corner, watching the activity around me. Orderlies and nurses rushed about, making sure to put everything in order. One pushed a mop across the floor, blending the smell of urine with the sting of disinfectant.

Another guided Stewart to a chair in front of the television. Helped him sit down, drool running down his brown sweatshirt, to watch a children's show without the sound on. Raw, pink flesh stretched tightly across his protruding cheekbones. Gray stubble covered his face and head.

He wouldn't have any visitors that day. He never had. I wished they would just let him stay in his room.

Family members entered the room. I watched them, trying to imagine what it would be to have my loved ones visit. I reminded myself that I never wanted Dot to come to this place. I didn't want her to see me like this.

Edith sat crumpled in her wheelchair. Knees pulled up to her chin, legs crossed at the ankles, her face scrunched like she tasted something sour. Her brain refused to let her body straighten.

Her parents visited every week. They told her the news about family members, sang to her, read stories. She never responded to them. I wondered if she even knew they were with her. But they came all the same.

Wesley planted himself on the couch in front of the window. He held his brown body perfectly poised, broad nose pointed up in the air. He believed he was King Henry VIII. His wife sat, uncomfortable in the room among crazy people.

"I'm so sorry, Cora. I hate being late." I heard Lisa's voice as she walked up behind me. "I can't even begin to tell you how crazy today has been!"

"That's okay," I said, half turning toward her.

Standing next to me, she pulled a can of soda from her bag.

"You want to share this with me?"

"That would be nice. Thank you."

Lisa got a waxy paper cup from the nurses' station and poured half the can into it. I watched her walk back to her seat. She interacted with everyone in the room. I felt small in comparison. She was everything I wasn't, everything that I had always wanted to be. Confident, outgoing, kind.

She seemed an unlikely chaplain. Her curly, out-of-control brown hair was pulled back into a wild ponytail. She wore jeans and T-shirts most days. Had I not known better, I would have thought she was a college kid.

I couldn't remember when Lisa had started visiting. But as the hospital chaplain, she'd heard that Stewart and I never had visitors. So she came to sit with us each week. Stewart refused to speak with her. I didn't mind getting all of her attention.

Lisa made her way back to me. Her bright smile never leaving her lips.

"So, tell me how your week's been." She lifted the paper cup and took a sip.

She always let me have the can.

4

"Darn it, Peace!" Mercy screamed from the upstairs bathroom.

"What the heck is your problem?" Peace yelled from the kitchen, where we sat at the table. She looked at me and rolled her eyes.

"Were you the last one up here?"

"Yeah."

"Well, if you use the last of the toilet paper you need to get another flippin' roll!" Mercy's voice carried through the vents to the rest of the house. "I guess your flower lovin', hippie mama never taught you that kind of stuff. It's common courtesy!"

Lola had a strict "no cussing" policy. For each swear word that slipped out of our mouths we had to pay a dollar to the building repair jar. Grace was the main contributor. She had a mouth on her that would make a sailor blush.

"Golly, Mercy!" Faith said from the living room. "Get off your bumper and find a roll for yourself, you lazy puppy."

"I'm gonna kick your rear end, you smarty pants!" Mercy had some trouble keeping her temper under control. Maybe that's why Lola gave her that name.

Everyone who moved in received a nickname from Lola. Some of the girls came with names that reminded them of awful times in their lives. They had names given by parents who abused or abandoned them. A few of the girls were even sold by their parents for a rock of cocaine or a week's worth of groceries. Other girls used their street names, names their pimps thought up. And those names never held good memories. Not even one.

My name, however, remained the same. My dad named me Dorothea. It was all I had left of him. My name held wonderful memories.

My childhood was very different from the other girls in the house. Even happier than Lola's childhood. When I told stories of my family, Mercy, Peace, Faith, and Grace gathered around and listened like little girls hearing a fairy tale. I only told them the good parts of my life. I wished that all my eighteen years had been perfect.

It didn't feel right telling them about the dark turn my life took. Only Lola knew about that. And only because she found me and helped me out. Something in me knew they understood something had happened to me; otherwise I wouldn't have been living in the house with them.

When I thought about the rough stuff that happened in my life, I tried to remind myself that God could use it. Something good could come out of all the pain and loss.

"Someday you will understand," Lola told me over and again. "I promise, it will be made right. All of it."

I'd had people make promises to me for a lot of years. But Lola's promises were different. She always kept them. Every single one.

I grew up in the suburbs of Grand Rapids, Michigan, only about ten miles from Lola's house. A neighborhood full of middle-class, hardworking families. Good kids. Nice schools. Safe from the outside world. At least that's what we thought.

We lived in the house with yellow siding and a wrap-around porch. Neighbor kids came over to play in our backyard. Running circles around the house, trying to avoid tromping on my mom's flowerbeds.

Inside, the house smelled of cookies baking. Bread rising. The aroma of my mom's love for us. She created goodies that all the other mothers envied. And my mom guarded her baking secrets. But she promised to teach me as soon as I got a little older.

I spent many nights at Lola's House dreaming of my childhood. I dreamed that they'd never ended. But then the next morning, waking up, I'd realize that it was all gone.

Those days were buried in two coffins beneath six feet of impossibility.

After all the guests left and we ate dinner, I returned to my room to read a little before turning off my light.

Night was always the worst time for me. The deafening sound of nothing filled the halls throughout the institution. I found it unnerving. Sometimes Stewart cried out in a dream if they hadn't given him enough medicine to make him sleep.

I despised my hard bed. It made sleep even more elusive. My muscles ached for something soft, something I could sink into. The nights when I couldn't sleep, memory returned. One fragment at a time.

I'd been living in Lansing, Michigan, for six years. It took several months for me to work my way up to a secretarial position in a law firm downtown. I'd worked very hard to achieve that job. Considering my lack of education, it hadn't been easy. The paycheck remained unimpressive, but it paid the rent and bought groceries.

One summer morning, an especially heavy rainstorm hit Lansing. I went about my routine, not wanting to be late for work. After pulling out of my apartment complex, I realized that I couldn't see very far in the deluge. Suddenly I drove into a flooded part of the road. The water rose up past the wheels of my little car. I pulled to the side of the road. But then the engine quit. I didn't know if I would be able to get myself out of the car without the water flowing in. Anxiety rushed my brain.

Someone knocked on my driver side window.

"Hey, ma'am!" the deep voice spoke loudly over the sound of heavy raindrops. "You need help."

It wasn't a question. And he was right. I needed help in so many ways. I couldn't think of an area of my life that didn't need a good dose of help.

"Ma'am, I'm going to need you to open your door. I'll help you get out."

"I can't." I tried to keep my voice under control. "The water will get in. It'll ruin my car."

Panic took over. The car seemed safer, stuck in the middle of a rainwater lake that grew each moment, than in opening the door and trusting a stranger. Especially a man.

"Well, you can't sit there all day," he said.

"Why do you care?"

"Because I don't want to watch you drown!"

Through the rain I could see his blurry image. It appeared that he wore some kind of uniform. Not a police officer, I could tell that much.

"I don't know you!" I yelled, rolling the window down a crack. "How do I know you aren't going to hurt me? Or steal my purse?"

"Oh for goodness sake, ma'am! I'm just trying to help you! Would you please just let me help you?" He straightened up and pointed to a small, round pin on his shirt. "Do you see this?"

"Yes."

"It says that I'm a Marine chaplain." He lowered his face back down to the window. "I'm a military minister. My name is Steven Peter Schmidt. I was born in Oregon to a family that went to church every single Sunday. After boot camp I went to Bible college. Then I reenlisted for the job I'm doing now. Now you know me. If you need a list of references, I'll take you to a phone and you can call my CO."

"I don't even know what a CO is!" I stalled, trying to think of how to fix my problem without his help.

"Commanding Officer." He looked across the street. His strong jawline was attractive, even if obscured by the rain-soaked window. "Listen, I'll take you to that little diner. You can use the phone there if you want to call for help."

I looked at my feet. A puddle formed on the floor mat.

"Fine," I conceded.

"Ready?" he asked, hand on the door. "You have to unlock the door first."

"Sure." I pulled up the lock.

He opened the door and, in a flash, swept me up and out. I found myself in his truck. He climbed in through the driver side door. My first good look at him made me speechless. He turned and smiled at me with his off-center grin. His chocolate brown eyes crinkled in the corners. Too charmed, I had to look away.

"Okay, let's get you to that phone," he said, starting up the engine.

We were dripping wet when we walked into the coffee shop. I tugged at my clothes, worried about how the water caused them to cling to me. We sat in a booth.

"You kids get stuck in the rain?" The waitress glared at us from across the room.

"She did." Steven pointed his finger at me. "And I saved her."

"Well, ain't you just a knight in shining armor."

"It's sure hard to pass up a damsel in distress. Especially when she's this pretty."

I looked at him. He winked. I turned away.

"Well, after you're done eating I'll have an awful mess to clean up." This with a teasing tone. "You wouldn't want this old lady to work that hard, would ya?"

"What old lady?" Thick, syrupy charm. "I'll tell you what. You bring me a mop before we go and I'll take care of the whole floor for you."

"Oh, you don't have to do that. It's not your job, young man." She pulled a pad of paper from her apron pocket and walked toward us, licking the point of her pencil. "Now, what can I get the two of you to eat?"

"Just coffee, please," I said, embarrassed. I only had enough money for that. And not even enough for a tip.

"Gosh, you know, I think I'll have the special." He pointed to a picture on the menu. "That any good?"

"Best in town." She answered. "How you like your eggs?"

"Sunny side up. And sourdough toast, please."

"You got it." She wrote on the paper.

"And can she use the phone?" He nodded toward me.

"Sure thing, sugar." The waitress motioned for me to follow her. "It's over this way."

At the counter, I dialed the number for my office. The receptionist answered.

"This is Cora," I said.

"Cora, where are you?" she asked.

"I got stuck in the rain. My car broke down."

"Do you think you can get here? Mr. Jones told me if you don't show up soon, he'll fire you."

"Then I quit. I can find something else." I sighed. "Just tell him that I'm done."

"What about your things, from your desk? Do you want me to bring them to you?"

"No. Just throw it all away."

I gingerly put the receiver down, wondering at the words I'd spoken. I'd worked so hard for that job. I couldn't understand why I'd been so hasty to quit. Anxiety choked me.

"Where's the restroom?" I asked the waitress.

"Down that hall," she answered, pointing.

The dimly lit bathroom made my panic worsen. Digging a safety pin from my purse, I made a small slice on my arm. The cut took the edge off my nerves.

The waitress walked in. I pulled my sleeve down quickly.

"I needed to fix my hair." I moved toward the mirror.

"Here, honey." She handed me a few hair pins. "You need a little help?"

"Thank you."

She twisted my wet hair, rolling it into a loose bun. I watched her reflection as she pushed the pins into my auburn hair. She stuck her tongue out the side of her mouth and squinted her eyes in concentration.

"My little girl hates having long hair. If I don't get it cut she'll take my shears to it herself." She smoothed the front of my hair. "I never get to play with anybody's hair."

"Thank you," I whispered. Her motherly touch soothed me in an unfamiliar way. It put a lump in my throat. It had been so long since anyone helped me with my hair.

"Now, what happened on the phone? You seemed upset."

"I quit my job."

"Well, it must not have been worth having. Everything'll work out for you. Pretty girl like you'll find something new in no time." She patted my shoulder. "And that fellow out there. He's sure to take good care of you. He seems to really think a lot of you."

"Well…" I wanted to correct her, but she didn't let me.

"Well nothing. I bet your folks are plenty proud of you. And a military man, too." She washed her hands. "Any wedding plans?"

"We aren't really—"

"Well," she interrupted me again, "the way he looks at you, I bet he'll pop the question soon enough. That wouldn't surprise me at all."

After drying her hands, she patted my cheek and walked out of the bathroom.

"But I just met him," I said out loud after the door closed behind her.

I gazed into the mirror for quite a while. Part of me hoped Steven would leave before I got back to the table. I didn't want to let anyone into my life, even for a few hours. When I got involved with people it always ended in heartache.

A different part of me wished that he would stay. I had to remind myself that he was just a man who helped me. Nothing more.

"I am so lonely," I whispered. "Lord, I need somebody."

Even after years of determining that God didn't care, I still prayed occasionally. Superstitious, hoping for good luck prayers.

I walked out to the table just after the waitress set two plates down. One was in front of my seat.

"I didn't order this." I sat, looking at the eggs, bacon and toast. "There must have been a mistake."

"Sure was." The waitress placed rolled up silverware on the table. "That old cook back there just made up too much food. Don't worry, honey. It's on me."

"Oh, thank you."

"Ain't no thing, darling," she said. "I'll leave the two of you alone now."

She winked at me before walking away.

"That was nice," Steven said, taking a bite of toast.

"It was." My stomach grumbled at the promise of the warm breakfast. I poked at my eggs, bursting one of the yolks on the white plate. After dabbing at it with my toast, I took a bite.

"So, what's your name?" Steven asked. "Oh, sorry. Of course I asked right after you take a bite. Let me see if I can guess." He rubbed his chin with thumb and index finger. Looking at me, he pulled his eyebrows together in thought.

"Let's see here." His squinted his eyes. "Is it Peggy?"

I shook my head.

"Greta?"

"No."

"Oh. Could it be Wilhelmina?"

The giggle coming out of my mouth caught me by surprise.

"I'm horrible at guessing."

"Clearly."

"Okay. Then you're just going to have to tell me your name."

"My name is Cora."

"Cora? That's a nice name." He sipped his coffee.

"Thank you."

"What does the name Cora mean?"

"Maiden," I said. "I looked it up in a baby name book at the library."

"The lovely maiden Cora."

"What does Steven mean?"

"Crowned." He wiped his mouth with a napkin. "Like a king. My parents wanted me to have a healthy self-esteem, I guess."

"Well, I guess it's fitting. You're the king and I'm the lowly maiden."

"I really doubt that there's anything lowly about you, Maiden Cora." His eyes held a gentleness I'd never seen in a man before. "You seem to be full of the grace and kindness of a queen."

We talked for hours. I'd never been so interested in what anyone had to say before. He told me stories that made me laugh. Deep down, from the stomach laughs.

When the rain let up, the waitress brought Steven the mop. He made quick work of cleaning the floor, whistling the whole time.

"You did a very nice job." I smiled at him.

"Good old Marines. They had to teach me a few things before I was able to grow up. And one of those things was how to mop. It was kind of a punishment for me."

"Mopping as a punishment?"

"Yeah. I was pretty self-centered when I first enlisted. They had to break me of that." He returned the mop, paid the bill, and led me out to his truck. "How about we go for a drive?"

"Where would we go?"

"I don't know. Maybe see what kind of damage the storm did." He looked at my car, safely parked across the street. "I promise I'll bring you back."

"I'm not sure." I looked down at my hands. "I don't make a habit of getting into cars with strangers."

"You have my word. I will be a gentleman."

"Don't you have to get to work?"

"Nope. I'm off until tonight. I'm on third shift at the Veteran's Hospital." He held his keys, jangling them. "Oh, or do you need me to drive you to work?"

"No. I actually just quit my job."

"And still smiling?" he asked. "Must be a girl like you has the world eating out of the palm of her hand. I bet life's pretty kind to you."

"You think so, huh?" I took a deep breath. "Okay. Let's go for that drive."

We climbed into his truck. He drove us to a little park.

"Have you ever seen the rose garden here?" he asked.

I shook my head.

"Well, then I'm honored to be the first to walk through it with you."

We walked among raindrop-covered buds. I stooped to breathe in the aroma of especially large, yellow blooms.

"Wow! Look at that, Cora," Steven whispered.

A rainbow spread across the sky. He grabbed my hand and took me to the marble pavilion at the top of the garden. The colors bowed above us, so clear, so vibrant. Like nothing I'd ever seen. Breathtakingly majestic. All of creation seemed to take pause, reveling in the glory of it.

We sat on a bench. Steven hadn't let go of my hand. Some kind of energy moved from his hand into mine and up my arm. Heavy and comforting like a blanket. A protection. Teetering between fear and excitement, I reminded myself that he was still a stranger. That we'd only just met.

"Can I ask you a question?" He kept his eyes on the sky.

"I guess," I said.

"Do you believe in God?"

"Sure," I answered, a little stunned by his forward question. "Yes, I believe in God."

"Good. That's a good thing," he said, glancing at me. "I have this idea about God. Do you want to hear it?"

I nodded.

"Well, you know how God created everything? I think He could have made it any way He wanted to. You know what I mean?"

"I think so."

"He could have decided to make it all ugly or boring or just one color. Just drab. But He didn't do it that way. He made His world beautiful." Steven looked back at the rainbow. "He didn't have to, you know."

"I suppose He didn't."

"Nature reveals God's glory. He didn't have to do that. I wonder if that's just Him showing us a piece of His love." He looked at me and laughed. "There I go preaching. Sorry."

"It's all right," I said, smiling. "I liked it."

We sat, letting the silence settle between us.

"But what about all the ugly things?" I asked, so quietly, Steven had to lean closer to me.

"Excuse me?"

"Well, God made some really ugly things too. Like warts. Warts are ugly."

He laughed. "Yes, you're right. They sure are."

"So, what is God trying to say to us when we look at things like warts?"

"I have no idea," he chuckled.

The rainbow faded as the heat of the day dried out the air. We sat quietly again.

"And what about ugly people?"

"I guess beauty's in the eye of the beholder, right?" he said.

"No, I don't mean that kind of ugly." I hadn't intended for the weight in my tone. The thickness of it caused me to talk slower, deliberately. "I mean what about people who do ugly things? You know, bad people. Hurtful people."

"Wow. That's a deep question, Cora. It's good." He sighed. "There's a lot of evil in the world. It's a broken place. And too many people choose to give in to the evil and ugly part of life. I don't think that is from God at all. He never made people to be like that."

Even though the day grew increasingly hotter, a chill shivered across my skin as Steven spoke. Goose bumps raised on my arms.

Steven stood, stepped toward a railing that overlooked the rose garden. I joined him. Put my hand back in his.

From my bed, eyes closed, the flash of memory left me. All that remained were Steven's words.

These past years had been worse than drab. They had been ugly, I had been ugly. Had done ugly things.

Beauty...beauty was more than I deserved.

"Dorothea, wake up, please," Lola whispered, shaking my shoulder.

"Lola, what the heck?" I grumbled, looking at the alarm clock. "It isn't even five a.m."

"Yes," she said, zipping up her jacket. "You are correct."

"Then why are you waking me up?" I whined. "I hate waking up."

"I need you to make one of your big family breakfasts."

"What's going on? Are you going somewhere?" I rubbed my eyes.

"The hospital called. A young lady delivered a baby a few days ago. She is set for release this morning and needs a place to live with her new son. The maternity ward can only allow her to stay for a few more hours. So I'm going to pick her up. We can't let her go back to the streets." She finished putting on her mismatched socks. "I would like her to have a great welcome."

"Okay." I sat up. "What do you want me to make?"

"The works. We have all the ingredients." Lola put her hand on my cheek. "You are a precious princess for getting up early to make breakfast for Jesus."

"Yeah, yeah. It's too early for that kind of chipper talk." I stood, stretched and tried to smile. "Did you happen to make coffee?"

"I surely did," she said.

In the kitchen, I started frying up bacon, baking coffee cakes and cinnamon rolls. I cut thick slices of homemade bread for toast. Sourdough. My mom's favorite. She used to bake it for my big brother and me. The smell of that bread brought memories of her pulling the loaves out of the oven. It made me miss her.

Whenever I cooked I felt connected to my mom. She spent most of my childhood in her kitchen whipping up something. She let me help. Taught me all the basics. Never got upset when I made a mess of her kitchen. Those were loving, warm memories.

About a year after I moved to Lola's house I started making breakfast every Saturday. I always wore the apron my mom made for me. By the time I finished cooking, I'd get it dirty with smeared egg or dusted with flour. Somehow my mom's apron never got dirty no matter what she was making. I could never figure out how she did that. Or why she even needed to wear an apron in the first place.

"Sugar, you need some help makin' breakfast?" Peace yawned, entering the kitchen.

"Yeah, that would be great. Thanks." I handed her some eggs and a measuring cup of milk. "Would you please whisk those up for me?"

"It ain't Saturday, is it? Don't you only do these breakfasts on Saturday?" she asked, grabbing a mug of coffee.

"Nope. Lola's bringing home another girl."

Nodding her head, she stirred cream into her coffee. I always thought her skin looked like milky coffee. She wore her dark brown hair twisted into tight cornrows. Her brown-green eyes were framed by the longest lashes I'd ever seen.

A tattoo marked up her neck. Her pimp's brand. So ashamed of it, she hid it whenever she could. When she felt like someone was looking at it, she covered it with her hand.

"Hey, you want me to add cheese to these?" she asked, beating the eggs.

"Sure. Thanks."

A few hours later we all sat in the living room, stomachs full and the dishes washed. Lola on her rounds to deliver leftovers to our neighbors.

Promise, the new mother, sat in a recliner. She held the baby, Nesto, loosely in her arms. A receiving blanket tucked around him tightly in a swaddle. Yellow ducks and green frogs all over the soft fabric. Every few minutes he'd squawk, spitting out his pacifier. Every time, Promise shoved it back into his mouth.

"So, what's it like?" Grace asked. "I mean, bein' pregnant?"

"It ain't fun, you know," Promise said, chomping on a piece of gum. "You get all fat. I got stretch marks all over my belly now. Ain't gonna be wearin' no bikini no more."

"But it was worth it, right?" Grace asked. "I mean, you got a baby."

"I guess. I didn't want to have no baby. But I didn't know I was knocked up till it was too late to get it aborted." She stood up. "Listen, I gotta go get a nap. I'm gonna put the baby in the swing down here. If it cries, just give him a bottle or something."

She went up the stairs and to her room. The rest of us took turns holding Nesto. He was a sweet baby. We gladly welcomed him into our home.

Holding Nesto in my arms, I remembered my dad. Climbing up into his lap.

"Daddy," I would say, snuggling up to him. "Tell me about when I was a baby."

"Well," he had said, wrapping strong arms around me. "You were beautiful. Just like you are now. But so small."

"Tell me the story about my name," I would beg. "Please, Daddy."

"Again? Aren't you tired of that story?"

"No. Tell me."

"Oh, okay," he had said.

Listening to the story, I would bury my face in his chest, smelling his cologne.

My dad drove their station wagon home from the hospital. My mom sat in the back with me. He'd never driven so slowly in all his life. Not even when taking my big brother Pete home. Something about a baby girl seemed more fragile. Made him more cautious.

Two-year-old Pete met us at the door. My grandparents, from Oregon, had our apartment decorated with pink balloons and streamers. A banner, hung across the living room, read Welcome Home, Baby Girl Schmidt!

I didn't have a name yet. They couldn't think of anything they both liked.

Dad held me so that Mom could eat. I slept so deeply and stayed so still he kept checking to make sure I was breathing. Every once in a while I smiled. He knew it was gas, but that didn't make it any less special to him.

"What are you going to name that baby girl?" my grandmother asked, plopping more mashed potatoes on my mom's plate. "She can't go on forever without a name."

"Well, we just aren't sure yet." My mom pushed the extra food away.

"What about my name? Delores. I think that's a nice name." My grandma pushed the plate back to my mom. "Why don't you name the baby Delores? Wouldn't that be special? And, Cora, if you don't start eating more your milk's never going to come in."

"I'm full," my mom had said, picking up the plate and putting it in the kitchen sink.

"You know, I would be honored if you named the baby Delores."

"Delores means sorrowful, painful," my grandpa said, flipping through a baby name book. "That's not a nice name."

"Nobody would know what it means," my grandma had snapped. "Normal people don't carry those ridiculous name books around. Besides, I've lived my whole life with that name."

"And you've lived up to it every day." Grandpa turned to the next page. "Oh, how about Dorothy? It means 'gift from God.'"

"I don't know. I like the meaning, I'm not so sure about the name," Dad said. "What about Dorothea?"

"That's a pretty name," my mom said, taking me into her arms. "Dorothea Schmidt."

"It says here the nickname is Dot," Grandpa read. "That's cute."

"Well." Grandma slumped into a chair. "I think it's awful."

Nesto in my arms, I tried to imagine being held again by my dad. The thought made my heart achy and my eyes water. I kissed the little baby boy on the forehead, hoping for happiness and love to enter his life.

I hated Wednesdays in the institution. Every Wednesday morning, the art therapist showed up for an hour filled with silly activities. She reminded us weekly that art helped us connect with our emotions. The only emotional connection I made in that class was frustration. I sat at the table in the dayroom, waiting for the class to be over.

"Time to let you feelings breathe," sang Sunshine Ruffman. She danced around the room passing out large pieces of paper to each of us. "Art has the power to heal the soul!"

She swirled, art supplies flying from her hands like so many seeds. Crayons here. Markers there. Her long scarf flowed behind her in a ballet of colored drawing implements. Tightly ringed black hair bounced as she pirouetted. At last, she perched on a stool, crossed her legs and inhaled deeply. She closed her eyes and let her fingers wiggle in the air.

"Friends, the time has come." Her nostrils flared. Her hands clapped together and she opened her bright blue eyes. "Create!"

Wesley scribbled, using dark crayons to create distorted, terrifying images. Stewart made stick figures with large, misshapen heads and limbs that sprouted from the chin and where ears should have been. Edith didn't move, didn't make a noise.

I sat before my paper each week wishing I could make something beautiful. I longed for my hand to craft pictures of family or rainbows or flowers. I yearned deeply to put the beauty I remembered into a piece of art. But all I could manage were dark, thick, ugly lines. I couldn't make a single pretty thing.

Steven and I married on a beach along the shore of Lake Michigan. I had convinced him to run away with me. Sunbathers witnessed our vows which were officiated over by a chaplain friend of Steven's.

Throughout the short ceremony, I couldn't take my eyes off him. It didn't matter to me that the sun peeked perfectly from behind thick clouds. Or that the waves dared to reach just up to our toes on the sand. I credited the perfection of the day to one thing—that Steven Schmidt loved me.

On that day, I determined that I would never need anyone else. He became sufficient to fill all my desires, all that I required.

After the ceremony we walked down the beach, scuffing our bare feet in the soft sand. I grabbed hold of his arm, knowing that as long as he lived, I would be safe. Protected.

I turned my face up to look at him. Only a year before, I'd seen that off-center smile for the first time.

"I can't believe we just got married," he said, eyes wide. "We should call our parents."

"Your mother will be shocked, won't she?" I laughed.

"She's going to be furious, that's what she'll be. She has always wanted to plan my wedding." He kissed my hand. "I'm glad we ran away to do this. It is so much more peaceful this way."

"Is she really going to be angry?" I wanted her to like me. "Will she blame me?"

"Yes. Probably. But she'll get over it. She'll have plenty to do when she plans our reception."

"She'll do that?"

"It's the least we can have her do." He laughed. "It will be insane. Way too many people and way too much food. And the presents will be overwhelming."

"I wouldn't have it any other way."

He stopped and kissed me. "I love you so much, Cora Schmidt."

"Oh my goodness! That's my name now, isn't it! I'm never going to be able to get used to it."

"You know, I feel pretty bad. I never thought I'd marry a girl without asking her father's blessing first."

"Well, life sure can have some surprising twists." I gazed up at him. "Don't worry about all that. Trust me. It's better this way."

"Could we at least give everyone a call? It would make me feel better."

My heart contracted with anxiety. I didn't know how to tell my husband of one hour that our elopement had a purpose. That I would never call my father. And, so, I chose not to burden Steven with the information.

I turned him to face me, put my hand on his chest and made eye contact.

"How about we just let this be our day? We can worry about telling everybody else later. I think we should spend today enjoying each other. Maybe we could find a hotel room?"

"I guess so." He looked at me, raising his eyebrows. "We have waited all this time."

We spent the first night of our marriage in a small cottage. I learned the tenderness of the man who loved me. He was the only man I willingly gave myself to.

If Steven had a fault, it was that he didn't expect more of me. He never asked about my family again. Never tried to dig deep into the place where my secrets lived. He let himself become the only person in the world that I needed. And then he was gone. And, just like before the day I met him, I had to survive alone.

"Hey, Grace, tomorrow's the room check," I said, stepping over a pile of her clothes on the floor. "Can you please make sure your stuff is picked up?"

"Oh." She looked at me, confused, sitting on her bed. "We have a room check again?"

"Yeah." I nodded. "We have them every single Tuesday. Just in case you haven't noticed."

"I guess I just don't really keep track." She turned her eyes back to the magazine she held in her hands.

"Listen, I really need you to clean up your stuff." I kicked a solitary shoe toward her. "The room's kind of overflowing with your junk."

"Yeah, sure, Dorothea. I'll do it," she said, not looking up.

"Really? Will you?"

"Yup. I swear. I'll get it done this time." She cussed under her breath.

"'Cause we've failed every week since you moved in."

"I know."

"Grace, I don't have another dollar to pay for failing this week."

"Gotcha, Dorothea. I'll take care of it." She didn't move.

I opened our bedroom door. Not all the way. A stack of papers and books sat behind it.

"I seriously could not imagine a worse roommate, Grace. I'm not kidding." A harsh growl resulted in my attempt at keeping my voice low. "You are so inconsiderate. I don't think you're capable of thinking of others. Are you? And so frustrating. So very, very frustrating."

I rushed out the door, flinging it behind me. I'd intended on slamming it. But a sweater sleeve jammed against the door frame, muting my effort. I screeched in exasperation.

"Lola, I'm about to beat the daisies out of Grace." I huffed into the kitchen.

"Really," she said in her normal, calm voice.

"Yes, really. She's the biggest slob I've ever seen."

"Oh, my. I'd never noticed, Dorothea. Go on." Her sarcasm didn't help my mood.

"You know exactly what I mean, Lola."

Lola washed the dishes with her sleeves rolled up. She wore her long, gray hair in the usual braid down her back. Her glasses rested on the tip of her nose.

"Are you okay, Dorothea? You're looking at me in a most peculiar way." She pushed the glasses up with a sudsy finger.

"Yeah. Sometimes you just look like someone I used to know."

"Oh, really. Who would that be?" She placed a plate in the strainer.

"It isn't important. Stop trying to change the topic."

"You changed the topic, dear," she said.

"Don't use your smart little mind to confuse me." I balled up my fists, putting them on my hips.

"Terribly sorry."

"Anyway, we need to talk about Grace."

"How ironic."

"What's ironic?" I asked, flustered.

"Nothing, really. Just noticing the interesting word play."

"Whatever. Who are you, Shakespeare?"

"Forsooth, I know not of which you speak," she said with a fake English accent.

"Can you please take this seriously, Lola? Gosh, what is up with you today?"

"Just feeling a little cheeky."

"Yeah, I can tell." I stepped closer to her. "Listen, you have to move Grace out of my room."

"I cannot to do that, Dorothea."

"What are you talking about? You can too!" I knew my tone inched toward disrespect, but I just couldn't seem to keep it in check. "Faith has been asking for Grace to move to her room. What, are you just against me right now or something?"

"Dorothea." Lola's voice had a tone of warning. "I am not going to move Grace from the room you share. Yes, share. It is no longer just your room, dear. And mind your tone, please. You are on the edge of disrespect."

"Sorry." I cleared my throat. "Can you please put Grace with Hope?"

"Nope. Can't do that."

"Please, Lola. I'm begging you for mercy."

"Oh, I can't give you Mercy. It would be far too crowded with you and Grace."

"Ha, ha. You're so funny." I tried to soften the sarcastic edge of my voice.

Lola continued putting dishes into the strainer, making me wait. Over the years she had become an expert at that kind of thoughtful pause. I couldn't tolerate them.

"Lola, this is serious. You have to do something."

She turned toward me, drying her hands on a towel.

"Dorothea, does Grace's lack of cleanliness truly bother you that much?"

"Yes, as a matter of fact, it does." I sensed vindication. I anticipated a victory. "It really bugs me a lot. It drives me nuts. My mom would have never allowed such a pigpen. It's horrible."

"Then clean it yourself."

"What?" I knew that my mouth dropped wide open. I didn't care. "What did you say?"

"Pick up her things and put them away." She turned from the sink and let her light green eyes lock with mine.

"But that isn't fair. It isn't right," I whispered.

"Dorothea, did it ever occur to you that Grace never had anyone teach her how to clean?"

"Well, no. I didn't even think of that."

"She didn't have one single person spend enough time to show her how to organize things or pick them up. Your mother did a good job of that. Didn't she?"

I nodded, too ashamed to speak.

"Well, dear, Grace's mother left her when she was eighteen months old. She stayed with her uncle who only taught her to service his friends. And then, when he grew tired of taking care of her, he sent her out on the streets. That was how she was raised." Lola put the towel on the counter. "She didn't have a childhood. She's had to learn so many things on her own. There are a lot of gaps in her life. Cleanliness is the least of her issues."

Leaning up against the counter with my arms crossed over my chest, I listened to Lola, knowing that I had been wrong.

"So, if you really want her to keep things picked up, you will need to teach her."

"Oh, great." I slapped my hand on my thigh. "Now I feel like dog poop."

"You should." She smiled. "Now take that feeling and use it for good."

She turned back to the sink to finish the dishes.

I climbed the stairs to my room. It occurred to me how different Grace and I were. It wasn't her fault that she'd been dumped on by her parents and uncle and all the other adults that came in and out of her life.

Why had my childhood been so much better? I wasn't a better person than she was, God didn't love me more. It just had to do with the choices that our parents made. My mom and dad made good choices, they spent a lot of time with my brother and me. They wanted us to have good lives. Grace's family chose the way of selfishness. And she paid the price for their decisions. That wasn't just unfair. It was unjust.

I moved toward the bedroom door, still ajar for the sweater sleeve. I heard Grace moving around inside. I opened the door slowly. It creaked. All the doors in that house opened noisily. I think that had to have been on purpose.

Grace looked at me when I walked into the room, her eyes red. She rubbed her face on the shoulder of her shirt, wiping away tears, but smearing her mascara.

"Dorothea, I swear, I'm so sorry. I know you're really flippin' honked off at me right now." She sobbed as she tried to fold her clothes. "I'm a bad person. Just please don't hate me. I promise, I'll throw everything out. Just don't hate me."

"Oh my goodness, Grace! I don't hate you!" I walked to her and helped her sit on the edge of her bed. I sat next to her. "Stop, just stop folding that for a second. I want to talk to you."

"What's wrong with me, Dorothea? I just don't know how to clean up my crap." She dropped the jeans in a lump on her lap. "There's junk all over the place. I know what I need to do, I just can't seem to get it done. I don't know how."

"Don't cry, Grace," I said. "I'm not that mad about it."

"It's like it's the only thing I can control. You know? Like, I've never been allowed to make one single decision for myself. Not ever. But I can choose to throw my clothes on the floor or whatever. Sometimes I think I'm crazy or something."

She let her head fall heavily on my knee. I patted her silky, blond hair, soft and smooth, like the hair of a china doll.

"You know, I'm just the opposite," I said. "I try to keep everything picked up and looking perfect so I can feel like I'm in control. Funny, huh?"

"I guess." She sat up slowly. "Was your mom really clean?"

"Yup. She was crazy about it. Seriously, she'd always find something to scrub no matter what. She never even gave dust a chance to get on things."

"I don't remember my mom," she said. "She left when I was really little. I used to have a picture of her. She was pretty young when she had me. Lola's kind of the only mom I've ever had."

"You could do a lot worse." I patted her knee. "She loves you."

"You think so? Sometimes I feel like I'm such a big problem for her. She never acts like I am, but she has to be really annoyed with me all the time. I mean, all the cussing and attitude and stuff."

"You think cussing would make Lola not like you?"

"I don't know. Wouldn't it?"

"No way. And you aren't a problem."

"But sometimes I'm a huge brat." Grace pulled her legs up, sat criss-crossed.

"Um. Do you remember how bratty I was to you just now?"

"Yeah. But I kind of thought I deserved it."

"You didn't. It was wrong of me to be like that." I stared at the floor. "I was just being dumb. I'm really sorry."

"Yeah. I forgive you," she said. "Hey, can I tell you what really worries me? I'm so afraid that I'm going to do something to make people leave me again."

"I know. It's scary, isn't it?"

Grace nodded her head.

"You know I've been here for a long time, right?"

"Yeah. Like four years or something."

"Five." I cleared my throat. "That's a long time."

"Yeah."

"And you know what? In all that time I've never seen Lola stop loving anyone. No matter what they did."

"Really?"

"Yes." I smiled at her. "And trust me, you're the best at cussing, but you aren't the meanest."

"Well, I guess I'll just have to work on that." She looked around the room. "Man, this is so embarrassing."

"You think so?"

"Yeah. Like, I wanted to talk about it in our group therapy. But I was just way too ashamed."

"You're seriously ashamed of this?"

"I know. It's really stupid. I mean, I've told them all about every-thing else that happened in my life. Like the old days with my uncle and then with my pimp. And that's some pretty nasty stuff. But a bunch of clothes on the floor is what embarrasses me."

"Well, you shouldn't be embarrassed." I grabbed her hamper. "How about we just try and clean up one thing a day. We'll start slow and move to something different tomorrow."

"I can try that." She reached for a pile of clothes. "I just need to make sure I don't get overwhelmed."

"Okay. That makes sense."

"It might not be easy. I might freak out big time. I might cuss a lot."

"That's fine."

Grace snorted in laughter.

"You know what, Dorothea? That was the longest I've gone with-out cussing. I'm pretty proud of myself."

She followed that with a ten-dollar string of expletives.

I decided I wouldn't turn her in.

Thursday. Visitor's Day. The weeks often moved slowly between Thursdays. Between my times with Lisa. I couldn't let myself think about what it would have been without the visits from her. I spent my Wednesday evenings in anticipation of seeing the one person in the world who actually came around for me.

Lisa arrived a little earlier than usual. She walked straight to the head nurse. The two of them stood behind the observation window. Their discussion became heated. Lisa made a call from the telephone on the desk. After a moment she handed the phone to the nurse, smiling smugly. She made eye contact with me and gave me a thumbs up.

"Good morning, Cora," she said after a few moments. She was breathless with excitement as she crossed the room toward me. She sat opposite me at the table.

I looked down at my hands.

"How have you been this week?" she asked, her eyes beaming. "Good?"

"Oh, I suppose so," I answered.

She pulled two cans of diet soda from her bag. "Here ya go."

"Thank you." I accepted the can. "How long have you been coming to visit me?"

"A few years."

"And in those few years I have never known you to bring two cans of soda."

"Well, I thought you might be getting sick of sharing with me. I figured you'd like your own." She smiled. "Besides, we have something small to celebrate today."

My heart pumped. Blood rushed to my face. The sound throbbed in my ears. I had very little to celebrate in nine years. Whatever Lisa had to tell me would change me, I could tell. One couldn't go for so long in mourning just to have a celebration that wasn't life altering.

"You have some mail." She placed a large manila envelope on the table in front of me.

I popped open my can of soda and took a long sip. It burned as it went down my throat. My eyes never left the envelope. I didn't recognize the handwriting on the envelope.

"It took me a couple phone calls and a near fist fight with Nurse Naomi to get permission to give these to you."

"What is it?" Nervousness crept into my voice.

"Why don't you open it and find out?" A smile lit up her entire face.

I opened the flap and closed my eyes as I pulled out the contents of the envelope. The slick, stiff stack of paper in my hands, I opened my eyes. Flipped through the photos.

Steven and me at our wedding reception.

My handsome husband kissing my pregnant belly.

Pete an hour after he was born.

Dot's first birthday cake smashed all over her face and in her hair.

I flipped through them, barely able to see through the tears.

Pete on his first bike.

Steven in his uniform holding Dot.

All four of us standing on the porch the day we moved into our house.

"I thought these were all lost." I whispered for fear that I would break to hear my own voice. "How did you know?"

"Know what?" she asked.

"That this was all I've wanted. I never thought I would see these pictures again."

Delight consumed me. The images of my loved ones moved me well past gladness. Laughter filled my soul and erupted from my mouth.

A smile lifted my face. I'd not really smiled in years. I breathed in the refreshing air of joy that the pictures had brought me. But then the laughter broke into a sob. Lisa put her hand on mine.

"I know you love your family very much," she whispered. "Why don't you tell me about them?"

I found the picture from my wedding reception. Steven, again, donned his dress uniform. I wore a light blue sundress. My red-brown hair cascaded over my bare shoulders. The two of us stood by a large cake, posing just before cutting huge slabs to feed each other. Memory overwhelmed me.

"Steven's parents came from Oregon the week after we eloped." I shared the picture with Lisa. "His mother threw a reception for us."

"You eloped? The two of you must have been a very spontaneous couple."

"Well, sometimes spontaneity helped me avoid certain unpleasant situations."

"What would that have been?"

"Oh, there were just a few people that I would have rather not had at my wedding. It's not something I like to talk about. Anyway, I arranged things in such a way that there was no one to invite. And with the reception, I simply left the invitations up to my mother-in-law." I looked at the picture. "I never gave her a list of guests to invite. She was so absorbed with how she wanted everything, as usual, that she didn't give me a second thought."

"And what did your parents think about your elopement?"

"It didn't matter," I said, waving off the question. "The reception was wonderful, but exhausting. So many people came, all with presents for our new life together."

"When you look at that picture what do you see? What does it make you think?"

"I see a couple of naïve kids. I only wish I could warn them about what was headed for them."

"Would anything have been different if you'd known about all that was going to happen to you?"

"I don't think I would have allowed myself to be with him. I would have run off and just been by myself." I looked at the ceiling, trying to hold back the tears. "Sometimes it's safer being alone."

"Interesting." She paused. "Do you think Steven would have felt the same way?"

"No. I don't believe he would have changed a thing. He would have wanted to be with me no matter what the future held for us."

The other visitors began walking into the room. I quickly slipped the pictures back in their envelope, not wanting to share the goodness with them.

Lisa and I talked about life. I told her about art class. She told me about the construction on the house she was having built. We talked about novels and movies and music.

Small talk.

We had shared a moment so filled with emotion and then only shortly afterward we talked about trivial things. Maybe I just needed to talk about a few things that didn't matter. Those were always the easier topics of discussion for me. The difficult, the complex—those were the things that had the power to break me into bits.

Lisa got up to leave. She gathered the empty cans.

"I wanted to make sure you understood that those pictures are yours to keep." She slung her tote over her shoulder. "There's a note in your case file. Dr. Emmert thought they would help you with some of the healing process."

"He's a kind man." I stood. "Sometimes I worry that he feels he's wasting his time and efforts here. At least with me. I can't seem to open up to him."

"I think he understands that. He says nothing but great things about you." She held my hand briefly. "He's impressed by your intelligence."

"Well, that's very nice of him."

"Cora, have a blessed week."

"Thank you. I shall try."

As she walked out of the dayroom, I realized I hadn't asked how she came about the pictures. I supposed it didn't much matter.

Later that evening I took the envelope to my room. I studied the reception picture. Behind the cake was a mountain of gifts. We took several trips in Steven's truck to bring them to our small apartment.

I lay on my bed, closed my eyes and remembered the gifts.

The day after the wedding reception, Steven's parents went back to Oregon, and I could finally breathe. We decided we would spend our day sorting the gifts in our new apartment. We had moved to Grand Rapids when we returned from our wedding and honeymoon.

We hadn't had a chance to register for gifts. The guests simply purchased whatever they thought we needed. We ended up with four toasters, six sets of sheets in various sizes and colors as well as multiple collections of all things useless.

Steven and I worked to stack the dishes in cupboards, arranging spoons and forks and knives in the drawer by the sink. Bed sheets and bathroom linens found a home in the hallway closet. Duplicates or things we didn't want went into the center of the living room.

It looked like a house-wares department exploded in our apartment.

"What are we going to do with all this stuff?" I asked, plopping down on the sofa, pulling my feet up under me. "Your family went just a little bit overboard with the gifts."

"I told you they would." Steven reclined next to me, head in my lap. "They love you."

"That's nice." I rubbed his short, fuzzy hair.

"You're about to make me fall asleep."

"Don't even think about it." I pushed him up into a sitting position. "We have to figure out what we're going to do with all this."

"Do you just want to have a garage sale?"

"We can't do that. What if your Great Aunt Beatrice comes and sees the hand-monogrammed towels she gave us marked at a quarter for the set? It would hurt her feelings."

"You make a very convincing point." He lowered his head back down. "I think I would have a better idea of what to do after a nap. I'm exhausted."

"No! I can't function with things this messy. We have to figure this out right now."

"It's not messy. It's really just organized chaos."

"Chaos makes me nervous, Steven." I stood and looked at the pile. "This makes me crazy. You really don't want to see that."

"Okay, okay. But once we get this all taken care of, I am going to need a nap. And ice cream." He smiled at me. "Those are my conditions of surrender."

"You are such a little boy," I teased. "I accept your conditions."

Steven stood next to me and surveyed the towels and small appliances. He looked over the glasses and dishes and sheets and blankets. So many nice things, but far too much for us.

"Let's just give it all away," he said.

"Just like that?" I asked.

"Yup." He rolled up his sleeves. "We don't need all this. We don't even really want it. And we certainly don't have any room for it. Let's find someone who can put it to good use."

"Okay. Who should we give it to?"

"Well, that's the problem. I don't know."

"Why don't we ask someone at the church on the corner? That's a Baptist church, right? They might know someone who could use it."

The Baptist church was the place of worship for a hundred dark brown, smiling, well-dressed people. Loud singing and preaching and exclamations emanated from that building every Sunday from early morning to mid-afternoon. They served soup every day of the week to anyone who came through their doors hungry. They were sure to have an idea of who needed all our extra gifts.

"Well, look at Mrs. Genius." He put his arm around my waist. "I'll walk down there and see if the preacher's in the office."

"I'll go with you."

The pastor gave us the address of a brand new mission downtown that would use our donations. We returned to the apartment and packed the bed of Steven's truck.

"Can I ride along with you?" I asked.

"I'd rather you not. It looks like it's in a pretty rough part of town." He kissed me through the open truck window. "I would feel better if you just stayed right here."

"Really?"

"Yes. I just don't want to take the risk."

"But aren't you worried about going there by yourself?"

"Hon, I'm a Marine. I think I can take care of myself." He patted his seat. "And if anything gets a little scary I have Genie loaded and under the seat."

"I hate Genie." His gun made me nervous.

"Don't worry, Cora. You'll always be my favorite girl."

He put the truck in reverse and drove away. I imagined all the terrible things that could happen to him. My mind played through visions of muggings and robberies and violence. For the two hours he was gone, my mind spun a web of anxiety.

At last, I heard the rumble of his truck pulling into the apartment complex. I exhaled, my fear dissolving. I looked out the window. The truck bed was empty. He waved and smiled. "Greetings, Maiden Cora!" he called as he walked through the door. "It's ice cream and nap time! Well, not at the same time. That would be messy. I'll take the ice cream first."

"Wait. First you have to tell me about the place you took everything," I said, relieved and curious.

"It was a shelter." He sat on the couch. "And, for the record, I was right. It was a really bad part of town."

"And?" I asked, my hands, palm up, in front of my face.

"And they were really glad to have all the things. They're just starting out. And they've got nothing." He put his hands behind his head. "It was like Christmas for them. The lady that runs the place kept saying that over and over."

"Oh, good. I'm glad all that stuff can be used."

"You want to know the weirdest part?" He looked at me, a little puzzled. "The woman there was a dead ringer for you. I mean, I had to keep looking at her to make sure it wasn't you. I think she must have thought I was crazy or something."

"That's strange." I said, my mind starting to wonder. "What was her name?"

"Gosh, like I can ever remember names." He scratched his head. "I know your name. That's a pretty big accomplishment for me."

"Oh, you'll probably think of her name as soon as you fall asleep tonight."

"No, babe, you're the only woman I think of in my sleep." He winked at me.

"It's a good thing, too." I walked toward the kitchen. "I think you deserve two scoops of ice cream."

"Sounds great!" He looked at me. "You're beautiful. You know that, right?"

"I guess."

"You are."

"But I'm a mess. Look at this mop!" I felt the frizz of hair on my head.

"It doesn't matter." He stood and walked toward me. "You could be bald and wearing a garbage bag; you'd still be the most beautiful thing in the world to me."

He pulled me toward him, kissing my forehead.

"You're the only thing I need," I whispered.

"I know."

"I ain't writin' that stupid essay," Promise pouted. "I didn't come here to do no homework. I never wanted to be here in the first place."

She sat in a chair, her arms crossed over her chest. She and Nesto had lived with us for three weeks. She didn't want to do anything.

"Promise, you don't have to do any homework," Lola said calmly. "But your grade will reflect that. And your case worker might have something to say about a poor grade."

"Whatever, you know." Promise pulled her long blond hair into a ponytail. "I really don't give a—"

"Watch it, Promise," Mercy interrupted.

"I do ask, however, that you maintain the same level of respect that is expected of the other girls." Lola pushed her glasses up the bridge of her nose. "You are a smart girl."

"Yeah right." Promise pulled together her perfectly plucked eyebrows and pushed out her full lips. Her skin was flawless, her hair shiny, her body far too mature for her fifteen years. And she didn't have an ounce of baby weight on her. She looked like she came straight from a modeling job. "You don't know nothin' 'bout me."

"I know more about you than you realize. Now, please sit quietly so I'm able to complete the lesson for the others."

"You think you can tell me what to do?" She stood. "I don't know who you think you are. Just 'cause you took me in don't give you the right to boss me around. I'm outta here. Ain't nobody gonna tell me what to do no more."

She stormed out of the room, leaving Nesto asleep in his swing.

"Oh, fiddle faddle," Faith murmured. "Go on, Lola."

"Thank you, Faith." Lola passed around a stack of papers. "Take one and pass it on."

"What's this?" Mercy asked.

"Your assignment. I want each of you to write a memory. Perhaps you will write about an embarrassing moment or a painful time in your life. Others of you might choose to write your earliest recollection. You may write anything you choose."

"Anything?" Grace called out. "You might not want to open that can of beans."

"Worms," I corrected her. "Can of worms."

"That's stupid. Why would there be worms in a can? That's just gross."

"Ladies, I'd like you to disperse to write." Lola made her way out of the room. "And no talking."

We all took our papers and pens and moved into different corners of the house. I sat at the table in the kitchen and stared at the paper. I couldn't think of a memory I wanted to write down.

"How's the writing coming?" Lola asked, walking into the kitchen. "I figured you would enjoy this assignment. You are a gifted writer."

"Right," I answered.

"Are you having difficulty?"

"Yes," I answered. "Remember, no talking."

"You are correct. My apologies." She started chopping vegetables. "I hope this racket doesn't bother you."

"No. It's fine."

"Oh!"

"What?" I jumped up, hitting my head on the light over the table. She spun around. "I almost forgot. I set up a college visit for you."

"You what?" I rubbed my head as I sat back down. "I thought you cut your finger off."

"There's a college in Lansing."

"Right, I remember."

"Well, next week is a campus visiting day. We're going together."

"Great." I didn't cover the sarcasm in my voice.

"They called a few days ago. They would like to give you a very generous scholarship."

"Is it a pity scholarship?"

"Actually, no. It's for your academics. They know nothing about your past."

"Oh." I scribbled on my paper.

"We have a meeting with the dean of students."

"Do I have to tell him about my life?"

"Not unless you wish to." She continued chopping. "And, incidentally, the dean is a she."

"Fine."

"Good. I'm glad you see it my way."

"Listen, Lola. The only reason I'm going on this visit is because I know you wouldn't leave me alone otherwise."

"Oh, and I've been praying about this for you."

"That, too. But it doesn't mean I have to go to school there. Besides, I have a lot of time before I have to make a decision. I've still got a whole year of high school to make up."

"Whatever you say." She used the broadside of a knife to pound a clove of garlic. "But you can't make me stop praying."

"I know that. Nobody can. Now, may I please get started on my writing assignment? I wouldn't want my teacher to get upset."

"Please do." She smiled at me.

She hummed, off key, as she cooked. I couldn't place the melody, but assumed it was some old hymn. What she lacked in talent, however, she made up for in enthusiasm. As she stirred the soup in her stock pot, she swayed her hips, pumping one hand in the air above her head.

Listening to her, smelling the simmering soup, touching the rough table, I allowed my brain to travel back to a memory. From my familiar, comfortable place, I moved my pen across the paper.

When I pushed aside all that clouded my mind, I could see the beauty of my childhood. I strained my memory to see the earliest moment I could find.

My brother Pete was two years older than me. I invaded his world, but he never complained. He was more than happy to share his family, his toys, and his bedroom with me.

Before we moved into the yellow house, we lived in a small apartment. Pete and I shared the only bedroom. Our parents unfolded the couch into a bed each evening.

I must have been three years old. I woke up in the middle of the night and feared the darkness of the room. I'd had a nightmare that I couldn't put into words. Frightening images flashed through my sleeping brain. I cried out.

"Dot?" Pete's small voice called from his bed.

"Petey! I had a bad dream!"

"It's okay, Dot. What happened?"

"I don't know. I'm scared."

"Do you need a hug?"

"Yes," I cried so quietly.

Pete left the warmth and comfort of his big-boy bed and climbed into my toddler-sized cot. He wrapped his arms around my neck and snuggled his head close to mine.

"Jesus is with you, Dot. He's going to make it all better. Don't be scared. Jesus loves you," he whispered into the dark. "No matter what happens Jesus will never let go of you."

He sang Sunday school songs to me until I fell asleep.

The comfort of my big brother, his soothing words, his gentle hug. All things that I missed after he was gone. Things that wove a memory of peace that couldn't be undone. Not by anything.

The schedule of the institution rarely differed from one day to the next. Each week we were fed the same menu. Each day we woke and ate and slept at the same times. It wasn't unusual for me to forget what month or year it was.

On occasion, I looked out the window, shocked that life outside seemed to be constantly changing. The shifting seasons scandalized me. The audacity of God to progress with time while I sat to gather dust.

One day I peered out the window in the dayroom. I'd gotten good at looking through the grid built into the glass. I focused my eyes on the vibrant hue of the crimson maple below. A familiar form walked toward the entrance below the window. Lisa used her key, opened the heavy door and disappeared from my view. I knew she worked in an office somewhere in the building. Still, I hoped that she stopped upstairs to see me.

"What day is it?" I asked one of the nurses as she walked past me.

"Monday," she answered.

I tried to mask my disappointment. That day I needed a friend.

A minute later Lisa walked into the dayroom and sat next to me on the couch.

"It isn't Thursday," I said to her.

"I know. I hope you don't mind me coming up for a few minutes," she said. "I just felt like popping in to see how you were doing today."

"I don't mind at all. It's nice to see you." I pulled my bathrobe tighter around my neck.

"Gosh, it sure is getting cold out there," she said, blowing on her chilled hands. "And so gloomy."

"That's Michigan for you," I said. "It always comes as a surprise, though."

"I know. I never look forward to it." She clapped her hands and rubbed them together quickly. "I dread the cold setting into my bones."

"You are far too young to be talking about cold in your bones."

"I'm not as young as you think." She smiled at me. "I bet this weather is hard on you. You're from the South, right?"

"Excuse me?"

"Your accent. It's Southern, right?"

Even my husband had never picked up on the accent that I worked so hard to cover. I didn't want Lisa to ask any more questions. Too much of my past was tied up and stuffed in the back of my mind, covered over with layers of deception. I tried to think of a diversion.

"Do you mind if I ask you a question?" I asked.

"I don't mind at all."

"Has anything bad ever happened to you?"

"Sure," she answered. "Bad things happen to everybody. I don't know of anyone who hasn't had some kind of hardship in their lives. It's all part of living on this broken earth."

"What happened?" As soon as the words left my mouth, I regretted them. "I'm sorry. You don't have to tell me. I just assumed too much."

"Don't be sorry, Cora. That's a fair question. Friends open up to each other, right?"

Friends. The word warmed my heart. "I think so."

"Well, the year before I graduated from seminary my husband and I had a baby boy. He was born with some problems. He died when he was just three months old. He never got to come home with us." She cleared her throat. "The stress turned out to be too much for our marriage. My husband left me shortly after the funeral."

My heart ached for Lisa. "I'm so sorry."

"I am too."

"How did you survive it?"

"All I had was my faith. As shaky as that faith was at times. I just refused to give up on God because I knew He wasn't going to leave me."

"But didn't it feel like He gave up on you?"

"What do you mean?"

"He let your baby die. And He let your husband leave."

"Well, those are good points. But I think God's heart broke when Luke died. You know, I felt peace knowing that God held my baby. That was one thing I never doubted." She wiped a tear. "I still have a hard time making sense of why Luke couldn't have lived longer or why he wasn't born healthy. The hope that has kept me sane is that one day I'll get to see him again."

"What about your husband?"

"Well, I know God had nothing to do with Matt leaving me. Matt made that decision on his own."

"But isn't God in charge of everything and everyone?"

"Yes."

"Then why didn't He force your husband to stay?"

She inhaled, her eyes narrowed in thought. "Because God gave us all free will. He could force us to do things, but He doesn't. It's important that we make the right decisions on our own."

"But if He really cared for us at all, then why wouldn't He protect us?"

"Oh, He does protect us. From much more than we will ever realize."

I paused, thinking about what she'd said.

"Do you pray a lot, Lisa?" I asked.

"Yes. Not as often as I should. But I spend time praying every day." She pushed a stray curl out of her face.

"Does it ever feel like He's not listening?"

"Sometimes. And that can be pretty frustrating."

"Why does He ignore us?"

"He's not ignoring us. Sometimes, though, I think He's waiting for the perfect time to show us what He's going to do." She smiled. "And sometimes what He has planned is completely different from what we ask or expect."

"What if He decides not to reveal Himself?"

"I don't know that He would do that." She looked into my eyes. "Someday He will show you the ways He's making all this work for your good."

"Has your son's death ever made sense? Or your divorce?"

"Little by little. But you have to trust Him first, you know. If you don't, then you'll have an awfully hard time seeing His work."

"I still believe in Him, I suppose." I could hear the tone of my voice flatten. I looked at the floor. "Sometimes I feel like I can almost see Him. I nearly feel Him. But He's so far from me. And if I even tried to reach out to Him I would tumble down the space between us. The risk of belief seems much greater than my need for Him."

Her eyes moistened. She, a woman who overcame deep sadness and now basked in the warmth of God's love; I, a woman shivering in the cold of His indifference. Her concern brought a sob to my throat, choking me.

I cried because of the darkness and the loneliness and the void in my life. Lisa rubbed my back, causing more tears to flow in a river down my face.

"'Save me, O God,'" she said into my ear. "'For the waters have come up to my neck. I sink in the miry depths, where there is no foothold. I have come into the deep waters; the floods engulf me. I am worn out from calling for help. My throat is parched. My eyes fail, looking for my God.'"

Psalm 69. The Psalm my mother read over and over. So many times and with so many tears. She never found Him. He never came to rescue her from drowning. Or, if He did, she didn't reach out to take His hand.

The words of David brought a flood of memory. Visions of people in my life. Some of them people who loved me, others who hurt me.

Graves, cribs, homes, shacks.

Images of life went spinning and tumbling and turning. My body went numb. I felt like I was falling, out of control.

Later that night I woke on the couch in the dayroom, covered by a thin, hospital-issue cotton blanket. The lights were still buzzing overhead.

Lisa sat, sleeping in a chair at my side.

For the first time in years, I knew I was loved.

The day was unusually warm for fall. I decided to nap in the hammock on the porch of Lola's House. It turned out to be a short nap. After only twenty minutes I woke with a start. Yelling from the street jolted me awake.

"Hey! Get back here! You hear me? Come back here right now." A deep voice boomed up the street. "Did I tell you to walk away from me?"

I lifted my head. Promise walked quickly toward the house, pushing Nesto in his stroller. Fear, anger, hate, and shame blended on her face. The man following her jutted his face forward, his eyes squinted. He had his shoulders pulled back, his chest puffed out.

"Must'a forgot who your daddy is." The man spat at her. She kept walking, not wiping the spit off. "I told you from the start, if you tried to leave me I was comin' to find ya. Well, here I am. And you're comin' with me now!"

"I ain't," she said, continuing in the direction of Lola's House.

"What you say? You say you ain't? Who says you got a choice?" He laughed. "I don't know why I want you back for. You ain't good for nothin' but trouble. But somethin' about you drives them guys crazy. They been askin' for ya."

"Lola!" I called, struggling to get out of the hammock. "We got trouble!"

Bare feet slapped against the hardwood floors. The screen door swung open.

"What that tat on your arm say? Huh?" He reached forward, grabbing Promise's shoulder and spinning her around. The stroller nearly tipped over. "Jenny, I'm talkin' to you! What that say on your arm?"

He took her arm and pushed up her sleeve. He beat his chest with one fist.

"It say you belong to me. You're my property. That mean you gotta do what I say and go where I tell you."

"Oh, Jesus," Lola whispered, slipping on the shoes I'd kicked off before my nap. "Jesus, give me strength. Holy Spirit, give me Your words."

"Jenny, what you think you is now? Huh? You think just 'cause you had a baby that you somethin'?" He flung his arms into the air. "What you gonna do? Who gonna hire you? You gonna put whore and stripper on your application? You used up piece of—"

"Excuse me, young man," Lola interrupted him. "I would like to have a word with you."

Promise's face became even more terrified. "Best leave this one alone, Lola. I can take care of this by myself."

"That's right, Lola." The man put his arm around Promise's waist. She tried to pull away, but his fingers dug into her side. "This is my girl. You ain't got no right to keep her from me here in this house. She's my belonging."

"This young lady belongs to no one but Jesus." Lola's words were strong and confident. She walked down the porch steps slowly and with purpose. "Now, very kindly, be a gentleman if you are able, and take your hand off her."

He held her tighter.

"I see." She walked forward. "You wish to negotiate?"

"What do you care about her?" he asked Lola. "You know what she done? You know she been dancing naked for me? She been lettin' them do all that nasty stuff with her?"

"Yes. I know that."

"Then you know she ain't worth nothin'. She's dirty."

"No more dirty than you or I."

He spat on the ground. "You can believe whatever you want about Jenny. But she ain't comin' back into that house today or ever. Just toss her stuff out the window and we'll get outta here."

"Interesting. You know, sir, I don't believe that she wants to go with you."

"It ain't up to her."

"Actually, yes, it is up to her." Lola turned to Promise, her voice reassuring. "Dear, I would like for you to go inside. Nesto needs his bottle."

Promise moved slowly from the man's grip. He lunged, taking hold of the stroller. Nesto cried.

"Jenny, you wouldn't leave this little baby boy with a man like me. You know what I'd do to him, don't ya?"

Grace and Mercy rushed past me. Grace carried a baseball bat. Mercy had a broom stick.

"That's for the building fund." Grace handed me a twenty dollar bill. Her face set with resolve. "I'll pay the extra later."

A string of colorful words flowed from her mouth, far more than the twenty dollars' worth. She cocked the bat behind her head, ready to attack. Mercy held the broom stick like a sword.

"Ladies," Lola said gently, but firmly. "Please put your weapons down. We don't need either of you spending the night in jail again. I would hate to see this young man end up like the others."

"What you girls gonna do? You really think you scare me?" He looked them up and down. "Or do you want me to find you work too? I can tell you both had plenty experience."

"Just let me take him out, Lola. Jail don't bother me none." Grace tightened her grip on the baseball bat.

"Probably just a no count, small time pimp wanna-be," Mercy said. "Right? Working for somebody else and peeing your pants over losing a girl."

"Listen, I ain't got no problem with y'all here. I just want Jenny to come back with me. I gots to get business goin'. I got bills. And Jenny's body sure brings in the cash."

"Oh!" Lola clapped her hands together. "Now I understand. This is about money. See, I misunderstood. I was under the impression that you wanted Promise back because you missed her, not because you missed the money she earned for you."

He pushed his lips together into a cocky smirk. "Do you even know how much guys would pay to see her? And that ain't nothin' like what they pay to get with her. It wasn't all bad for her, neither. She got half the cash." He spat again. "Then she went and got herself knocked up. You know, them johns would still pay a good price for her then, too."

"You sick pig!" Mercy yelled at him.

"Thank you, Mercy. But I really would rather you kept the commentary to yourself." Lola paused. She looked at the man. "I need to apologize. With all the excitement I have forgotten my manners completely. What's your name?"

Caught off guard, he stammered. "It's Taz. My name's Taz."

"I suppose I should have been more specific. What is your given name?"

"Um. Antonio. But my ma always called me Tony." His guard fell slightly.

"Well, Antonio, that is a fine name. Much better than Taz." She walked closer to him and extended her hand. "I'm Lola."

As she shook his hand with her right, her left hand pushed Nesto's stroller toward Grace and Mercy. The two quickly wheeled him up to the house. Antonio didn't notice. He seemed to be under some kind of trance.

"Promise, dear, I would like for you to go feed Nesto now. He must be very hungry. I have a few things to discuss with Antonio."

"No," Promise mumbled stubbornly. "You don't know how dangerous he is."

"Don't worry about me, sweet soul. Your concern is very kind. But you really need to let me take care of this. I have had these discussions before. Do you understand? I may not know Antonio yet, but I have known many others like him. I assure you that there is nothing new under the sun." Lola smiled tenderly at Promise. "Do you trust me?"

Promise nodded her head.

"Besides, we are being watched." Lola pointed to all the houses around her. "Do you see them?"

Promise and Antonio looked where she pointed. In the doorways and windows our neighbors stood watch.

"Every one of them is waiting for me to cry out for their help. And I can tell you that they are all well armed. But I would rather not get them involved."

Antonio's face turned from confident to nervous. He released his firm grip on Promise, and she ran to the house.

"Come, Antonio, let's sit ourselves down on that bench under the tree. I'll have one of my friends get us a cup of coffee. Do you like coffee?"

"Yeah, sure," he said, walking with Lola to the bench.

"Do you take cream and sugar?" I asked from the porch. I tried to see him as Jesus. Or at least to heap burning coals on his head.

"Yup. Both. Lots." He looked at me, confused. "Please."

"Okay." I retreated to the house.

I walked past Promise on my way to the kitchen. She sat on the steps feeding the baby. Her tears splattered on his T-shirt. The other girls were huddled near the window, silently watching Lola.

Trying to control my shaking, I poured coffee into two mugs. Shallow, wheezy breaths caused my head to spin.

"Don't be anxious," I whispered to myself.

Walking back out to the bench, I forced steady streams of air deeper into my lungs. Intentional steps delivered me to Lola's side.

"Oh, thank you," Lola said, not looking at me as I handed her the mugs. "Next, would you please get the building fund jar? I believe a few contributions were made to it this afternoon."

"She only put twenty dollars in. She'll have to pay back the rest next week," I said, my voice trembling.

"Right. Well, can you please get it just the same? Also my purse."

Fear attacked my vision as I returned to the house, making each barefoot step blurry. I gripped the railing as I climbed the stairs to Lola's room. Inside her room, the jar sat on her dresser. Her purse hung in the small closet. I grabbed them both.

Walking back down the steps, I blinked my eyes hard, trying to clear up the frazzled feeling of terror that spread through my whole body. I feared for Lola. That the man next to her hid a knife or gun in his pocket. That by the time the neighbors came to help, it would be too late. I rushed down the remaining steps and out to the bench.

I placed the purse and jar in Lola's lap.

"Now, Antonio, you said that Promise had great earning power. How much would it cost for you to leave her alone?"

"I don't know," he answered.

"How is it that you don't know? You seemed quite certain only a few moments ago."

"I said I don't know," this time with more force.

"Okay. How about a ballpark figure. One hundred? Two hundred?"

He eyed the jar. Then he looked at the house.

"You see," Lola spoke quietly. "Promise deserves to be free. She doesn't need you coming around here making trouble for her and Nesto. She is a new mother and she is trying to start her life over. She needs peace and calm."

"I understand that. But you don't have any idea what she brought in every night for me."

"Then just tell me what it is you want and I will pay your price."

"One thousand," he said quickly. "And I ain't gonna get talked down just 'cause you got your thugs out there with me in their sights."

"Well, then. One thousand it is."

My panic deepened, thudding in my gut. There was no way we had one thousand dollars. Not even close. We'd just used most of the building fund to put toward a new water heater.

Lola started counting the money. She pulled out dollar by dollar. It looked like for every bill she removed another took its place.

"Well, how about that. Nine-hundred and forty-two bucks," she said, beaming.

"That ain't enough," Antonio said.

"No, Antonio, it isn't. Please be patient. Let me see what I have in my purse."

Lola took all the money out of her wallet, even emptying her change purse. Fifty-eight dollars.

"That's one thousand dollars exactly." She shoved all the money into the jar. "And you may keep that container as well. I doubt all those bills would fit into your pockets."

"Oh." Antonio took the jar and looked around again.

"Antonio, I have to tell you something. That money means that you may never, ever talk to our Promise again."

"Yes, ma'am."

"And you can never come to this neighborhood again. All of my friends out there will remember you and they will take your life if they see you here. You are aware of that, right?"

"I think so."

"And I really want you to live a full life. I would love to know that you have done wonderful things in this world."

I heard him sniffle. He turned his head from Lola.

"You were not born to pimp or hustle or exploit women, children, or anyone else. You were created to do something beautiful for Jesus. And you need to let Him do that with your life. If you let Him, He'll help you figure out what that something beautiful is." She put her hand on the nape of his neck. "You need to go see my friend at the mission on Division Avenue. You know that one with the cross?"

"Yes, ma'am."

"Good. Go there right away. Ask for Russ. Tell him that Lola sent you. I trust you will go." She patted his back.

"You know that baby in there? Jenny's baby?" His voice trembled.

"Yes. Nesto."

"I think he's my kid."

"You think so?" She spoke to him with much love in her voice. "And this was the first time you've seen him?"

"Yeah." He wiped his eyes. "I don't know why I'm tellin' you all this."

"It's okay. You can trust me." She took her hand off his back. "How does it feel to be a father?"

"I don't know. A man like me shouldn't have nothin' to do with a baby. I ain't fit to be a daddy. Well, you know, that kind of daddy. I'd just turn out to be like my father was."

"What was your father like?"

"He was a pimp. He let his friends hurt me. You know, touch me and stuff." He pounded his leg with his fist. "I don't want that kind of thing to happen to Nesto."

"I'm very sorry that happened to you, Antonio."

"Yeah. And my ma was a hooker too. I guess it was just the family business."

"I'm glad you want more for your son."

"Yeah."

"That's a very unselfish thing for you to desire. I'm proud of you."

"I ain't worth that."

"You are."

"I don't know how to clean up my life, Lola." He looked at her, his eyes red. "I don't know how to fix what I've messed up."

"Talk to Russ at the mission. He'll be able to help you. And I will pray for you every day for the rest of my life."

"Thank you."

"There will be days when you will be less than thankful for my prayers. God is going to work amazing things in your life. But they won't be easy changes for you. Just don't resist Him. He can be quite persistent." She stood, taking Antonio's hand and pulling him up. "Let me walk you to the end of the street. I'll make sure nothing happens to you."

"You could have called the cops on me." Antonio cradled the jar. "You're too nice."

"Oh, I'm not all that nice. Believe me."

"But you were nice to me. And you didn't have to be."

"Antonio, I see Jesus in your eyes. And the Jesus inside me helps me to be nice. See, we aren't too different, you and me. We both need Jesus to work in our lives. The only difference is that you still need to learn that He is what is best for you."

"Nah. I'm too bad. Jesus don't want me."

"Oh, son, He does. He desperately does." She smiled at him. "Now, you use that money for good. No drugs, no women. You understand?"

"Yes, ma'am."

They walked to the corner, hand in hand. She let their arms swing in rhythm with their steps.

I wished that she was my mom. Then I instantly felt horrible for that thought. But there were moments, many of them, when I would look at Lola and see glimpses of my mom from before everything went wrong.

Lola walked alone back to the porch. Only when her feet were back on our steps did we allow ourselves to sigh in relief. Exhausted, she smiled and went straight to Promise, hugging her.

"I'm fine," Promise said, releasing herself from Lola's arms. "I could' a took care of it myself."

Lola looked at her and smiled. "Well, I'm glad we won't have to find out."

"I swear I ain't never seen nobody talk to Taz like that. You're either stupid or ballsy."

"Hey, Promise. Why don't ya try a little appreciation. Lola just saved your butt," Peace said. "Say 'thank you.' Ain't so hard."

"Whatever." Promise handed Nesto off to Grace. "I'm tired."

She walked up the steps. I watched her, fists clenched, my fingernails digging into the palm of my hands.

"Let's go make dinner." Lola turned toward the kitchen, seeming not to notice Promise's attitude. "I'll teach you all how to make pot pie."

Somehow, the tension broke as we cut up vegetables and rolled the dough. Lola pushed the tray of pot pies into the oven.

"Man, Grace," Mercy said, wiping the counter. "We totally had that punk. Lola, you should'a let us take him down."

"Heck, yeah!" Grace laughed, still holding the baby.

"I, on the other hand, am perfectly pleased with the way God handled the situation." Lola set the timer.

"Yeah, He used Grace's filthy mouth to save Promise," Faith said. "I guess He can use just about anything."

"Naw, I ain't never said that many cuss words in all my life." Grace laughed. "Well, that might not be totally true."

"Don't forget, my dear, you still owe about fifteen dollars." Lola smiled. "And thank you for your contributions to the building."

"There ain't a jar no more," Grace said.

"Ah, very true." Lola opened the pantry and pulled out another large canning jar. "However, I believe this will do well enough."

Together, we set the table before eating our dinner. Then cleared and cleaned the dishes. Like a family. Eventually, we all split up to go about our evening.

Lola sat at the kitchen table with her Bible and a notebook. I poured two cups of coffee. Put one in front of her before I sat in my chair.

"Thank you, Dorothea." She sipped. "The perfect cup of coffee."

"What a day, huh?"

"Indeed. On days like these I am ever grateful for the protection of the Lord." Lola flipped a page in her Bible. "And He has never failed to provide for our needs. I feel like it's Thanksgiving in my heart."

"How did all that money get in the jar?" I asked. "I know it wasn't Grace."

"The only way it could have gotten there was by God's provision. I was praying that He would give us enough to satisfy Antonio so he would leave Promise and Nesto alone."

"Oh, I don't know, Lola. That kind of stuff doesn't really happen, does it?"

"Well, it isn't unprecedented. After all, He did feed five thousand people on two separate occasions. I would think that a few hundred dollars is a much easier feat to arrange."

"And you really think that He wanted to do that for us?"

"I do. He saw that we had a need and that we were willing to share. So, He made it happen, right here."

"Is paying off a pimp the same as being willing to share?"

"Oh, I think we'll see something come from this. I have a feeling that Antonio is going to undergo some pretty significant growth tonight. You'll see." She finished off her coffee and got up for more. "You'll see, Dorothea."

The next morning Peace found the jar in the mailbox. All the money still inside it. A small piece of paper was folded up among the bills.

"For Nesto. Tell Jenny I'm sorry."

Lola didn't come out of her room until ten a.m. Very late for her. She'd been up all night. I knew she spent all that time on her knees for Antonio.

The returned money didn't surprise her at all. She simply took the jar to the bank and opened a college fund in Nesto's name.

An orderly guided me down the hallway toward an open door. He led me with a hand on my elbow past the dayroom, the nurses' station, the shower room.

Dr. Emmert peeked out the door, waiting for me. He smiled warmly and with his eyes. I looked away instantly. I most certainly didn't want to be smiled at. Not on that day.

It had been nine years to the day that I watched Steven board a plane. The last time I saw him. I would have rather spent the day in my room under heavy medication. However, I had little choice in the matter. The meetings with Dr. Emmert were required.

"Cora! How are you today?"

"Fine," I mumbled.

"Would you please come in? Have a seat." The psychologist welcomed me into the small room and directed me to a chair.

"You all set, doc?" the orderly asked.

"Sure am, Ryan. You may come back for Mrs. Schmidt in one hour."

"Yup." With a grunt, Ryan strutted away.

The doctor held my chart in his hand. He also held the power to recommend my release to family for at-home care.

I never wanted that. I would only be a burden to Dot. She needed to be busy with college and planning her future. She didn't need to be hindered by a mother who needed constant care and support. I'd already done enough to her. I couldn't stand the thought of her becoming the mother and I the child.

"Cora, you are looking well this morning."

"Thank you." I blushed. Compliments were rare in that ward.

"Are you ready for our little chat?"

"Yes." I appreciated how he called our sessions "little chats." Dignity was also hard to come by.

He lowered himself into a chair by the table and glanced casually at the open folder. It contained all the events, medications, episodes, and visitors I'd had in the last month. My file must have been the most uninteresting thing to read.

"I understand that you received some family photos." He looked up. "Lisa consulted me about that matter."

"I know," I answered. "She told me."

"How have you felt while looking at the pictures?"

"They make me miss my family." I tried to suppress the sob that threatened to break through. I cleared my throat. "They make me happy for the good times I had."

"That's healthy. If you didn't miss your family, it would be cause for concern." He closed the file and put it on the table. "How do you feel about discussing your childhood? Are you at all interested in that?"

"No. I'm not comfortable with that."

"What if I asked you to speak with someone else about it?"

"Who would you want me to tell?"

"Lisa." He glanced at me over his glasses. "You seem to be comfortable with her. If I'm correct, I would say that you actually trust her. And she says the nicest things about you. She told me that the two of you are becoming good friends."

"She did?"

"Of course." He smiled. "How does that make you feel?"

"Very nice. Very, very nice." I folded my hands in my lap. "I don't think I have ever had a true friend. I mean, one who really cared about me without the chance of getting anything in return."

"Well, I think that's a good reason to trust her. Don't you?" He put his hands, palm up, in front of him. "Unless, of course, you would like to tell me about your story. However, I believe that it would be more beneficial for you to discuss it with Lisa. You need to open up to some-one in order to become well."

"I would rather tell her. But it has to be on my terms and at my pace."

"I think that's fair." He opened my chart, made a note. "What would you like to talk with me about today?"

I liked having the little taste of control. I didn't have many oppor-tunities to make decisions.

"My hair," I said. "I'd like to talk about my hair."

"Okay. Let's talk about your hair."

"I need to dye my hair." I fingered the long, gray locks. "I looked in the mirror yesterday and nearly fell over. It's become so awful."

"What's so bad about it?"

"It's gray. Completely gray."

"And you think that's a bad thing?"

"Yes, I do."

"What do you think that the gray in your hair says about you?"

"It says that I'm old."

"I see." He allowed for a thoughtful pause. "And is being old bad?"

"Well, not for everyone. But it is bad for me."

"What about me?" He touched his pure white hair. "Clearly I'm old. Is that bad?"

"Absolutely not."

"So, it's only bad because it's you?"

"Yes. I guess so."

"Okay. I see. What do you think other people think when they look at you?"

"They think I'm a crazy old woman." I scratched the scalp beneath the offending hair. "And they think that's the reason I'm all alone."

"First off, Cora, you aren't crazy."

"But of course I am."

"You most certainly are not."

"But I'm here, aren't I?"

"You are. But don't you think I would know crazy when I saw it?"

"I don't know, I guess you would."

"You have difficulty with depression and anxiety." He caught my focus. "That doesn't make you crazy."

I looked away from him.

"Additionally, graying hair is a natural progression of life. Everyone eventually develops signs of aging." He smiled. "Wrinkles, creaky joints, liver spots. That's all just a part of what happens to our bodies."

I sighed. "I just don't think I look right."

"What else?"

"I look like someone who has lost everything." I paused, sighed. "I look like my mother."

"And you don't want to look like your mother?"

"No. That is the last thing I want. I'm already acting like her. I don't need to look like her, too."

"Interesting. Go on."

"I look like I've let myself go. And that, of course, is true."

"Okay." He tapped a pencil on his chin. "How do you think people viewed you before? When you felt that you looked more youthful?"

"Perfect." I swallowed hard. "They thought I was perfect. And I looked perfect."

"Like Mary Poppins."

I nodded, the corners of my mouth tempted to curve upward.

"How did it feel when people thought that of you?"

"It was a conflicted feeling. Half wonderful and half stressful."

"Meaning that you worked hard to keep up that impression?"

"Yes." My memory tried to sweep up under me. "I worked so hard. I would stay up all night to get everything done. And I worked all day to keep things perfect. It was extremely exhausting, but I couldn't ever let anyone see that. It really was a compulsion I'd been doing my whole life. I felt that if I let anything go it would have shown my weakness."

"It was important for you to seem perfect?"

"No. I wanted to be perfect."

"I see." He put the pencil on the table and cupped his chin with his hand. "Are you aware that it is impossible to be perfect?"

"Well, I don't know."

"You are far too hard on yourself, Cora" He crossed his arms. "I don't hold that standard for you. I doubt your husband did, either. And certainly your daughter would never expect perfection from you. Lisa seems to enjoy your company, gray hair and all."

He allowed for a pause.

"Cora, I'm not saying that you are not to color your hair. Many healthy women do so. I would actually like to see you do something that made you feel feminine. However, you need to understand this; you don't have to be perfect. You are loved regardless."

"But I feel this constant compulsion to make up for what I've done." A round tear rolled down my face and splashed on my lap.

"What do you feel that you should make up for?"

"For what I did to my father."

"What did you do?"

"I don't want to talk about it."

"Okay. Let's redirect this. When was the last time you felt that life was perfect?"

"The day before I knew that Steven would be deployed."

"I want you to think about that day. Think about the details of it. Perhaps make a list of what it was like to have the illusion of perfection and then see it fall apart." He closed my file. "We can talk about that next time we chat."

"You don't want me to discuss it right now?"

"No. I want you to really contemplate it before you put it into words. You need to build yourself up for that kind of revealing discussion." He put his hands on his knees. "Now, how are your medications working for you? Anything you would like to decrease?"

We talked about medication, art therapy, my visits with Lisa, my lack of appetite. But all during our conversation I thought about that day, the day that my perfect world dropped into a pile of rubble. Thousands of lives were destroyed that day.

And God sat back, a spectator to it all.

"Dorothea, we need to leave in fifteen minutes!" Lola called up the steps.

"All right!" I yelled. A little louder than I needed to. I blamed my nerves.

I'd tried on every outfit in my closet. Nothing looked right. I wanted to look cool and smart and casual all at the same time. But I couldn't seem to put anything together.

"Are you seriously thinking about going to this college?" Grace asked, sitting on my bed, thumbing through a course catalog. "All's they got is Bible classes."

"That isn't all they have, Grace." I pushed my head through the turtleneck of a sweater. "They have a lot of classes. I'm just checking it out today. It doesn't mean I'm going there."

"Well, I think you should."

"Really? Why?"

"Yeah. I mean, how many people get the chance to go to college for free?"

"Almost free. I have to figure out room and board." I slipped my feet into the ugly brown dress shoes I bought at the thrift store. "Man, all my shoes are ugly. Gosh!"

"Yeah, you need to let me do all your shopping." She laughed. "Just because something's three bucks at Goodwill doesn't mean you need to buy it. You have to try things on first."

"Shut up."

"But you really should go."

"To Goodwill? Grace, I don't have time! Lola's going to make me get in that hunk-of-junk van in the next seven minutes no matter what I have on! There's no time to go shopping!"

"Chill, Dorothea. Goodness. I mean you should go to that college." She got up. "I bet you ten bucks that you'll love it. You won't be able to wait for next year."

"We'll see." I turned to her, tugging at the black cardigan over my gray turtleneck. "How does this look?"

"Honestly?"

"Do you even know how to lie?"

"Not really. You look like a librarian. And not the cute kind of librarian. You look like the old, stinky kind." She scowled. "No more pleated pants, Dorothea."

"What the Howdy Doody am I supposed to wear?"

"Just wear that long, black skirt and my pink sweater." She tossed the catalog onto my bed. "I told you twenty outfits ago that you should wear that."

"Thanks." I changed into Grace's choice.

"So, are you going to go to that college or what?"

"Grace! I don't know! I'm not sure what I want to do!"

"Is it really about what you want to do, Dorothea?" Grace did her best Lola impersonation.

"Yeah. I guess Lola always does get her way."

"No." She began picking up the heap of clothes from the floor. "I'm pretty sure it should be more about what God wants you to do."

I hugged her.

"What's that for?" she asked.

"I don't know." I let her go. "Sorry."

"It's all right. But if you wear those shoes I am going to smack you," she said. "Wear mine. They're in the closet."

My time was up. I slipped on Grace's black shoes and carried my backpack down the steps where Lola waited for me.

"Oh, that's a nice outfit." She smiled. "Grace picked it out, right?"

"What, you don't think I'm capable of dressing myself?"

"Actually, no."

"Yeah, it was Grace."

"She has an eye for putting things together."

"Well, you should have seen the room. It looked like our closet threw up." I swung my backpack onto one shoulder. "But you'll be happy to know that she's up there hanging everything back up."

"Good for her." She zipped up her jacket. "Excited?"

"More like totally nervous."

Lola and I got into the old, rusted-out minivan that someone donated only a few weeks before. She had a gift for making things work until something else came along. She would use anything.

But the problem was that Lola never second-guessed a gift. No matter how broken down and nasty the gift might be. And that was my fear, getting into the old, rusty van. I had some serious doubts until she turned over the engine.

"Well, I guess that's a good sign." I laughed.

"Oh, this perverse generation! Always in need of a sign."

I rolled my eyes and shook my head at her paraphrase of Jesus. "Nice, Lola."

As we pulled away from the house, the van coughed up a huge, black cloud. I made sure to buckle my seat belt.

15

Back in my room, I let my memory slip back to nine years before. The images of that day haunted me. At first I wanted to fight off the memories. But after the persistent nag of recollection I gave in. I indulged in the remembrance of the day my perfection died.

I woke up that day as normal, after only a few hours of sleep. I made breakfast and fed the kids before sending them off to school. I filled a thermos with coffee for Steven and kissed him good-bye at the door. After they were all gone, I started on my household rituals. Everything started out typical. The sun shined brilliantly on that early fall morning.

I scoured the kitchen floor on my hands and knees. Dot called this "Cinderella mopping." Such a creative little one. To the average eye I scrubbed an already spotless floor. But I saw the streaks, the crumbs, the germs. I had to clean. I really didn't have another option. I glanced up at the tiny black-and-white television on the kitchen counter.

"What channel is this?" I wondered out loud. "Isn't it a little bit early for this kind of movie?"

Smoke billowed out of a sky-scraper. Suddenly the building's identical twin erupted in flame. I left my bucket of water and moved to the living room, turning on the bigger TV.

The reporter spoke about airplanes crashing into buildings. Fire and smoke and fear filled the sky. I couldn't understand much after that. But I knew that many, many people stayed, stuck in those buildings.

"Cora?" I heard Steven's voice as he came in from the garage. "Where are you?"

"I'm in the living room," I called back.

"I left work as soon as I heard. This is awful."

His face pale, Steven didn't hide his terror. I'd never seen fear on my husband's face before. He sat next to me, holding my hand.

The towers in New York City had the attention of the entire world. Then came reports that the Pentagon was hit, too. And one plane made a fiery crater in the countryside of Pennsylvania. All of these things at the same time. How could that have happened?

"Oh, Jesus, are You coming back now?" Steven whispered. "I can't see how this will end well."

One building crumbled, straight down, into the ground. I felt more than heard the scream that broke from my body. All of those people. And now they were gone. All of them. Just like that. I had watched them all die from my comfortable couch.

Then the next building fell the same way.

A numbing spread through my arms and legs. I'd been horrified just moments before. But then, as if a switch was flipped, I felt nothing. A few words broke through my tingling detachment. Terrorists. War. Iraq. Bin Laden.

War. Had I heard the word "war"?

"They won't send you," I said to Steven, trying to talk myself out of believing he would go. "They wouldn't do that, would they?"

"They might, honey." He turned off the television. "They probably will."

"But you're just about to be discharged."

"I know. It doesn't matter. The military can stop that."

"But I thought you'd be discharged and become a pastor. In a church. In a safe ministry."

"I know. But they aren't going to discharge me right now. They're going to need me."

"No. That's not fair," I said, desperate. "I need you. The kids need you, too."

"I know that, Cora."

"Could we get away? Move somewhere else? You wouldn't have to go if they couldn't find you."

"Babe, I can't do that." He took my hands in his. "I love you. And I love Pete and Dot. Part of my job as a husband and father is to make this world a better place. It's a hard thing. But I know it's what God has called me to do."

He started to pray. He prayed for our country, our leaders, our soldiers, the families that lost loved ones, the people stuck in the buildings. He prayed for our family. He asked that we would be able to forgive those who attacked us. He prayed for me.

And I felt nothing. I kept my eyes open, refusing to pray.

It seemed as if God was in His heaven and all was wrong with the world. And He didn't show any concern at all on that day.

After his prayer, Steven left to get the kids from school. I retreated to the kitchen to make cookies. I couldn't think of anything else to do. Pete and Dot needed something to comfort them. And I couldn't bear to just sit and wait for them to get home.

My large, glass measuring cup slipped out of my hands. It shattered on the floor. Picking up the shards, I pricked my finger, drawing a small bead of blood. The sharp pain broke through my numbness. An adrenaline rush hit my body. Some kind of strange relief overtook me. That familiar feeling. One I hadn't felt in years.

Something in my mind told me that it was a bad feeling, to cut myself. But another, much louder, much more demanding voice told me that I needed something to break through the zombie-like feeling I had. I took a sharp piece of the glass and cut my arm. Just a small slice, like a paper cut.

And God didn't stop me.

16

The sixty-mile drive to Lansing in the van terrified me. I didn't know that a moving object could shake that much without falling apart. And we didn't exactly make any friends going forty in a seventy miles-per-hour zone on the highway. Somehow, though, we made it to the college.

"Only half an hour late!" Lola said as she pulled the van into the parking lot. "It's a good thing we left so early."

"And only twenty-five near-death experiences." I rolled my eyes.

"Oh, who's counting?"

"Well, me for one."

Lola parked the van. When she turned off the ignition, the engine made a sinking, exhausted grunt. A puff of something came from the vents.

"I don't think that's very good, Lola," I said.

"Oh, don't be such a sour puss. It will be fine." She opened her door and hopped out. "Let's go."

"Hey there!" One of the college girls greeted us at the door. She wore her hair pulled back into a tight, peppy ponytail and a too-bright-pink T-shirt. The print on the material read, "Hi! I'm Shannon! I'm so glad you came!"

"Hello," Lola said, shaking Shannon's hand. "This is Dorothea Schmidt."

"Oh, my goodness! What a pretty name! I mean the Dorothea part. Not so much the Schmidt part. Not that it's an ugly last name or there's anything wrong with it. But it just isn't as pretty as Dorothea. You know?" The words came faster than I could follow. The corners of her mouth lifted so wide that I thought her smile would jump off her face and give me a hug. I found myself wishing for a paper towel to soak up all the extra enthusiasm that leaked out of her.

"Thanks," I whispered. "I think."

"And you." She turned to Lola. "Are you her mom?"

"Well, no. I just came along for the visit today," Lola answered, trying not to open the door for questions. Not because she would have been uncomfortable, but for my sake.

"Oh. Well, where are your parents, Dorothea? At work or something?"

The bad part of my heart wanted to tell her that my dad was dead and my mom lived in the nuthouse, if she needed to know so very badly. I blinked, several times, trying to think about what I should say. I attempted to see her as if she were Jesus. Even the bad part of my heart wouldn't let me talk to Jesus like that.

"Nope. I just came with my aunt today." I hadn't meant to lie. The words just came out of my mouth.

I looked at Lola. She tried to hold back a laugh.

"Aw, that is so sweet! Isn't it great to have an aunt who's so supportive?" Shannon cooed, I thought, near to tears. "Well, I really thought she was your mom. You two look so much alike."

Lola and I looked at each other again.

"I don't see it," I said.

"I guess I'd have to look at a picture of me when I was your age to compare." Lola smiled.

"Oh, my goodness! You guys are just too cute!" Shannon squealed.

The girl's sticky sweetness just about gagged me. I coughed a little instead.

"Okay, you two cuties! Let's get you registered for the visit and into a class before lunch starts."

As Lola and I walked to the tiny room that held the literature class, she put her arm around me.

"Way to go, Abraham." She chuckled.

"I know. I know. I'm sorry. It kind of just slipped out."

"Well, my dear, I would be mighty proud to have a niece like you." She removed her arm. "You know, you could pass as my niece. Had my sister ever given birth to a daughter, I am certain that she would have looked like you."

"I didn't know you have a sister."

"Oh, well, I guess I shall have to tell you about her sometime." She dramatically wiped her brow in mock relief. "But there is your class. I sure did dodge that discussion."

"Are you avoiding something?"

"Absolutely." She nudged me toward the classroom. "That is a talk for a different day. Enjoy your class. I want to hear all about it. But for now I will be in the pursuit of coffee."

I walked into the classroom, completely intimidated. Only one seat remained unoccupied, lucky for me, in the back of the room.

A few students turned in their chairs to introduce themselves, to welcome me. They told me about the class, the college. Asked me a few questions. Then the professor began class. He lectured on Richard III. I couldn't have been more impressed. I drank in every word. My expectations exceeded, an excitement covered my unease.

When I caught up with Lola for lunch I hugged her.

"I gather your class went well," Lola said.

"It was awesome." What I wanted to tell her, what I couldn't figure out how to say was that college was a dream that I'd given up a couple years before. But sitting in that class, I knew it was possible.

One of the last pieces of hard shell around my heart cracked.

17

The afternoon lull allowed for me to sit in the quiet of my room. I flipped through the pictures Lisa had brought me. The emotion of memory exhausted me. Closing my eyes, I leaned my head against the wall.

Someone screamed from the hallway. Shrill and full of fear.

It was one of the nurses. "Somebody call nine-one-one! We need an ambulance!"

I stood and opened my door.

As I looked out, the afternoon nurse ran past me, crimson staining the bottoms of her white shoes and smudged on the hem of her yellow pants. She ran away from Stewart's room. A trail of red footprints followed her.

The few days before, Stewart had seemed almost happy. He interacted with the rest of us, laughing and telling stories. He talked about his family. He met with Lisa, asking her to pray with him. A smile plastered itself across his face and brightened the entire ward.

He had even made a telephone call to his family. The first contact he'd made to anyone in years. Then he bragged to us about how well his children were doing in school and in sports. I knew that Stewart had done something to himself. On that afternoon I realized that his cheerful disposition hadn't been a sign of his healing, but rather of resignation to ending his life. I understood how peaceful the thought of an end could be.

I stuck my head out the door of my room. I didn't see anyone in the hallway. A horrible and strangely familiar smell thickened the air. My heart thudded in my chest as I walked slowly down the hall. My pulse thumped in my ears. Stewart's door stayed wide open from when the nurse left him. After a deep breath, I walked in.

Blood pooled around him, his body half on his bed, half on the floor. Pinched between his finger and thumb, he held a small razor blade. The weapon he used against himself. Such a small thing caused so much life to flow from his body.

I stepped inside the room, the sock on my foot soaked up a bit of the cold blood. I crouched next to his face. His eyes were open, but dull. They looked like marbles, irises swirled with green and brown. Using my fingers, I pushed his lids closed.

His hand, the one still holding the razor, rested on his chest. How had he gotten it? Could he have taken it form the nurses' station? The art therapist's supply box? Did he pay an orderly for it? How long had it taken him to die? Had it hurt? Or did a strong enough determination rush through him to cover the pain of the slices?

I gently took the blade from his fingers and wiped it on his shirt. I pressed it lightly on my wrist. It had been so long since I'd been able to cut myself. From deep inside, a longing burned, moving rapidly through me. That well-known soothing feeling took over my body. Fear accompanied it, making the urge stronger. I pushed the edge harder. A strange sensation swept over me, a numbness coupled with longing.

"This is it, Jesus," I whispered in prayer. "This is Your last chance."

I moved the blade slowly and gently across my flesh. Just enough to form a scratch.

A dark and frightening voice inside me cried, "More! Deeper! Harder!"

The voice I'd heard the first time I cut myself so many years ago.

I pressed harder, drawing a thin ribbon of blood.

The voice called out louder for more pain, lusting for more blood.

I lifted the blade to find a better spot to cut. Ending my life seemed a comfort. I no longer controlled my hands and arms and brain. Automatic movement.

Suddenly, right before I lunged into my own flesh with the blade, a peace warmed me. It started from my heart and radiated to the rest of me. Not the false calm of moments before. Rather, true comfort and relief.

A hushed, gentle voice whispered. "Cora, I love you. Live for Me."

I'd never heard a more beautiful voice. The words hugged me. For the first time in my life, I experienced what seemed wholeness.

I wanted to live.

Closing my eyes, I stood, longing to maintain the comfort of being loved.

But blood soaked my bathrobe and pants and socks. The nurse would be back and I didn't want her to find me like that. I stepped over Stewart's leg to leave the room. The razor blade dropped to the floor with a sharp clink.

18

Our day on the college campus ended far too quickly. I attended a handful of classes, ate in the cafeteria, met students. For a few hours, I forgot about my past and felt comfortable and excited. I saw, right in front of me, a chance to move away from everything that dirtied my memory. I could step out of the ugly shoes of a girl who had suffered and become the girl with a promising future.

At the end of the day, Lola and I walked to the van together.

"I'm not excited about this ride home," I said, opening the rusted door.

"Oh, Dorothea, admit it, you like this van," Lola said, turning the key in the ignition. "Lord, start her up, please."

Nothing.

She worked the pedal, rubbed the dashboard, opened the hood.

Nothing. Nothing. Nothing.

"Okay, well," she mumbled. "Now what?"

The sky darkened. I had no idea what we were going to do. We wouldn't be able to stay at a hotel. We barely had enough money for the gas to get home. The thought of sleeping in the rust-trap of a van made me cringe.

"Lola, we have to get back home," I said. "What if something happens? Like, what if Antonio comes back?"

"Don't worry about that, Dorothea. I arranged for the pastor's wife to stay there as long as we're gone. Besides, I heard from my friend at the mission. Antonio has been meeting with him every day. He won't be bothering us. Isn't God amazing?"

"Right. Yeah." I just wanted to focus on getting home. "What exactly do you think we're going to do tonight? We can't sit here until this stupid van magically starts up."

"Are you nervous?"

"As a matter of fact, yes, I am."

"Well, don't be. Every situation is an opportunity to see the Spirit move in His ways. He can be a pretty adventurous God if we just watch out for what He's doing."

"Oh, boy, Lola. Please, don't do anything weird."

"Ha! Dorothea. It won't be me. It will be the Holy Spirit." Her eyes sparkled. "I actually have a feeling that there is a little excitement headed our way. Let's go find out what it is!"

She patted the van with the heel of her hand and headed back to the college building.

"Here we go," I muttered, preparing myself for the embarrassment that I knew would follow. I walked behind her, shuffling my feet.

Shannon stood near the entryway picking up brochures and business cards.

"Oh, hi!" she screeched. "Are you guys going to spend the night? There's an extra bed in my dorm room and I can always find a couch or something, too! It would be so much fun! We could watch movies and order pizza and just chat all night!"

"As fun as that sounds, I'm afraid that we won't be able to. But thank you for the very kind offer. Perhaps next time," Lola said. "It seems, however, that we are experiencing some vehicle problems. It is behaving very cantankerously."

Shannon squinted at Lola. "I'm sorry, but I have no idea what you mean."

"Our van won't start," I said.

"Oh!" she said, getting it. "Do you need someone to take a look at it for you?"

"That would be most helpful, if there is anyone who is able," Lola said.

"Oh, my goodness! There sure is!" She pulled a small cell phone out of her pocket. "We'll just call Paul. He's like some kind of car genius. For real."

She pushed a few buttons and then held the phone to her ear.

"Hey, it's Shannon!" She giggled. "Um, I have a few friends here who need some car help. Do you think you could come up to the administration building? Awesome. See you in a few."

She hung up the phone and smiled at us, even perkier than before.

"He's great," she said, red faced.

Lola touched Shannon's hand. "Thank you so much, dear."

"So, Dorothea, are you going to come here next year?"

She'd remembered my name. I felt badly for having disliked her earlier. "Well, probably not. I have another year of high school to finish up," I answered. "But there's a chance I could graduate earlier if I work really hard."

"There's no doubt that you could do just that," Lola moved a wisp of hair from my face. She smiled at Shannon. "Dorothea is especially bright."

"Cute, cute, cute!" Shannon hopped and clapped with each word. "That would be so awesome! I hope you can get it all done! I think you would really fit in here!"

For just a second, my chest tightened. The pressure of fitting in scared me. It meant covering up the bad things and pretending to be like everyone else. I'd never be like them, I would have to act for at least four years. I couldn't catch my breath.

Lola put her hand on my shoulder. "I think Dorothea will blossom here," she said. "God will use this place to make her grow."

At Lola's words, I relaxed. She had that way.

Shannon looked toward the door. The giant smile and bright red blush returned to her face. I turned my head to see what could have that effect on her. A guy walked toward us, carrying a toolbox. He was, of course, tall, dark, and handsome. I looked away from him. The last thing I needed was to develop a crush.

"What's going on, Shannon?"

Shannon went from bubbly to nothing less than volcanic at his arrival.

"Hey, Paul!" she squealed, leaping to give him a hug. "So, these guys came for the visit thing today."

She continued to tell the tragic tale of our minivan trouble in rapid-fire speech that left us all dizzy.

"Well, I'll take a look," he said, shifting his weight. "Where is it?"

We took him to the parking lot.

"Wow. What year is this?" he asked, putting the toolbox on the ground.

"I think it's about twenty-five years old," Lola answered.

"Okay, it's a little older than me."

"Don't make me feel like an old woman," Lola teased.

He smiled at her. Oh, boy, it was a nice smile. I tried not to stare.

He inspected the engine, tried the ignition, checked the fluid and on and on. As he looked, he pointed out several major issues. Lola nodded her head as if she understood. I knew there was no way she got it. She did understand, however, that each problem cost more and more money. Much more than the van was worth.

"Well, I don't know what I can do to fix all this tonight. It's getting a little late. I'll need to get some parts." He wiped his hands on a bandana from his pocket.

Lola pushed her glasses up her nose with one finger. "First, before you do anything to it, I need to know how much it will cost."

"I think I can do it for free," he said. "My roommate's dad owns a junk yard around here and I can always find extra parts there. I'll just take this on in my spare time. It's kind of a hobby of mine."

My cheeks burned with embarrassment. He'd known somehow that we were different. We didn't have money to have a nice car or even to fix our old one. Fear smacked me when I considered what he would tell his friends about us later.

"Can I give you ladies a ride somewhere?" He packed up his tools.

"We need to get to Grand Rapids," Lola said. "I know that God will provide a way."

"Where in Grand Rapids?"

"Just southwest of downtown."

"Well, we're practically neighbors. I grew up a few miles south of town."

"How about that?" Lola said, pleased. I could almost hear the gears turning in her head.

"You know, I have some stuff I could do at home tonight. I bet I could get a few things packed in about ten minutes. Do you mind getting a ride from a stranger?"

"Well, you're hardly a stranger, are you?" Lola put her hand on his shoulder. "If you're able to take us home we will gladly go with you."

"You could always, um, drop us off at the bus stop on Division and, uh, Forty-Fourth," I stammered. I didn't want him to see where we lived.

"This late? No way I'm letting two ladies ride the bus. It's not safe downtown this time of night. It's not a good idea."

He didn't know Lola and my history with those streets, the dark alleys. If he had known, then he might have been more afraid of us and less afraid for us. We'd met the danger in those nights. It hadn't killed us because God kept us safe.

"We will let Paul drop us off at home if that would make him feel more comfortable," Lola said.

Ten minutes later Paul opened the car doors to let us in.

"What a gentleman. Thank you." Lola sat in the front.

I rode in the back, trying to figure out how mortified I would be when he saw our neighborhood. If he thought the bus would be too dangerous, he would be shocked by our street.

My chance for a fresh start seemed to collapse. I imagined him telling his roommate all about our neighborhood, what kind of place I came from. I would have a reputation before I even enrolled. I'd never be able to cover it all up.

I lay on my bed, Stewart's blood still on my hands and clothes. No one had seen me go in or out of his room. What I'd seen had exhausted me. It seemed that choosing life drained my energy. So I just put my head on the pillow and rested. I dreamed without sleeping. The images that moved through my mind were vivid, color-soaked daydreams. Painful images. I remembered things, long ago tucked into the back of my memory.

My mother, lifeless and cold, in her bed.

Titus, face stained black from coal dust, his chest torn open by lead.

Marlowe, body bleeding, screaming for me to get away.

My father, rage contorting his face, hate seeping from his pores.

And then I saw Steven, knocking on my window in a rainstorm, offering to help me. He was the one person in the world who protected me. And yet his body, blown to pieces, spread among the desert sand, could no longer offer security. His dog tags were the only thing left of him.

Pete, his eyes were so green. I'd forgotten. They'd stayed closed for so long I couldn't remember the sparkle of them.

Dot's crying. She found me after I lost hold of myself. She screamed. So loud and so long. Terrified by me. Her own mother.

How had all of that happened in my life? I couldn't understand what I did to deserve such wrath from God. He punished and hurled pain at me, but never once grabbed hold of me to pull me back up. After His anger was spent, He left me with so little.

And yet He wanted me to live for Him. Hadn't He said that? But what did I have to offer Him with my life?

I had nothing left, save for Dot, the only one who survived being around me. But I didn't know where she lived. My only hope was for her safety. Her happiness.

My memory took me to her laugh, her smile. The way she danced around the house, swirling her skirt and singing songs about Jesus, warmed my heart. She mourned her father so deeply. And then she mourned her brother. Her eyes were so red, so sore from crying. I couldn't bring the laughing dancer back to my daughter's heart.

From my bed I prayed. A stumbling pleading to God. I couldn't think the words loud enough to reach His ears, so I mumbled them.

"I know You want me to live for You. I have no idea why You want me. But I feel like You do. I don't know how. I'm just too far gone to change my life now. But I beg You to take my daughter. Take care of her and keep her safe. Let her be loved. And let her forget about me. Give her someone who can become her family."

I gagged, grief forcing its way out. The tears felt good. Releasing the sorrow lightened my load, if only slightly.

I got out of bed, removed all the blood-stained clothes, and tried to rub the red off my hands and feet. I put on a long-sleeve shirt to hide the fresh cuts.

No longer did I doubt that I would survive. I'd made it to that point. Life would continue on, and I would ride the waves of the storm. Somehow I knew that God spoke to me in Stewart's room. I needed nothing else.

"I'm starving," Paul said, pulling out of the college parking lot. "Have you eaten dinner?"

"We have not," Lola answered.

"Do you like burgers? It's on my mom and dad," he said. "They won't mind."

"That would be lovely. Thank you," Lola said.

Paul took us to a drive-thru only a few miles from the campus. He ordered our food, passing a burger and fries back to me.

"What a Good Samaritan," Lola said, hungry and yet trying to eat like a lady.

"Oh, I don't know about that," he said. "I think a real Good Samaritan would have taken the two of you to a nice steak house or something."

"Well, I think this is very nice, indeed. Don't you, Dorothea?"

"Dorothea?" Paul asked, looking at me through the rearview mirror. "Gosh, I guess I was so busy with your van I forgot to ask your name. Sorry about that."

"No problem," I answered. "Thank you very much, by the way."

"You're welcome." He looked back and forth between my reflection and the road. "It's kind of funny. I used to know a Dorothea."

"Huh. I used to know a Paul." His attention caught me off guard. He looked at me in a different way. Not how I was used to men looking at me. He looked at me without lust, without expectation.

"Everybody knows at least one Paul. We seem to be everywhere." He turned his head and smiled at me.

For the rest of our trip, Lola and Paul carried on with different streams of conversations. I couldn't keep up with the pace of their discussion. Exhausted from the day, I snoozed for the second half of the drive.

I woke up when the car changed direction. Paul backed up into a driveway. Sitting up, groggy and disoriented, I looked out the window. We weren't at Lola's house, but the neighborhood looked strangely familiar.

"What are we doing here?" I asked, looking up and down the street.

"Paul needed to do a few things at his parent's house before dropping us off," Lola answered.

"It'll only take a minute," Paul said, putting the car into park. "But come on in and meet my parents. They'd kill me if I didn't introduce you."

We climbed out of our seats and into the brisk air. My heart fluttered and I gasped for breath. I looked across the street at my childhood home.

"Paul, what's your last name?" I asked him.

"West," he answered.

Paul West. Pete's best friend. Our neighbor. His family watched out for us through the really tough times. I dug my thumbnail into my arm, feeling the small sting of pain. I was awake.

"This way." He led us through the open garage door.

I followed, trying to keep myself together. Trying to calm my nerves and breathe through the panic. Part of me longed to be welcomed back into their family. Another hoped they wouldn't recognize me. I feared the questions they might ask.

"Mom, Dad! I have a couple people with me!" Paul's voice sounded through the house.

"Oh, good. Do they need food?" a woman's voice called from another room.

"Nope. You bought us burgers."

"That's nice of us. I'll be right there." After only a moment, Paul's mother entered the room.

Mrs. West. She looked almost exactly the same. The warm caramel tint of her hair, her welcoming smile, the brightness of her eyes, were all as I remembered.

"Oh," she gasped as she looked at Lola and me. "Paul, where did you find them?"

"They were visiting the college and had some car trouble. They live downtown. I'm giving them a ride home."

She walked closer to us. I was quivering.

"Norman!" she called, her voice full of urgency. "You need to come down here!"

"Mom, are you okay?" Paul asked.

She touched my face. "I just never thought I'd see the two of you again."

"You remember me?" I whispered, a tear dropped from my eye.

"How could I ever forget you, Dot?"

"Dot?" Paul said. "Oh my word! Dot!"

"You really remember me?"

Mrs. West turned to Lola.

"And you. All you've been through."

Lola looked confused. I must have, too. She looked at me, a little concerned.

"I'm sorry. I don't believe that I've had the pleasure of meeting you before." She smiled warmly. "But I have been told that I have a familiar face. Some kind of hippie meets grandmother."

"Are you sure you aren't Dot's mom?" Mrs. West looked at me. "Is she okay? I mean, after the breakdown?"

I nodded. "My mom's still in the institution."

"Oh, I see. You thought I was Dorothea's mother." Lola struggled to put us at ease. "I am not. I haven't been blessed with children of my own. But Dorothea has been like a daughter to me for the last five years."

As Lola spoke, something seized my nerves. I couldn't put my finger on it. Then my brain shut off. My body slumped to the floor. And darkness.

Lisa arrived at the same time as the ambulance after Stewart's body was discovered. One of the nurses must have called her right away. She rushed to the nurses' station. I heard her voice from my room.

"Who found him?" she asked.

"Naomi," an orderly answered. "She was just checking on him. Guess she had a funny feeling or something."

"How's she doing?"

"Not so good."

"Has anyone called Dr. Emmert?"

"Not yet. You were the first person we thought of."

"Okay. Could you please give him a call? I'll start checking in on the residents."

I walked into the dayroom as quietly as I could. Ashamed that I'd been in Stewart's room, I hid behind a large, plastic tree. Lisa sat with Wesley.

"I don't know why he would'a did that." Wesley wept.

"I don't understand it either, Wesley." Lisa cried right along with him.

"I'm just so sad, Pastor Lisa."

Lisa handed him a tissue and looked into his eyes. "I don't think I will ever know why someone would take his own life. It breaks my heart."

"Mine too." Wesley's body shook with sobs. "I just want Stewart to come back home."

"I know what you mean, Wes. I understand that." Lisa held Wesley's large, chocolate-colored hands in her small, cream-colored ones. "I do too. I'm going to miss him. And it's okay to feel that."

"My mama told me one time that anybody who kills theyselves goes straight to hell." He looked at her with childlike eyes. "Is that true?"

"I don't know." She sighed, putting a hand on his shoulder. "I believe that God can have mercy on anyone He wants."

"Do you really think so?" He smiled sweetly. "I really hope that's true. And Stewart wouldn't have to be so sad all the time. He had a sad life, didn't he?"

"Yes. He did."

"I'm so tired, Pastor Lisa. Crying makes me so sleepy." Wesley rubbed his eyes. "I think I need to rest for a little bit."

"I think that would do you a lot of good, wouldn't it?" She helped him to his feet. "I'm glad I got to talk with you today. You are a really wonderful person."

"Thank you. That's very kind of you." He walked with her to the hallway that led to his room. "Pray for me, would you? Sometimes I feel like I've got nothing going right for me. I don't want to give up like Stewart did."

"I know. I pray for you every day. I promise I'll keep that up."

"Thank you. You're a real nice lady."

The new orderly, a young man with tattoos on his forearms, walked over to Wesley. He reached up to put his skinny arm around the large man.

"Come on, bud. I'll help you get into your bed." The orderly's voice was gentle and kind.

Lisa went to Edith next, putting her hand on Edith's short hair, caressing it. She spoke soft words into Edith's ear. Then she kissed her on the cheek.

Lisa looked around the room. She spotted me behind the dusty plant. The look on her face spoke of her concern for me.

"Cora?" She walked toward me. "Do you feel like talking to me?"

"I suppose," I answered.

She pulled a chair around to my hiding place to sit with me. Her grief mingled with peace created a tangible shift in the air around me. She possessed such conflicting emotions. I feared that the two would react like magnets repelling one another. I couldn't understand how they coexisted in her soul. Lisa confused me.

"Are you doing okay?" she asked.

"No," I said, ashamed. "I went into Stewart's room. I closed his eyes."

"It was pretty gruesome, wasn't it?"

"Horrible." I held my eyes shut tight to hold back the image of the blood puddle around his body. "But his face was peaceful."

"You've seen a dead body before, right?"

"Yes." I opened my eyes. "That's why I'm here, isn't it?"

"Is it?" She pushed a stray hair behind her ear. "Cora, do you remember why you're here?"

"Yes. But, I don't want to talk about it today." Guilt swept through my body. "It's just too hard to think about right now."

"I'm sure it is."

She looked at me. She had bags under her eyes.

"Stewart had a razor blade." I pulled at my sleeve to cover my wrist. "He did?"

"How could he have gotten it?"

"I don't know. I'll make sure the nurses know about that."

"Do you think he felt a lot of pain?"

"I really have no idea."

"His face looked so peaceful." I realized that I repeated myself.

"I'm not sure how to feel about that. I don't know if that should make me feel better or worse." She tapped her fingertips against her knee. "I have to call his family after we're done talking."

"Have you ever made that kind of call before?"

"A few times. I always wish I could just go and actually spend time with the family, in person. They're in Texas." She looked at me. "I don't think I could get there, though. It isn't the kind of thing you want to find out over the phone. Especially the way he died."

"I understand."

We sat, quiet, for a moment.

"Wesley asked about suicide sending a person to hell."

"He did."

"What about other things?"

"I'm sorry, Cora, I don't think I understand what you mean."

"Well, you said that Jesus has grace, and that He understood Stewart." I looked at the floor. "If Jesus could have mercy for a man who killed himself, what about other sins?"

"I believe He is able to forgive any sin."

"But what about murder?"

"Yes, even murder." She looked at me, concerned. "Why do you ask?"

"Because of what I did. To him. To my father."

"What did you do to him?"

"Don't you know? I think it's in my case file." The words came from my mouth more rapidly than I'd anticipated. "I murdered my father. I killed him. Shot him with a handgun. He found my picture in the newspaper and tracked me down. I didn't want him to hurt us, so I murdered him."

"You shot him, right?"

"Yes."

"And he was threatening you."

"I don't know." Suddenly my memory was blocked. "I don't know. I can't remember what he said."

"Cora, you aren't a murderer."

"But I am. I know that I did it."

"You may have killed him, but it wasn't murder."

"How do you know?"

"Because, you're right, it's all written in your file."

"And what does it say?" I sat on the edge of my chair.

"That you were defending your kids."

"That's not right, is it?"

"And you shot him to keep him from hurting your daughter."

"I did?"

"Yes. He had a gun." Lisa's forehead wrinkled. "That was right before the accident."

"Yes. When Pete got hurt." Small pieces of recollection inched closer together in my mind.

"Right. And after a year of dealing with everything you had an emotional breakdown. And that's completely understandable. You lost so much." She touched my arm. "Do you remember now?"

"No," I sighed. "I don't know."

"You suffer from a panic disorder. The stress caused your mind to shut down. That's why you're here, Cora."

"But he's dead. Right? My father is dead?"

"Yes, he is."

"And I killed him."

"Yes. But not the way you remember it. It was completely unavoidable. It was either him or you and your kids. You did the best you could do."

"So, this isn't jail?" I licked my lips quickly. Suddenly I felt so dry. "I mean, a jail for crazy people?"

"No, Cora. This is the state hospital. You're here to get well so one day you can return to living your normal life."

"But I'm not getting better."

"Actually, you've improved quite a bit. It's happening just a little at a time, but you are getting better. Dr. Emmert told me that when you first came you slept all day. And at night you'd scream and tear your hair out. You were always scratching at your skin. The last few months you've made huge progress."

"I'm so confused right now."

"Sure. I understand. You've had a very draining day."

"I think I need to rest and think for a while."

"Are you going to be okay? Would you like the nurse to give you something to help you sleep?"

"Yes. I think that's a good idea."

She nodded.

"Come back tomorrow or the next day. I think I'm ready to tell you about a few things," I said, weary. Exhausted from fighting to keep my secrets. "And bring pictures of your little baby, if you have a few. I think I remember you said his name was Luke, right?"

"Yes." She smiled. "People never ask to see his pictures. I think they assume it would be too hard for me. Thank you for wanting to see them."

Lisa left after praying for me. A nurse came and gave me several pills to swallow before leading me to my room. I fell asleep on top of my blankets, trying to make sense of Lisa's words.

If I wasn't a murderer then what was I? I'd believed that I was for so long. I was almost certain that I had killed him in cold blood.

I woke up in the Wests' extra room. Walking to the window, I rubbed my head. It throbbed. I needed coffee.

Looking out the window, I viewed my old house. The flowerbeds in the front yard had been dug up. The yellow siding painted brown. I didn't even want to think about all the changes on the inside. Closing my eyes, I tried to imagine it the way things were when I was younger. Then another memory took over.

Pete and I decided to walk home from school. In the November afternoon air, our breath steamed in front of our mouths. The gray sky made for a gloomy and overcast day. So typical of late fall.

We turned the corner to our street. I ran my gloved fingers through the needles of the old pine tree that grew by the street sign. It was my very favorite part of the neighborhood. I knew exactly where to crawl between the boughs in order to find the hideout underneath the tree.

Paul sat on his front porch, waiting for Pete. Paul went to the Christian school and always got home before us.

"Hey, Pete!" he called, punching an old baseball into an even older mitt. "You wanna play catch?"

"Sure. But I gotta check on my mom first," Pete said. "I'll be out in a few minutes."

Dad had been gone for nearly a month. Mom wasn't dealing with it very well. She never let herself stop moving. Keeping busy helped her to stay sane.

"You think she made cookies?" Paul asked.

"Probably. All she does all day is cook and clean," Pete answered.

"Why does she do that?" I asked, tugging on Pete's sleeve.

"It keeps her mind off Dad being gone."

"Hey, Pete!" Paul called. "If she made too many cookies, bring some over. I'll eat them! I love cookies."

Just then a dark car pulled onto our street. The turn signal blinked slowly as it moved into our driveway.

"Who's that?" I asked.

"No," Pete said quietly, not hearing me.

The tone of his voice made my stomach hurt. I couldn't figure out why.

"Pete? What's going on?"

"No." Again.

My heart beat faster and faster. Everything I saw went slower and slower.

Two men in Marine dress uniforms stepped out of the car. One man, the younger one, turned to look at Pete and me. He tripped over a loose cobblestone in the driveway and righted himself. The older man quietly scolded him.

"Marines," Pete whispered. "Oh, please, no."

The two men stepped onto the porch. The older one knocked on the door.

My mom opened the front door, a beautiful smile on her face. She was so pretty. She'd lost weight since our dad left, her clothes hung off her. But she was still pretty. Her smile faded as she realized who stood at the front door.

"No," she said, her face pleaded with the men. Then she just kept screaming. "No, no, no."

The older man held her upright and helped her into the house.

I grabbed Pete's hand, not knowing what else to do.

"What's wrong?" I asked. "Why is she screaming?"

"It's Dad. Something happened to Dad," Pete answered. "I have to help Mom."

He ran toward the house, my hand still holding his. I fell to my knees before letting go. The sidewalk ripped through my tights and blood quickly soaked the thin cotton.

Pete made it to the younger man. He helped Pete sit on the porch. The man spoke a few words. My brother covered his face and his body shook. The man put his hand on Pete's back.

I got myself up off the ground. My scraped-up knees hurt. Running to the pine tree made the pain worse. I crawled into the canopy. The needles stuck to the blood on my legs. I didn't care. It didn't matter.

I sat under the cover of thick, green branches and hugged my arms around my shins. Eyes shut as tightly as I could, I scrunched my whole face and tried to ignore what I knew was happening. Something bad had happened to my dad. I couldn't understand what was going on. I only wanted to hide from the news, to block it out.

"She's in the tree. Dot went in there." I heard Paul's voice, weak and scared. "You have to crawl to get in."

The clip clop of footsteps on cement grew louder as the man got closer. A shuffle of branches and needles and dress uniform brought the young soldier into the tree.

"Do you mind if we talk for a minute?" he asked, his voice deep and comforting. "Is that okay?"

Without opening my eyes I said, "Okay."

"My name's Chuck."

"I'm Dot."

"I like that name."

"It's really Dorothea, but everybody just calls me Dot." I opened my eyes.

Chuck had smooth, brown skin. His shoulders were broad. He looked strong. His face seemed kind.

"Well, my real name is Charles."

"How did they get Chuck out of Charles?"

"Probably the same way they got Dot out of Dorothea." He smiled. "Just for fun, I guess."

"Probably." I scratched the back of my neck.

He coughed. Adjusted his jacket. I could tell that he was uncomfortable. The way he had to slump under the branches.

"Dot, do you know why I'm here?" he asked.

"Did my daddy get hurt?"

"Yes." He looked down. "He did."

"Then does he get to come home?" I asked.

He shook his head. "No. I'm afraid not."

"They can't make him stay there if he got hurt."

Chuck didn't look up at me.

"What happened?" I asked. "Did he die?"

"Yes. I'm so sorry, Dot."

A large part of my life ended. No more trips to the beach. No more building snowmen and forts in our front yard. No more hugs or smiles or kisses. I would never have my daddy again.

I cried. The pain didn't all come on right away. That kind of loss only comes on a little at a time.

Chuck reached into his pocket for a hanky. He very gently wiped tears off my face and pushed back the overgrown bangs from my forehead.

"I can't breathe," I gasped, trying to regain my breath.

"Just relax."

Deep breaths in and out. I tried to be strong. Tried to settle. Calm.

"I want him to be alive. Why can't he be alive?" I asked.

"I know. I miss him, too."

"Did you know my daddy?" I asked between gulps of air.

"I did. He was a very good man."

"Was he nice to you?"

"Always. I don't think I ever saw him being mean."

"Did he help you?"

He nodded.

"What did he do?"

"Well, I had a really hard time when I first joined the Marines. So I went to the chaplain's office for some advice. That's when I met your dad."

"And then what?"

"He told me about Jesus."

"Really?"

"Yes." He cleared his throat. "A lot of us became Christians because of your dad."

"That's really important, isn't it?"

"It sure is. The most important job there ever was. And your daddy was good at it." Chuck looked at the ground. "He was a good friend of mine."

"Me too."

I heard my mom's screams coming from inside our house. I wondered if Pete was okay. How hard was he crying? I couldn't think about it too long. I felt my heart shattering.

"I need to go home now," I said.

"I think that's a good idea. You three are really going to need one another."

"Can you carry me? My knees hurt real bad."

As Chuck cradled me and walked to my house, he whispered in my ear. "It's going to be okay, Dot. One of these days, God's going to heal your heart. Don't ever give up on God. He won't ever give up on you. I promise."

I stood in the Wests' house, years after my father's death, looking out the window. I took in the sight of my childhood home and realized that I still waited for Chuck's promise to come true.

Lisa came the day after Stewart died. I sat, looking at the can of soda she brought for me.

"It's hard to get started sometimes, isn't it?" she asked.

"I just don't know where to begin," I said.

"Cora, I know this is a huge stretch for you." She put her hand on my knee "And I don't want you to do anything you aren't ready for."

"I know. Thank you." I sipped my drink. "Did you bring the pictures of your baby?"

"I did."

Something within me needed to know that she understood what it meant to suffer.

Lisa reached into her purse and pulled out a small photo album. I looked at the pictures. That child never saw the sunshine or spent the night sleeping on his daddy's chest. Lisa wasn't woken up at three in the morning to feed him. Instead, he lived all of his life in a sterile room. Inside an incubator to keep the germs off him.

"He was a really special little guy," Lisa said, beaming with motherly pride. "He cooed at me whenever I came to the hospital to visit him. The nurses told me that I was the only one who got his sweet singing."

"That's a beautiful memory for you." I continued to flip through the album.

"You know, I still miss him. I spent every day at that hospital. I was there so often that the nurses always had a coffee ready for me, just the way I liked it." She frowned thoughtfully. "After he died I would end up in that part of the hospital. My body was just automatically drawn to that place. I couldn't help it. I guess part of me forgot that he was gone."

My heart ached for her. Her story resonated with familiarity. More than she knew. We sat in silence, still looking at the pictures of a baby hooked up to tubes and IVs and respirators. Both of us had sons that died.

Her suffering convinced me to trust her. She wouldn't pity me. She wouldn't judge me. She would understand.

"I grew up in Tennessee," I said, breaking the silence.

"You did? What region?"

"In the mountains in the east." I closed the album. "This is a messy story. But it's true. Do you think you're ready to hear it?"

"I'm ready. Are you?"

"I am."

When I was a child, we lived in a small, broken-down building. Scrap wood pieced together the walls of the shack. The windows and doors were poorly insulated, fitting loosely in their frames. Chill and snow seeped through in the winter. The tin roof radiated heat in the summer. Every part of the structure leaked. Rats and insects outnumbered the five people who lived there.

That square of wood and tin and glass was set so far back from the road that the occasional passerby would have completely failed to see it behind the thick trees. It was easy to ignore. And most people wanted to forget we were there.

The light blue paint peeled from the walls. I hated that the most of anything else in that shack. It chipped off the warped paneling, exposing the rotting wood beneath. So ugly, so wrong. As a child I prayed for paint, for buckets of it, so that I could cover over the decay of the house.

God never sent the paint.

My father slept in the one bedroom. When he felt generous he would allow my mother to stay in the bed with him. My brother, sister and I slept on cots in the living room.

When I was small, before my sister was taken away, my mother kept the house as clean as she possibly could. She scrubbed and swept and mopped and dusted. She could never get it clean enough.

How could one woman keep a house clean when it held such dirty secrets?

"Hey, Dot, it's me," Mrs. West said, knocking on the guest room door. "Do you mind if I come in?"

"Just a second," I called, wiping tears off my face. I stepped away from the window, straightening the plaid curtains. Before sitting, I pulled up the green comforter to cover the pillows. "Come in."

"I made you some coffee," she said, walking in. "I hope it's right. Lola told me how much cream you take."

I took the mug. It steamed, and rich aroma filled the room. "Thank you so much, Mrs. West."

"Oh, please, honey, call me Kristi."

"I really don't think I could. It would be weird."

"After all these years, Dot, you should be able to."

She took care of Pete and me when our mom couldn't. She was more of a mother to us in those months. And she never made us feel like we were a burden.

"Are you hungry? We've got all kinds of cereal."

"No. Thank you, though." I sipped my coffee and sat on the edge of the bed. "This is really good."

"Oh, I'm so glad."

"And thanks for letting me sleep here last night. I have no idea what happened to me."

"No problem, Dot." She sat across the bed from me. "You know we have always loved to have you here."

"I'm just kind of embarrassed. I've never passed out like that."

"You have nothing to be embarrassed about." She looked at me intently. "I hope you don't mind me asking, but do you have panic attacks a lot?"

"Sometimes." I paused. "There are times I just get overwhelmed or nervous. You know. That's when I kind of lose it a little."

"They're pretty scary, aren't they?"

"Yeah. But at least I know what's going on and what to do when they hit. The first time it happened I thought I was dying."

"I've heard that from people." She patted my hand. "But it seems like your life is treating you a little better these days."

"Yeah. Lola takes really good care of me." I smiled.

"By the way, Paul drove her home last night. He said he's happy to take you there as soon as you're ready. No rush at all, though."

"Okay. Thanks."

"Honestly, I really thought she was your mother. I guess I just assumed that if she was with you, well, that it made sense."

"You know, there are times when she reminds me of Mom. It's kind of funny, I guess."

"Sometimes I wonder if God does things like that because He knows we need something to comfort us. Either that or He just really enjoys irony."

"Maybe." I smiled. "I think it's pretty crazy that Paul ended up being the one to rescue us yesterday."

"Oh, he was so excited to have found you." She pushed up her sleeves. "When we were denied custody of you, he was just brokenhearted."

"I don't understand," I said. "You tried to get me?"

"Of course. But they said there was some kind of conflict of interest because of Norman's position. You know. As the executor of your mom's money."

"You really tried to get me back?" I leaned forward, nearer to her. Hoping that I heard her correctly.

"Yes, honey. We fought pretty hard. Norman even hired a lawyer. But then we heard you ran away." She looked at her hands. "We couldn't find you anywhere."

"I didn't know anyone cared enough to look for me."

"The hardest decision we ever made was to stop searching." Her eyes, so full of remorse, met mine. "It killed us."

"Why did you give up?" I asked, my voice just a whisper.

"We figured you were gone. That you left the state." She reached over and grabbed my hand. "I have regretted that decision every day. We should have done more."

"You couldn't have helped me," I said, tears in my eyes. "But thank you for trying. That actually means a lot to me."

"I'm so sorry," she said, frowning.

"Don't be. I'm okay now." I forced a smile, my go-to defense. "It's nice to finally be found."

Lisa came to see me every day to talk. It felt amazing to have someone care for me again. It had been a very long time.

She listened to me describe my childhood home. She let me tell
that portion of my story several times. I seemed to sputter on and on
about the small details. The floor board that hid my small treasures,
the piece of wood on which my mother charted our growth, the outhouse and all its spiders.

"Thank you, Cora, for sharing all of that about your home," Lisa
said after days of listening. "Do you think you're ready to talk about
some of the things that happened inside that house?"

"I don't know." I looked at her. "I thought it would be easy. I was
sure I was ready. Now I'm just not sure I can do it."

"Why's that?"

"Oh, I don't know, Lisa." I took a deep, thick breath. The air burned
my lungs. My heart raced.

"It's okay, Cora."

"I've just never talked about this. Not ever," I whispered.

"Never? You never told anybody?" she asked. "Not even your husband?"

I shook my head. "Not even him."

"Okay. I didn't know that. You sure know how to keep a secret."
She handed me a can of soda from her bag. "Why didn't you tell Steven?"

"That is something that doesn't even make sense to me. It wasn't
that I couldn't trust him. Maybe I just didn't want to burden him." I
opened the can. "Or maybe I just didn't want to talk about it. I thought

if I didn't acknowledge it then it didn't really happen. Perhaps I hoped if I covered it under enough layers I could forget all about it."

"I can understand that." She nodded.

"And besides, trusting people can be risky."

"That, actually, is very understandable. I don't think you've had a whole lot of practice in trusting people. But you can trust me. I promise." She smiled. "You just go ahead and talk. If you need a break let me know. I can always come back another day. This might just get real exhausting."

I began to speak. Before, when I told her about the shack, I struggled with the words. My mind resisted releasing all the information. I stammered and strained to speak. However, that day was very different. It was as if some kind of unseen force dragged the words from my mouth and soul. And I couldn't stop the stream of memory.

Sunday mornings, my mother led my brother, sister, and me to church. My father stayed at home, passed out. My mother told us that we needed to go to church so we could learn about living like Jesus.

We learned in Sunday school that we should love our neighbors, obey our parents, and read our Bibles. We also learned all about what an evil man our father was. And how we would suffer the punishment for his sins.

That I understood. We bore the punishment for his sins every moment of our lives.

Each week, we took seats in the back pew to hear the sermon. I was grateful to sit behind everyone else. That meant they wouldn't glare at us. So that if they talked about us, they had to do it in front of our faces.

My family. The Yarborough family. The people who lived in the falling down shack on the ridge. Banker's daughter that got herself in trouble and had to marry a coal miner. A drunken, womanizing, gambling coal miner.

"Shameful," they would say of my brother, Titus. "That boy borned outta wedlock. Just shameful."

"Marlowe and Cora," they would say of my identical twin and me. "So much alike, them two. Can't never tell 'em apart to look at 'em. But if you hear 'em talk, well, then you'd know. Cora ain't such a nice girl. Sullen, that one. But that Marlowe's somethin' different. That Marlowe's just too good for the likes of them."

"I don't know why she don't leave that man," they'd say of my mother. "You see all three of them kids with the black eyes. And she herself don't look no better. Why don't she just get her some help?"

The walk back down the mountain, after Sunday services, we all shuffled our feet. Worn down. Beat down. Without a hope in the world.

One Sunday, after church, we walked home in the pouring rain. The thirty-minute trip took twice as long in our drenched clothes and feet that got stuck in the mud.

"Come along," my mother called to us, pushing the hair off her face. "We mustn't be too late. Your father could wake anytime."

"Will he whoop us?" Titus asked.

"He may if he's angry enough." My mother gathered us to the side of the road as a driver passed, splashing us with mud. The driver and passengers didn't look at us.

"We forgive you," Marlowe cried, waving.

"I don't," I said under my breath.

Eventually, we made it to the house. Before walking in, we heard rustling and crashing from within.

"Marlowe, stand behind me," Titus said. "Cora, you walk in the back."

"Why's father so hard on Marlowe?" I asked. "He's just plain mean to her."

"Because he can't abide the goodness in her," my mother answered. "Hush now."

"Why can't we just run away?" I whispered.

"Where would we go?" my mother asked. "We have nowhere else in the world."

She unlatched the door and stepped in. As I followed behind the rest, I saw a large fleck of paint that hung off the door frame. I grabbed it, held it in my tight fist. Like a talisman of protection.

The four of us stood in the doorway. We could barely step any further into the house. My father had torn the living room apart.

The couch lay overturned, its dingy cushions tossed across the room. Contents of bookshelves and drawers had been thrown, scattered and broken, on the floor. A puddle of vomit spread on the area rug. The smell of it burned my nostrils even from across the room.

"Where the blazes y'all been?" he roared as we stood huddled, watching him claw through a laundry basket of clothes. "Y'all get into this house right now."

We stepped over the debris and further inside. He watched us, readying himself to attack. A predator about to pounce upon his prey.

"Well, y'all gonna answer my question? Where all y'all been?"

"I took the children with me to church this morning," my mother answered, her voice trembling.

"Did you ask me my permission, woman?"

"No sir. I would have hated to wake you up."

"And did y'all think that maybe I'd like to come to church with ya?" he snickered. "Or y'all think you're too good of Christians to be seen with a sinner like me?"

"No, sir. That thought never crossed my mind," she answered. "We just thought you were tired. After how hard you work every day of the week, we just wanted to give you a rest this morning."

She knew he was ready to lash out at someone. She moved her slender hands to shield us. Titus turned toward us, making sure to stay in front of Marlowe.

"What's for dinner?" He plopped himself down in the creaking rocking chair by the front window. "I'm half to starved."

"I have some stew simmering. It should be ready by now. Just let me go check on it."

She led the three of us to the kitchen, just a small alcove off the living room.

I smelled the cabbage, potatoes, and carrots cooking together in gentle bubbles of watery broth. My stomach groaned from hunger. But I knew that most of the vegetables would need to go into his bowl. He demanded everything. And our fear proved stronger than hunger. We didn't dare keep anything from him. Weak broth would have to do for us.

My mother tied an old, faded apron around her waist. She ladled the thin soup and vegetables into a large, clay bowl. Reaching into her apron pocket, she pulled out the only sharp knife she owned. She cut a slice of cornbread, smothered it with butter, and returned the knife to her apron, concealing it from my father.

"Have her bring it to me," he growled. "Marlowe."

My sister carried the bowl gingerly to him. I held my breath as she walked, praying that she would deliver it without a spill. He took the bowl.

"Would you like anything else, Pa?" Marlowe asked with sweetness in her voice. Her kindness was a gift that he did not deserve.

Marlowe loved our father the way Jesus loved Judas. She knew he would destroy her but forgave him ahead of time and loved him just the same.

He slurped some of the broth and looked directly at my sister.

"Needs salt. Get me the salt shaker," he demanded. "Your ma is the worst cook I ever knowed. My pop always told me never marry a rich girl. Can't cook worth a barrel of manure."

My mother rushed to Marlowe with the salt shaker. She passed it along to our father. He shook the small white crystals into his soup. As he ate he hurled insults and obscenities at my mother.

"Should'a took up with that Mary when I had my chance. Ain't no one on this mountain can cook like that Mary. And she ain't no wisp of a woman neither. She got curves in all the right places. Not like you, Thelma. That Mary sure is pretty." He dripped broth down the front of his beard. "And she thought I was the best thing ever touched this mountain. But, no, I had to go and get you all knocked up instead. And didn't even get me no money from your tight-wad pa. That Mary went off and married herself to the preacher. I bet he don't give her what I used to." He touched himself, making an obscene gesture and laughing.

When he finished berating my mother and slurping his soup he put the bowl on the floor and belched. When he straightened back up in the chair he looked at Marlowe.

"Hey, come over here, girl," he said.

Marlowe walked to him, lowering her body to pick up the bowl.

"Naw, you ain't gotta get that. Let the other one worry 'bout that. You come sit up here on Pa's lap." He put his hands under her armpits and lifted her to sit with him.

"You're a awful good girl, ain't ya?" he asked.

"I try to be, Pa." Marlowe said with a voice so small, so unsuspecting. Her green eyes open wide.

"Ya always do as you're told?"

"Yes, sir."

"Ain't ya never disobey?" He scrunched his brow together.

"Sometimes, sir. But I try my hardest to do what's right."

"And you sure is gettin' purtier every day." He used his big, rough hands to move her smooth face from one side to the other. "How old is ya now?"

"Eleven years old, sir."

"That's fine. That's just fine." He grasped her firmly by the shoulders. "Now, listen here, girl. You'd do anything for this family, wouldn't you?"

"Yes, sir. Anything."

"Then you gotta listen up. Ya hear? I got somethin' real important to tell ya."

"Yes, sir." Her eyes searched his face.

"I owe a man some money. Name of Ducky. You ever hear of him?"

"Yes, sir."

"Where ya hear about him at?"

"Church, sir. Pastor doesn't speak well of Mr. Ducky."

"That's right. 'Cause Ducky's a bad man. And he do bad things." He looked at my sister right in the eyes. "And ya know what Ducky'd do to a fella that don't pay his debts?"

"No, Pa, I don't."

"He cuts his hands clean off. Right at the wrist. Then that man can't never work no more." He gripped her tighter. "And sometimes he kills the man's whole family. You wouldn't want that to happen to our family now, would ya?"

"No. No, sir. That would be awful." Her voice weakened.

"It sure would." He turned her head to look at Titus and me. "You wouldn't want your idiot brother and sister to get their head's bashed in, would ya?"

"No, Pa," she whimpered, close to crying.

"Then you got to do just what I tell ya. You gonna be the one to save this whole family. No questions, you hear?"

She nodded her head quickly, not taking her eyes off his face.

"Now, that's a good girl. Now you're gonna go pack up your things. You gonna live at Ducky's house now. You belong to him."

"Harold, no!" My mother cried, rushing to the rocker and grabbing his arm. "Let him have me. They can do whatever they want to me. She's just a little girl. Take me."

He used the back of his hand to smack my mother across the cheek. She fell to the floor, holding her face. She wasn't surprised by the hit. She must have expected it. His voice roared at her.

"Ducky don't want no used-up old bag of bones like you, woman!" He turned back to Marlowe and gently caressed her red-brown hair. "They lookin' for younger girls now. Say that's what sells now a days. And we gonna give 'em what they want, ain't we, girl?"

He dropped Marlowe to the floor. She looked at me, horrified. Together we ran to the corner where our belongings were kept. They'd been overturned along with everything else. We sat among our things and wept together in a small huddle on the floor.

"What y'all cryin' like babies for?" my father yelled across the room. He pointed at me. "You shouldn't be blubberin' about nothin'. You should be thankin' me for sparing you. You know how much Ducky'd pay for a couple twins?"

I knew he meant the words as a threat. A warning. One slip up and I would be sent to join Marlowe doing whatever those terrible men told me to do. I would have to watch out for myself or I would be sold off, too. The only way to protect myself was by being perfect.

"Boy, get your sorry little butt over there and pack up that girl's junk," he said to Titus. "No toys or nothin' like that. Just a couple a dresses is all she'll need."

My brother walked to us, his eyes full of tears that he wouldn't allow to fall. But I also saw anger in how he set his jaw. Powerless to save Marlowe, he built more hatred for our father.

"Please, Harold," my mother sobbed. "Just let me try to talk to Daddy. He could lend us the money you owe. We could pay it all off and not lose Marlowe. Please. How much is it that we need?"

"Don't you never say nothin' to me about your daddy again! I ain't no man to take a handout from nobody! And I ain't about to let no wife of mine to act the beggar to her father." He kicked her with his booted foot. "I'm the man around this place. I make the decisions. If ya don't like it then just take off. Go back to your daddy."

My mother curled up in a ball on the floor. "Yes, sir," she said.

"Beside, it don't matter. I'm still gonna take the girl to Ducky's. It's too late for me to go back on that now."

I stayed in the guestroom for awhile after Kristi left for work. A new feeling I barely understood sat heavy in my gut. Rescue had been so close. Sitting on the bed, I battled regret.

Eventually, I convinced myself to move out of the room. I needed to get back to Lola's house. I walked down the steps. Very little had changed since the last time I was there eight years earlier. The leather furniture, pictures on the white walls, gray carpeting. All of it the same. Paul's senior picture and a new recliner had been added. But for the most part it hadn't changed.

"Good morning, Dot," Paul said from the couch in the living room, watching a football game.

"Hey," I said, bleary.

"You need more coffee, don't you?" He switched off the television.

"You have no idea. Thanks."

We went into the kitchen. He poured coffee into my mug for me. Then he pulled a box of cereal from the cupboard.

"Is this still your favorite?" he asked, handing me the box.

"Yeah. How do you even remember that?" I looked at the red box with the picture of rainbow-colored marshmallows. Tearing open the box, I smiled.

"Well, when you guys were here a lot, my mom made sure to always have it in the house. And my dad and I weren't allowed to eat any of them. They were just for you."

"Please tell me this cereal isn't that old." I hesitated before dumping the cereal into a bowl.

"No." He laughed. "Mom ran out to the store this morning before you woke up."

"She didn't have to do that." Tears tried to spill over from my eyes. I willed them to stay put. "It's too much trouble."

"You know, that's my mom." He got the milk from the refrigerator and put it on the table. "She was just so excited that you're here again."

"So, your mom's working at the hospital now," I said. "When did that happen?"

"Oh, when I was in high school, she went to nursing school," he answered. "She loves it."

"That's cool."

I poured milk over the cereal in my bowl. So hungry, I shoved a spoonful into my mouth, dribbling all down the front of me.

"Oh my gosh. That's attractive, right?" I said, laughing.

He handed me a napkin. "You know, you always were a dainty eater. Do you remember the time we were eating pudding and Pete made you laugh?"

"Oh, yeah. It went shooting out of my nose."

"And right on my face." He shook his head. "It was chocolate. And so gross."

"You don't know how much that hurt."

"I'm sure it did."

"Thanks so much for reminding me of that."

"You're welcome. I have a whole file of embarrassing Dot stories I could pull out for you, if you'd like."

"No, that's all right. I'll pass. You can just keep those to yourself."

"Man, I'm so glad you're here, Dot," Paul said, eyes soft.

I knew that if I said anything, I would crumble. Being in that house, loved by the West family, missing Pete, regretting my past. All of the emotion left my heart raw, exposed. Keeping my eyes down, I avoided Paul's gaze. I didn't need to break down over my marshmallow cereal.

Then a new anxiety stabbed in my chest. Being alone, in a house, with a boy. A man, really. An old and very recognizable fear set in. I had to remember that Paul West wouldn't hurt me. Not ever. I looked up at him and tried to smile.

"We got to the point where we just never expected to see you again. Especially not after all the time we spent looking for you," he said. "I'm just glad we know that you're doing okay now."

"Thanks. That's really nice," I said, trying to dismiss him.

"We always wondered...."

The phone rang.

"You should get that. Right?" I asked, relieved for the distraction.

After I got myself together and collected what little I had with me, Paul drove me back to Lola's house. The whole way I asked him questions about the college, eager to know as much as I could.

"What's your major?" I asked.

"Christian Ministries," he answered.

"What is that?"

"It just basically means that one of these days I'd like to work in a church or on the mission field somewhere. You know, in ministry."

"Wow. That's cool."

"What are you thinking about studying?"

"Well, I guess I was kind of thinking about something in literature or writing. But I don't know for sure," I said, like a little girl talking about a far-off dream. "I might try to become a teacher. I was thinking that I might want to teach in an inner-city school."

"That's great. I think you'd be good at it." He looked at me for a second. "It'll be cool having you at college with me."

"Really?" I scrunched my face.

"Yeah. I would love to hang out with you."

"Well, I'm not completely sure I'll be coming. I mean, picking out a college is kind of a big decision."

"True." He smiled at me. "But I promise that I'd be really nice to you. I'd even introduce you to all my friends. I'd take care of you."

I kept my face straight ahead. He wanted to take care of me. I didn't know how I felt about that. Shoving those thoughts away, I smiled again, masking my anxiety.

"And I'd let you sit with me in the cafeteria, but only if you promise not to spew pudding out of your nose on my friends."

"Now, that is a promise I just can't make."

We drove onto my street and pulled in front of the house. Lola lounged in the hammock, reading a book. She looked at us, drowsy eyed, as we climbed out of the car.

"You know, in the daylight I can see a lot of repairs you need to have done to this place," Paul said to Lola. "The eaves are a little droopy, a few shingles need replacing, and I think I see some nails that should be hammered down on the porch. Not to be rude or anything."

"By all means, young man, be my guest. We're always looking for free repairs," Lola joked.

"If you insist," Paul said, walking back to his car for the toolbox. "Why don't you ladies go inside and get yourselves a cup of coffee and relax?"

Lola laughed. "You think that going inside is relaxing?"

"Okay," Paul said, confused. "What do you mean?"

"Wouldn't you like to know?" Lola linked arms with me. "After you're done with all this, just knock on the door. You can't come in, but you'll still see what I'm talking about."

"All right."

"Come along, Dorothea. Let's go have that relaxing moment."

Stepping inside, I heard all the other girls talking through the vents. Word spread that a cute guy was outside working on the house. Giggles bounced throughout the home.

"My goodness," I said to Lola. "All that noise for a boy."

"Isn't it a beautiful sound, Dorothea?"

"What? Them? No. It's annoying."

"Is it?" She cocked her head. "To me, they sound like teenage girls giggling over a handsome boy."

"Yeah? That's what it sounds like to me."

"It's a moment of innocence. They're changing, my dear. Victims don't giggle. But survivors do."

I sighed. "Doggone it, Lola. You can never just let me be a jerk, can you?"

"That I cannot." Lola walked toward the kitchen, pulling me along. "Let's make some brownies."

"You're the best."

Lola made the most amazing brownies. I unwrapped the cubes of bitter baking chocolate and dropped them in the double boiler, stirring constantly as they melted with the heat. I loved working in the kitchen with Lola.

"He certainly is a nice boy, isn't he, Dorothea?" she asked, measuring the flour.

"Who? Paul? Yeah, I guess." I tried to hold back a smile. "He was kind of like another big brother."

"Did you have a crush on him when you were younger?" she teased.

"Maybe." I forced an annoyed tone. "What little girl doesn't have a crush on her big brother's friends?"

"Oh, I don't know. My brother never had any friends."

I looked up from the pot, still stirring. She cut a rectangle of butter and placed it in a small pot.

"Brother?" I asked. "Seriously, Lola? You have a sister and brother?"

"Yes." She stood next to me and turned on one of the burners under the butter. "Could you please be a dear and keep your eye on this butter? Just turn off the gas once it's melted."

"I can't believe you have a brother and sister and you've never told me about them before."

"Actually, dear, had. I had a brother." She cleared her throat. "I guess I simply don't talk about my past much, do I? I'm more interested in helping all of you heal from what happened to you."

"But I've lived here for five years and I didn't know anything about them."

"Perhaps that is because you never asked. Besides, that was a very, very long time ago. Ages ago. It was a different life."

"Do you mind me asking what happened to your brother?"

"Well, Dorothea, it was horrendous. I watched him die. It was terrifying." She looked at me, her eyes severe. "Mind the butter, dear."

I turned off the burner.

"How did he die?" I asked.

"He was murdered. I held his head in my lap. It was a violent death. There was lots of blood." She shook her head. "Then he stopped breathing."

"Who killed him?"

"I shall save that disclosure for another day, Dorothea. I'm sorry. I don't know that I have it in me to share that with you today." She turned on the mixer.

"I shouldn't have asked. I'm sorry, Lola." I had to talk so loudly over the sound of the mixer. "You don't have to tell me."

I took off the top part of the double boiler.

"Is the chocolate ready?" Lola asked.

"Yes." I walked to her with the small pot.

"Fantastic." She poured the chocolate into the mixing bowl, scraping the pot with a spatula. "You want to know something peculiar? I am always tempted to lick this chocolate from the spatula. But I know that it's just far too bitter. It would be awful."

"I know. It smells so good."

"You are correct. It looks good and smells amazing. But it just wouldn't be exactly right yet. It will only taste good with the right amount of sugar and vanilla and melted butter. It isn't quite whole yet."

"When I was little, I stole a square from the pantry." I drew warm water into the sink. Added soap. "I took it up to my room. When I heard my dad walking up the steps, I shoved the whole thing into my mouth. It was nasty. Apparently, my dad thought the gagging was punishment enough."

"Ah, yes. I'm sure he figured you wouldn't make that mistake again." Lola chuckled, shook her head. "Dorothea, I am so thankful that you had a loving father. It warms my heart."

"You would have thought he was pretty cool." I wiped my hand on a towel. "I miss my family, Lola. How did it all get so complicated?"

"Life is usually pretty complex, isn't it? I cannot remember a time when life was smooth and easy." She put the pan of raw brownie batter into the oven. "I must admit that I often struggle with the grief of all those I'm missing as well. I still haven't discovered God's good work in all of the bad that has happened."

"I'm glad I'm not the only one."

"I think for a long time I harbored guilt for feeling that way. Like I wasn't relying on God completely." She set the timer. "But, you know, I have started to wonder if that feeling of a void wasn't the Holy Spirit trying to communicate something to me."

"What do you mean?"

"Well, perhaps those feelings of longing are a nudge for us to re-connect with someone who needs us. Or, just maybe, that person we're nudged toward is someone we need."

"Who's missing in your life, Lola?" I asked.

"Again, a topic for another day." She handed me the timer. "But for now I need to get a little rest. Would you please check on the brownies in about twenty-five minutes? Do the toothpick test on them to see if they're done. Thank you."

Lola went up to her room, the smallest in the house. She con-stantly insisted on the smallest, ugliest, most undesirable portion of all we had. She took the ugly winter coat from the donations. Chose to sleep on the lumpiest mattress. Took the thinnest blankets. Went last through the line at meals and ate the burnt piece of lasagna. And she was mortified if it was ever pointed out. We never talked about it, but I think it was the reason we all respected her so much.

I cleaned up the baking things, scrubbed down the counters and started a new pot of coffee.

I heard a knock on the front door. I flipped on the coffee maker and walked to answer the door. A scuffle of feet moved across the upstairs floor and toward the front of the house.

"I've got it!" Grace screeched, opening the door. Her blond curls bounced around the fair skin of her face. She looked so pretty. I tried not to be jealous.

"Hi," Paul said, standing in the doorway. "Um, do you mind if I talk to Dot for a minute?"

"Dot?" Grace asked. "Who the monkey breath is Dot?"

"Me." I nudged my way past her. "Dot was what everyone called me when I was little."

"Oh. That's kind of cute, I guess," she said, teasing.

"Do you need something, Paul?" I asked, ignoring her.

"Paul, huh? Now that is a nice name." Grace smiled at him, pushing herself back in front of me. "So, how does a guy like you know a girl like Dorothea?"

"Yeah. Well, we grew up across the street from each other." He held his finger in a bandana. A tiny spot of blood soaked through. "Listen, I know I can't come in or something. But I just need a clean wash rag or bandage."

"Oh my gosh! You're bleeding! Let me take care of that for you." Grace took him by the elbow and tugged him into the kitchen. "That's a lot of blood!"

"Seriously, Grace. You know he can't be in here!" I said.

"But he's about to bleed to death. Lola wouldn't be mad." She winked at me over her shoulder. "She would want us to help the poor guy."

"He's not bleeding that much." I walked quickly, following them. I didn't like her touching him. "He's fine, Grace."

She turned on the faucet. As she rinsed his hand under the running water she let loose a fury of her very best vocabulary. He turned his head and looked at me, unsure of how to handle her.

"I'll take care of it from here, Grace," I said. "Thanks. You may have just saved his life."

"Yeah, whatever, Dot." She smiled at Paul. "It sure was nice to meet you. I hope you come by more often."

"Thanks," Paul said.

Grace strutted out of the kitchen and to the stairs. Several pair of feet clomped up the steps. The group of chattering girls gathered in my room. I could hear every word they said. And it made me shake my head and smile.

"We don't really get all that many guys around here. We aren't always sure how we should act." I handed him a bandage. "I think you can figure out how to do that yourself."

"My mom's a nurse. I think I can manage."

Another wave of loud laughter erupted from upstairs.

"Oh, my." I said. "We'd better get you outside. You really aren't allowed in here."

"Fine by me." He started toward the front door.

"I'll meet you out there. You want a cup of coffee?" I called after him.

"Actually, a glass of water would be nice." He turned and smiled at me before walking out to the porch.

I poured my coffee and some water for him and headed out to Paul. The girls pressed their faces against my bedroom window. We could see them from the bottom step of the porch.

"Goodness." I said. "Could they be any more obvious?"

"Well, I have to be honest, I'm a little flattered. I don't get that kind of attention everywhere I go." He winked at me. "And all I had to do was catch my finger on a rusty nail."

His wink made my heart beat faster.

"Oh. I hope you're all up to date on your shots," I said, flustered, unable to think of anything else to say.

"I'm not a dog, you know." He laughed.

I smiled and handed him his glass.

"Thanks." He drank. "This is quite a place you have here."

"Well, it's Lola's house. We just live here."

"Are you all foster kids?"

"Kind of," I said. "Yeah. I guess you could say that."

"But why in this neighborhood? I mean, no offense or anything, but isn't this a dangerous area?"

"Only if you aren't from around here." I sat on the steps. "An unfamiliar face gets people a little touchy."

"Oh." He sat next to me.

"But don't worry. You're with us. That speaks well for a guy around these parts."

"How do you know that?"

"Because our neighbors keep their eyes on what happens here. You were helping out Lola. That earned you major points."

"Well, that's a relief." He wiped the beads of water from his glass. "What would happen if I wasn't 'okay' here?"

"Oh, they'd let you know. They don't waste time. If they don't like somebody it's pretty obvious. Your car would be stripped down or they'd beat you up."

"Yikes."

"Yup. I can't tell you how safe that makes us feel."

"That makes you feel safe?"

"Yeah. Hardly anybody comes around to mess with us."

"Well, that makes sense."

We sat and talked a little about the things he thought needed to be done on the house. He'd thought about asking a group of college guys to come do a work trip to our neighborhood. He dreamed about the possibilities of fixing up the vacant lot at the end of the street to create a park or neighborhood garden.

I felt a smile on my face as he spoke. Very few people would have been brave enough to come into this area, let alone want to change it for the better and for the right reasons. The fear of others from the college learning about my neighborhood had faded. I just sat in awe of his ideas for brightening up that dark place.

"I mean, just because it's a poorer area of town doesn't mean it shouldn't be nice and safe. You know?" he said, excited. I liked his enthusiasm. "We could do a whole lot of work here. I mean, not that

Lola isn't already. But we could add a whole different dimension to it."

"No, I understand what you're saying."

"I just think that Jesus would want us to bring more of Him to this street."

"The kids around here need to know how important they are."

"Exactly," he said, looking right into my eyes. "Seems to me a lot of people need to know they're special. Not just the kids."

"Wow." I turned my head, unable to keep his gaze, too caught up in an intensity that overwhelmed me.

"Well, enough of my dreaming for today." He stood, handed me his glass. "I really have to get going. I've got a class tonight. If I skip it one more time I might fail."

"That wouldn't be good."

I stood next to him. A few inches shorter than him, I had to look up at his face.

"Listen, Dot, it's really nice to know that you're okay."

"Well, I'm not sure I'm so 'okay,'" I joked.

"No, I'm not kidding. I mean it. I wondered about you all the time after you went away."

"Thanks."

"Listen, you just tell me if you ever need anything. I'll even skip a class. I don't care if it makes me fail. Seriously." He took a scrap of paper from his pocket and wrote his number on it with a small pencil. "Call me whenever you want."

"Okay." I took the paper.

"You know, I want to see you again. Soon. I feel like I just got you back in my life. I'm not ready to let you go again." He started walking to his car. "How about I pick you up tomorrow night at six for dinner. My treat. Unless you have other plans."

"No. I never have plans." Shoot. That was dumb. "I mean, I would really like that. As long as it isn't fast food."

"Then you pick the place." He reached his car. "Maybe you can give me the Dot Schmidt life update."

"Sounds great." I waved. "See you tomorrow."

He drove away. He was gone, but the flush on my cheeks didn't stop burning.

Then I panicked. What if Lola wouldn't let me go on a date? Was it a date? How could I tell him about my life? What would I wear?

"Oh, golly gee," I said under my breath.

I heard all the girls in the house tumble down the steps. When I walked inside they surrounded me.

We giggled together. The timer buzzed and I got the brownies out of the oven. We sat, eating the goopy, warm chocolate and chatting about boys.

Just like normal girls.

"I thought I'd bring you something different today. It's getting a little too cold for sodas," Lisa said, placing a lidded paper cup in front of me. "I just got you a mint mocha. Have you ever had one of those?"

"Oh, goodness, it has just been so long since I had good coffee," I answered. "All they give us here is the cheap, watered down stuff. It is horrible."

"Wow. That's something I'll have to bring up with Dr. Emmert."

I sipped the coffee. The espresso and milk and chocolate and whipped cream hit my taste buds with a richness of flavor that I had all but forgotten. I closed my eyes and exhaled deeply. "Oh, that is good. Thank you."

"I'm so glad you like it."

"I do. Very much." I sipped again. "If you're ever able to break me out of here I think I'd like to go get coffee."

"You would love it, Cora. They have a whole case of baked goods. Carrot cakes and muffins and scones." She licked her lips. "They even have cookies the size of your head."

"Really?" My stomach yearned for something decadent.

"Yes. Really. How about I bring you one of those cookies when I come tomorrow? They have just about any kind you can think of."

"Oh, I'm going to be real boring. I'd just like chocolate chip."

"I can get that for you."

"It's strange. You know, I haven't really wanted to eat since Steven died. You mention cookies and, all the sudden, my stomach starts growling."

"Well, I think that's a pretty good thing."

"Me too." I sighed, took another drink. "I'm ready to start. Where did I leave off yesterday?"

"Your father was taking Marlowe away."

"Yes. That's right."

After Titus packed up what few belongings Marlowe had, my father led her to his beat-up truck. She did not fight. She did not cry. She just went along with him. Like a lamb to the slaughter.

And all to save our family. But she didn't know at the time that her sacrifice wouldn't save a single one of us. Her leaving would simply be another step in our disintegration. It merely prolonged the inevitable destruction.

I stood on the porch, watching, as my father drove the truck away. She looked back one last time, her face framed by the rusted-out truck. Her hair still in two braids that I'd put in her hair before church. Fingering the braids she'd put in mine, I slouched. Frowned. Cried.

I watched the better half of me being taken to be ruined. I didn't know what went on at Ducky's. But I knew it was evil.

So evil that the pastor in the old mountain church called down fire and damnation on the establishment weekly. And yet the building remained. The pastor condemned the patrons to hell. And yet many of the men in the congregation crept away from their wives and children to play cards, get drunk, or spend time with the girls. The members of the church cried out their agreements of the judgment on the debauchery with many roars of "Amen" and "Preach it." And yet many of them gave most or all of their earnings to pay off bar tabs or gambling debts. The preacher called for all of us to shun Ducky, to walk to the other side of the street should we happen to run across him in town. Yet half of the pastor's income came directly from Ducky. He called it righteous penance.

Still on the porch, I heard my mother picking up the mess my father created in the living room. Titus retreated to the back and chopped up logs for firewood. As if their lives reset and Marlowe had never belonged with us in the first place.

I, on the other hand, couldn't carry on. All I could think was how I'd been cut in half. I've heard that some identical twins are able to feel each other's pain. My body and soul hurt all the time. Oh, what she must have lived through.

And I wondered if she could feel how I missed her. I prayed that she could know somehow and that it would comfort her in at least a small way. I didn't want her to think our lives moved right along without her.

My father didn't come home that night or the next. He spent more and more time at Ducky's. I didn't know if that was a good thing. But as for mother, Titus, and me, life became quiet, peaceful.

On rare occasions, he returned home to pass out on his bed. His stench took over every inch of the house with smoke and booze and sweat. Those smells had the power to make me nauseous well into my adulthood. To send me into a panic.

My father stopped going to the mines. And yet somehow he had cash. I wondered what happened at that horrible place. I wondered what Marlowe was doing and what he did to make so much money.

"Cora, are you okay?" Lisa asked.

"Yes," I answered, shaken from the memory. "Why?"

"Well, my hand."

I looked down at my hand, so tightly gripping hers that her fingers turned purple. I let go, horrified that I'd hurt her.

"I'm so sorry, Lisa."

"It's okay." She wiggled her fingers. "How about we stop there for today? We can pick it back up tomorrow. How does that sound to you?"

"That's fine." I paused. "You know, this may sound strange to you, but I actually look forward to telling you more tomorrow."

"Really?"

"Yes. I can feel a little of the burden lessening. It's as if I wasn't able to breathe before. Right now I just feel so much lighter."

"That's wonderful, Cora. I'm really glad to hear that." She stood. "And tomorrow will be just a little better with that chocolate chip cookie."

"I'm really looking forward to that, too."

"Lola! What the George Herbert Walker Bush am I supposed to put as my high school?" I asked, more than a little aggravated.

I sat at the kitchen table, filling out my college application. Every question made me more anxious than the last. My stomach turned and flipped and flopped. I was terrified that the smallest mistake would keep me from being accepted.

"Just put 'Lola's Fabulous Home School,'" Lola said. "And kudos for the old school President Bush reference. I didn't realize you were a Republican."

"Old school, Lola? Really?" Promise said, rolling her eyes.

"Oh, snap, young lady. I am far more hip to the fizzle than you think," Lola said, pushing up her glasses. "Don't let the washed-up hippie look mislead you."

"I can't put that on an application." I said, grumpy. "Stop trying to make fun of this. It's really important, in case you were wondering. I mean, this is kind of my entire flipping future here."

"No need to get so heated, Dorothea. You're taking it a tad bit too seriously. You're as good as enrolled. This application process is simply a formality." Lola reassured me, as always. I tried to not let it annoy me.

"I know. I'm sorry." I said. "I'm just kind of afraid that it's not going to be perfect."

"Well, I think that's a slightly too lofty goal. Don't you worry about tomorrow, Dorothea. Today has plenty of trouble of its own."

"Cite your source, please." I smiled.

"Yes. That was Jesus." She pointed to the application. "You would do well to simply write 'home school.' They may ask questions should they have any. And you don't need to worry. You are far more precious than the lilies or the birds."

"Okay." I wrote on the application. "I feel better now. Thanks."

"Very good. Now, this superfly chica needs to get back to the endless mountains of laundry in the basement." She put her fingers into a V. "Peace out, home slices."

She strutted out of the room, leaving Promise and me in the kitchen.

"She's insane," I said.

Promise grabbed a piece of cheese from the refrigerator and hopped onto the counter.

"Seriously, Promise. Lola would make you put a quarter in the pizza night fund if she saw you up there," I said.

She slid down and walked to Lola's chair. As I watched her move across the room, I envied her body. Curvy and pretty and tall. She looked older, more mature. Watching her, I sat up straighter, held in my stomach.

"Hey, so, can I talk to you for a sec?" she asked, sitting down.

"Sure." I looked back at my application.

"Do you think I'm a good mom? I mean, do I do a good job with Nesto?"

"I guess. I don't know. What would I know about how a mom should act?"

"The other girls say you had a good mom. Ain't that right?" She pulled her legs up under her on the chair.

"Yeah." I looked up at her. Her eyes seemed to see right through me.

"Here's the thing, I don't remember my mom being nice to me or nothing. So I don't know if I'm being a nice mom." She broke the cheese into crumbles before placing one on her tongue, never taking her eyes off me. "I thought you of all people would want to give me some help."

Her voice sounded strange. Kind of flat. I couldn't put my finger on what my instincts tried to tell me. Life on the streets trained me to sense danger. I knew that I needed to be careful.

"Well, Promise, I think all a mom really has to do is keep the baby fed and clean, right?" I looked at her eyes, trying to read what she thought. "What are you so worried about?"

"Everything." Her blue eyes were dull. I could tell she worked hard to keep emotion out of them. "I'm scared that I won't be able to help him grow up."

"You'll be fine." I looked back down.

"Here's the thing, though. I think I'm gonna give Nesto up."

"Give him up?" I put my pen on the table and leaned back in my chair. "What's that mean?"

"I'm gonna let somebody adopt him."

"Seriously? You know you couldn't ever get him back, right?"

"Yeah. And neither would his dad. And that's kind of the point."

"Have you talked to Lola about this?"

"Nope. And I ain't gonna." She pointed at me, threatening. "And neither are you."

"What?"

"Listen, Dorothea, I ain't sticking around here. This place just ain't for me."

"What's wrong with it?"

"I can't live with all these rules, you know? It's all holding me back and stuff. I feel like I went from having a pimp tell me what to do to having an old lady do it."

"That's stupid, Promise. Your pimp never loved you. You know that. And Lola does."

"How do you know Taz never loved me?" She raised her voice. Almost shrill.

We stared each other down. She maintained her tough attitude. I couldn't see anything but anger.

"So, what, you just want to go back to Taz?" I asked, breaking eye contact.

"Nah. He ain't husslin' no more. Besides, I think I could get more." She stood up. "There's a new place up north. They need dancers."

"You don't want to do that, Promise."

"Why not? They said I could make six figures the first year. You know what I could do with that money? It's better than the track."

"But it isn't worth it."

"Sure it is. It's only like four hours a day. And you keep all the tips."

"But you aren't even eighteen yet. You can't work there."

She snorted. "Like they even care. Nobody asks your age when they're sticking tens and twenties down your pants."

"It's just so dangerous."

"No it ain't. They got bouncers there if anybody gets too grabby. It's fine. Plus, I get all the drinks I want."

"Promise, I don't think you should do this."

"Shoot, what else do you think I got going for me?"

"You could finish up your GED, go to college, get a good job."

"I can't get a job making more than one hundred thousand a year. Seriously. A girl like me is made for just one thing." She moved her hands down her sides to her hips.

"That's not true," I said. "You're more than just that."

She moved closer to me, squatted down close to my face.

"I think you should come with me." Her voice changed. A sweet, coaxing whisper.

"No," I said, firmly.

"I'm serious." Her eyes moved up and down my body. I shifted in my seat, trying to shield my body from her ogle. I hadn't felt so uncomfortable since my days on the track. "You got the look, honey. Guys love the 'good-girl-gone-bad' look. You know. We could dye that dark hair blond. Put in some pigtails. A little makeup could really make them puppy dog eyes drive the guys crazy. We'd play up the school girl thing and they wouldn't even care that you're small up top."

"No." I crossed my arms over my chest.

"And you wouldn't have to ask permission to call your little boyfriend. I wouldn't even care if he stayed over so you guys could—you know."

"He's not my boyfriend." I looked away from her. "And even if he was, we wouldn't be sleeping together."

"Just a few nights of dancing a week, Dorothea, and you'd have your whole college bill paid off."

"But that's not a problem. I'm getting a scholarship."

"You don't really want to go to that school, do you? It's all Lola's idea. She's just trying to control you after you leave this place. You know they got a curfew there, right? Grace told me that."

"Yes. But that's kind of normal."

"And Lola's trying to keep you close. I don't know, I think she's got a strange thing for you." She put a hand on my knee. "She looks at you all the time."

"That's crazy."

"I've got a place already lined up. Two bedroom apartment, all the stuff's in it already. Couches, beds, everything. We could get a car. Man, can you imagine how free we'd be with a car?" She moved her hand on my thigh. "Come on, Dot."

"Don't call me that." I pushed her hand off. She put it back.

"We could sneak out of here tonight. Stay somewhere downtown till we can get a ride to that apartment. It'll be fun." She smiled. "I know a guy who'd let us crash at his place for a couple nights."

"That doesn't sound like a good idea to me, Promise."

"So, what are you saying?"

"No. I'm saying no."

Promise's knees cracked as she stood up straight. She put her fingertips on my forehead and shoved me.

"Whatever. I don't need you."

"What the heck, Promise."

"My name's Jenny," she said, her voice harsh. "I don't know why everybody around here has to get a different name. It's weird."

"It's not weird."

"And what about you? You're the only one that gets to keep her name. Don't even tell me that you ain't Lola's favorite."

"It's different."

"How? How's it different? Just 'cause you was raised rich? Huh? Or 'cause your parents weren't complete jerks?"

"I don't know."

"You're right you don't know. You don't got to know nothing. You're a rich kid who thinks she knows everything. Like you can fix everybody's problems."

"I wasn't rich."

"You think you're so much better than all us. Here I am, trying to help you out. Trying to get you a good job. But, no, that's not good enough for you. You're just too high and mighty for that. But it's okay for me to do, right?"

"No, I don't think you should do it either."

"Why? Are you jealous that I'd be making so much?"

"I don't want anything bad to happen to you."

"Right. Whatever."

"I'm serious."

Promise picked up my application and threw it on the floor. "You think you're so much better than everybody else. But you ain't any different. All you are is a washed-up old hooker just like the rest of us. Isn't that right? Maybe I should figure out a way to tell that cute little boyfriend of yours."

"Promise, not another word." Lola stood in the doorway, holding a basket of laundry. She spoke with a gentle firmness. "Let me make one thing very clear, your tone is completely out of order. I don't allow anyone to speak like that to another person in this house."

"What? You gonna make me put a quarter in a jar?" Promise asked, turning toward Lola.

"Excuse me, Promise, you need to be quiet and listen." Lola put the basket on the floor. "I don't know what this conversation was about. It's not my business unless either of you decided to discuss it with me. However, if you are struggling here, I'd like to know so that I'm able to help you."

"I don't want Nesto no more." Promise looked straight into Lola's eyes, put her hands on her hips. "I want to put him up for adoption."

"I understand that. First thing in the morning I'll take you to speak with my friend from Christian adoption services. She can walk you through the options."

"And I wanna leave."

"As for that, I'm afraid that option is completely off the table. You're under eighteen. If you left this house you'd be a runaway and that goes against the agreement you made with your case worker."

"I've been a runaway most of my life."

"And how did that work for you in the past?" Lola raised her brows.

"I did okay." Promise turned around, her back to me.

"Well, that's arguable." Lola went toward Promise. "How about this, Promise..."

"I want you to call me Jenny." She turned back around. "I hate being called Promise."

"Okay. I'm sorry about that, Jenny," Lola said. "How about we compromise a little? You agree to stay in this home for one more month. If you're still convinced that you should move along, I'll call your case worker in for a meeting. However, if you'd like to remain here I would be so very thankful for that. Either way, I will always have a special place in my heart for you. I know that you are so much more than this hard shield that you put up. You are a beautiful and wonderful daughter of God."

"Whatever. Yeah. I'll stay for one month. But that's it."

"Listen, Jenny," I said. "I'm sorry I made you feel like I thought I was better than you."

She looked at me and raised her middle finger, sneering. Then turned and walked out of the kitchen.

Lisa delivered, as promised, the biggest cookie I'd ever seen. She had me hold it next to my face for comparison and took a picture of me with her cell phone.

"Oh, this is a great picture," she said, turning the phone so I could see.

"I am so old," I said, looking at the wiry, silver hair and the lines on my face. I took a bite of the cookie in an effort to forget about perfection for a minute. It was delicious. I intended to eat the entire thing.

"If I ever bake again I think I'll try and make a batch of cookies this size." I spoke with my mouth full.

"Are you a baker? I guess I should have just figured that about you." Lisa bit into her cookie. "I can bring some ingredients with me tomorrow so you can make some giant cookies if you'd like."

"Oh, that's all right," I said. "What if I've lost my touch? It's been so long since I baked. I wouldn't remember any of my recipes."

"It might take a little practice. But that would be okay, wouldn't it?"

"I think it would make me so sad if they didn't come out perfect. It would be disappointing."

"Well, then you could just try again."

"I always forget about that option." It felt nice to have someone give me little nudges. "Are you ready to hear some more of my story?"

"I am. But first I wanted to ask you a question about Marlowe's removal from your home."

"Okay."

"Didn't anyone notice that she was gone? That's been bugging me since yesterday. How did no one figure that out and try to help you?"

"That's an interesting question, Lisa."

There was only one school on the mountain. It had a single classroom, which all the different age groups shared. The teacher was from Lexington. A young, inexperienced city girl who liked to think that she was making a difference for the Lord by reaching out to the poor mountain kids.

The children at that school were harsh, hateful and cruel. Nothing more than the reflection of their parents' prejudices and toxic ideals.

"Cora, that's a right fine dress ya wearin'," one of the girls would say, her friends giggling next to her. "Think I seen it before. Oh, I remember. I throwed that raggedy ol' dress out in my trash bin last week. Poor little Cora's a raggedy trash digger."

"Look at his bones all stickin' out." The boys hounded Titus. "You is such a sissy girl."

They called out insults at us all day long. During class, if we raised our hands to answer a question they made fun of our odor. At lunch they teased us for having nothing more to eat than fried dough. After school they ridiculed us for the holes in our shoes.

And the teacher, Miss Kendrick, did nothing to stop them. She believed peer teasing to be an important part of the educational process. A weeding out of the strong from the weak. We would eventually learn to submit to our betters. The other children would learn how to make their way ahead of everyone else in life.

School had always been a torture for us. Our mother allowed us to stay home for the first week after Marlowe was taken. When we returned to school we didn't know what to expect.

"Cora Yarborough," the teacher called the roll.

"Present, ma'am," I answered.

"Marlowe Yarborough." Silence. "Marlowe? Ain't she here?"

"No, ma'am."

"Well, you and Titus are here. Where is your sister?" she asked. Her voice spun through my head as she repeated herself. "Where's your sister?"

"She's dead," I answered. I had no control over my response. The words fell from my mouth. They were the words rehearsed several times. My father's commanded answer for any inquiry.

"Oh, dear." Miss Kendrick put her hand over her mouth as tears let loose in her eyes.

The rest of the class stared at us, eyes wide, mouths agape.

"What ever happened?" Miss Kendrick asked, hand still on her mouth.

"There was an accident. She's gone to be with Jesus." I looked at Titus. He nodded at me, his face solemn.

"Oh, dear, oh, dear, dear. I am so sorry. How terrible."

Word spread across the community of Marlowe's tragic death. Some said that she had been crushed under a tractor. Others said that she fell out of the truck's flatbed while our family made a trip into town. Most, though, just shook their heads. Such a sad thing for a child to lose her life so early. And such a delightful little girl she had been. The only good thing to come from the Yarborough family.

And not one soul asked a single question. People got sick. They had accidents. Children died. Death was a fact of life well accepted among the people on the mountain. Several of my classmates died over the years I attended school. Often the doctor was unable to reach the shacks positioned higher up on the ridges.

No one gave a second thought to Marlowe's whereabouts. And if they did see her at Ducky's they certainly weren't going to admit it. That would be confessing to the unmentionable sin of associating with the degenerates who spent time there.

My father forced Titus and me to bury anything of hers that remained in the house. We dug a shallow hole by the garden. I filled the pit with a small rag doll, a few rusty hair clips, a sundress she outgrew the year before. Titus formed a small cross from twigs and stuck it in the ground by the loosely packed dirt.

"Marlowe is alive," I'd whisper as I fell asleep.

Eventually we stopped going to school completely. Again, no one asked questions. It was common for children to stay home and help with the family or go to work in the mines. Part of me thought the teacher must have been relieved that we were gone. She could stop feeling badly about our "dead" sister and no longer had to witness our daily humiliation.

Titus got himself a job as an assistant in the coal mines. At the end of each work day he would return home, eyes shining blue amid the black coal that covered his face. His earnings paid a few of our household bills.

After a time, though, like all Yarborough men before him, Titus began to drink away most of his money.

I took over my mother's household duties. She refused to get up from Marlowe's small, vacant cot. I cooked, cleaned, washed, scrubbed, worried. She slept all day. When she did wake it was only to sob about her lost girl.

"He should have taken me. Not Marlowe," she'd weep. "Oh, God, help me."

She would cry for a bit before falling back into her wasting sleep.

I resented her nearly as much as I did my father. They had both failed us.

My dad knew that I loved yellow. For one of my birthdays, he covered my room with different shades of the color. My bed, dresser, carpet, walls—all a cheerful yellow. A reminder of his love for me.

I woke up in that room three days after I found out he was dead. After Chuck carried me home, my world collapsed and my brain shut off. I had slept the whole time. Nothing woke me up. I slept deeper than the noise, the chaos, and the worst days of my life to that point.

I slept through my mom tearing all the family pictures off the walls. Leaving dents and holes in the paint.

I slept through my dad's family coming from Oregon. Through them taking over the house, cooking and cleaning and crying.

I slept through all the reporters with their cameras and microphones and notebooks. Them trying to get a special interview with the war hero's mourning family. They wanted to boost their ratings with our misery. But the only thing they found was a woman, broken and distraught. A woman who didn't need them bothering her. Still they pushed and pushed to get an emotional reaction to put at the top of the six o'clock news.

I slept through the memorial service. Through the revelation that the roadside bomb left nothing of my daddy to bury. Through the American flag handed off to my mom, the Marine saluting her as she wept. Through "Taps" played woefully on the trumpet, the heart-wrenching rifle salute.

It wasn't until those three days were spent and gone that I woke up.

A stream of sunlight tried to break through the drawn blinds of my room. Nauseating warmth suffocated me. The comforter seemed so heavy as I pushed it off my body. Cool air washed over me, chilling me more because of the sweat on my arms and legs and face. Disoriented, my mind tried and failed to put together the pieces of the days I had missed.

I gasped, shocked as the wave of memory overtook me.

"Daddy's dead," I moved my mouth around the words. But without sound.

My mouth felt like cotton. My stomach growled at its emptiness. My heart throbbed, bruised. The damage of loss and grief strangled me. My muscles ached and my head spun.

Sitting up with a struggle, I tried to push myself up to standing. The weakness in my legs caused me to fold to the floor like a bunch of blocks. I didn't have the will to try again. My cheek to the yellow carpet, I cried.

All the sorrow attacked my gut. I heaved. Agonizing, empty retches. Like dust trapped in my throat.

I made my hand into a fist and hit my knuckles into the carpet. It hurt. But the pain couldn't match what I felt inside. I punched again and again. My fingers started to bleed.

I was only nine years old.

How could such a little kid know how to handle that kind of sadness? What's the right way for a little girl to grieve her daddy?

My door opened. Pete looked in. His eyes rimmed with red. Exhausted. Worn down. Burdened. It seemed that the whole time I'd slept, he'd stayed awake.

He tried to smile. But the joy was gone from his face.

He looked at my hand and rushed in, knelt down next to me. He held my battered fist and forced my head on his shoulder.

"Dot, we're going to be okay," he said. "We are."

Despite my weakness, I tried to push him away. I wanted to punish someone for the pain. He was just the one closest to me at that moment. My hands shoved against his thin, bony chest. My strength gone, I couldn't budge him.

"We'll be okay," he repeated, holding me tighter.

"No we aren't, Pete! We aren't okay," I whispered, my voice rough, my throat raw.

"We are, Dot." He pulled his head away to look into my eyes.

He had the kindest eyes I'd ever seen. Like our mom's. Deep green, soft and compassionate. He had the kind of eyelashes that women would die for. That day they were moist and stuck together.

"I promise. We are." He blinked, his lids heavy.

"But he's dead." The words came more as a whimper than anything.

"I know. And now he's doing pretty great. He's with Jesus. So we don't have to worry anymore like when he was in Iraq. We just know he's having a good time in heaven." He wiped his nose with the back of his hand. "He's way better off than we are."

"But I want him back." I tried to scream. It only came out as a pathetic cry. "It isn't fair!"

"I know." Pete sniffled. "You're right."

"Why'd he ever have to go to that stupid war?" I cried. "I hate war. All it does is ruin everything."

Pete used his careless boy hands to smooth my sleep tousled and snarled hair.

"Being mad isn't going to help, Dot," he said. "And right now we have to pray that God can make us be okay. We're going to have to learn how to live without Dad now."

"I can't live without him."

I wiped my face on my shirt, the same one I wore three days before. No one changed my clothes or washed my face. No one even put a bandage on my torn-up knees. The bloody tights still on my legs. My mom would never have let me go like that.

Then, I realized something else was missing. No noise of baking pans clanging or the washing machine swishing or the vacuum. No telephone conversations or off-key singing from the kitchen. I didn't hear the sounds of my mom.

"Where's mom?" I asked.

Pete let go of me. He sat back against the wall and rubbed his eyes.

"Well, she's in bed right now," Pete answered.

"Is it night?"

He shook his head.

"What time is it?"

"I think it's four or something."

"Is she taking a nap?"

"I don't know. She locked the door. She won't let me in."

"How long has she been in there?"

"All day. Dad's funeral was this morning. She went straight in there as soon as we got home."

"I slept through the funeral?" I cried. "Why didn't you wake me up?"

"We tried. You just wouldn't budge. Mrs. West stayed with you while we were gone." He patted my shoulder. "You want me to tell you about the service?"

I nodded.

He told me about all the people who came, the memories they had of our dad and the funny stories they shared. His eyes lit up. He seemed awake. As if just talking about the day energized him.

Eventually he ran out of words for the service. So he told me about the days I slept. I just sat and listened to him. Somehow I knew he needed to talk about all of it.

When he finished, his eyes became tired again.

"Pete, I'm really hungry," I said.

"I bet. There's a ton of food in the kitchen. People keep bringing stuff over."

"Really?"

"Yeah. There's lasagna, pizza, sandwiches...."

"Is there bologna?" I interrupted.

"Yup. A whole tray of meat and cheese."

I tried to stand. The strength just wasn't in me.

Pete leaned over me and lifted. He tried to steady me on my feet. I reached out for his hand. Then I saw that his knuckles were scabbed over. I hadn't even thought about all that he suffered. Chuck had been right. My brother needed me.

"Pete," I said, holding his arm to keep from falling. "I'm going to be okay. I swear. No matter what happens to us. I'll always be okay."

"That's good, Dot." He hugged me quickly and without the usual awkwardness of sibling embraces.

I looked at my brother. At only eleven years old, somehow he acted much older. He took on the weight of holding our family together. And he seemed to be doing a pretty good job in that moment. But it couldn't rest on him forever.

He carried that load until he couldn't any more. Then, without him as the foundation, it fell, shattering us to pieces.

We spent that afternoon and evening eating the food from family, friends and neighbors. We watched reruns of game shows until we couldn't keep our eyes open. We kept the TV on as we slept, curled up on the couch and recliner. We did this for days. Our mom didn't come out of her room that whole time. After a while it seemed like she was gone, too. Just Pete and me and the TV. Everything else seemed like a memory.

"I've been thinking about Steven a lot the past few days," I told Lisa, cracking eggs into a mixing bowl. "More than usual."

It was Wednesday morning. The rest of the residents scribbled away in art therapy. Dr. Emmert had given me a reprieve so that I could spend my time with Lisa. I appreciated the break greatly. Lisa had even brought ingredients to make cookies. The day had taken on an enjoyable shape.

"I think that's a really great thing, Cora. Right?" she said, sneaking a chocolate chip. "What kind of things have you been remembering?"

"Oh, just some of the little things about him. I'm almost embarrassed by the insignificance of what I've been remembering."

"Like what?"

"Well, one of the things I thought of was how he liked me to add cinnamon to the coffee grounds before I brewed it." I reached for the chocolate. "Leave some for the cookies, please."

"Right. Sorry." She handed me the bag. "You know, I think that sometimes the little memories are the most refreshing."

"Oh, and every night after brushing his teeth he would tap his toothbrush three times on the edge of the sink. It drove me nuts. I was sure it was unsanitary. I scrubbed that sink every day to make sure it wouldn't make his toothbrush germy."

Lisa chuckled.

I let the mixer whirl through the cookie dough.

"And he loved me." My voice barely above a whisper, hardly audible. "I do remember that. He loved me so deeply. I really believe he wouldn't have thought less of me for all that happened when I was young. And I know he would have forgiven me for keeping it from him."

I turned off the mixer, leaving the room quiet.

"So, have you forgiven yourself?" Lisa asked after the silent pause.

"Nearly." I kept my eyes on the spoon as I dropped lumps of cookie dough on the baking sheet. I raised my head and turned my eyes up to gaze through the window. "Look at that."

Lightning flashed bright against the darkened sky. The tree branches swayed, the leaves flapping wildly.

"It's going to be a doozy of a storm," Lisa said.

"And his favorite Bible story," I said. "I keep thinking about it."

"Let me guess." She squinted in thought. "The storm on the sea."

"That's right. How did you know?"

"Oh, just a lucky guess." She smiled. "I figured this storm made you think of it."

"As I remember it from Sunday school, Jesus slept in the boat through a deadly storm that His fishermen disciples couldn't seem to handle. I don't know how He could have slept through that."

"What else do you remember from the story?"

"Well, His friends were crying out to Him. Didn't they ask Him why He didn't care? Why He wouldn't do anything to help them?" I slid the cookie sheet into the oven.

"They did. They were terrified. And do you remember what happened next?"

"No. For some reason I can't recall that part."

"Jesus woke up."

"He did?" I closed the oven.

"Yes."

"And did He help them?" I stood upright, put my hands on my hips.

"He did help them——and so much more." She leaned against the kitchen counter. "See, I think that the disciples wanted Jesus to get His hands on an oar or pull a sail. Or, well, honestly, I don't know anything about boats. But the point is that they wanted Him to do something. But then, instead, He stood up and said three little words. He said, 'Peace, be still.' And with just those three little words the storm stopped. The water calmed down."

"So, Jesus didn't stay asleep?"

"No. Oh, heavens, no. He woke up and saved them."

I looked at Lisa. She grinned at me, seeming so sure of Jesus. So confident in His goodness.

"Why would He have done that?" I asked. "He didn't have to save them."

"He did it because He loved them."

I closed my eyes, letting the thought sink in. He saved me because He loved me. The smile on my face took me by surprise.

"Oh. Well, that changes everything, doesn't it?" A small glimmer of faith sparked in my soul.

I started telling Lisa more about my life. And realized that through the telling, Jesus calmed my storm little by little.

After Marlowe had been gone a year, life took on a new rhythm. Her absence became our new way of life. We'd accepted it. How devastating that humans could carry on with existence after something so traumatic. It must be the one way we could survive the horrid things of life.

My mother started to show small signs of improvement. She got herself up from the cot she'd slept on for nearly a full year. Most mornings she choked down a little breakfast. Some days she found small bursts of strength to help with a few of the easier chores. And every once in a while she could force her lips to form a slight smile.

"Cora," she called from her cot one morning.

"Yes, Mother?" I answered from my father's bedroom. I moved my mop over the last of a puddle of dried urine on the floor. He'd messed himself after he passed out the night before. His stinking clothes were piled in the corner. I would need to clean it all up before he returned. Whenever that might be. I carried the bucket into the living room.

"What day is it, Cora?" She sat on the edge of her cot.

She pulled her hair back into a thin, greasy bun. Her slip hung loosely from her shoulders. Bones jutted out under her pale, thin skin. She looked up at me, her eyes too big, sunk in deep in her face.

"Well, honey," she said. "What day is it?"

"It's Tuesday." I noticed a loose chunk of paint in the corner. I pushed it down against the wall, hoping it would blend in with the rest of the paint. It broke off and fell to the floor.

"Good. Just as I suspected. Cora, we are going to church this morning." She stood slowly and painfully. "Oh, I need to get up more often. All this inactivity is causing the most horrible ache in my joints. Please do not allow me to stay dormant like that again."

"Yes, ma'am."

"Now, where is that housecoat of mine?"

I retrieved her garment from the closet in the bedroom. I inspected it. I had just washed it the day before. I rubbed my fingertips over the blood-stained collar. All my scrubbing hadn't done much to erase it. Taking it to her, I hoped she wouldn't notice the tiny red drops. I didn't want her to be ashamed.

"It is Bible study day at the church," she said, slipping the housecoat over her head. "We are about the business of finding some help for your sister today."

"Marlowe isn't dead," I whispered, walking away from my mother.

"What was that, darling?" she asked.

"Nothing, Mother."

"Very well," she said, feeling under the cot with her hand. "Cora, do you happen to know where my shoes have gotten off to?"

"Pa burned them," I answered.

"Why would that man do such a foolish thing as that?"

"'Cause he didn't want you goin' nowhere."

She stopped. Pulled her hands up. Inspecting me with wide eyes.

"Cora, have you misplaced your beautiful grammar?" She looked around. "There must be some kind of footwear in this home that I may strap to these feet."

The only shoes we found were some old work boots that had once belonged to my father. He'd worn them to the mines.

"Perfect," my mother said as she slipped them on. The boots swallowed her dainty feet. She tied the laces as tightly as possible and stood in them. "They will have to do."

Watching her walk in those boots caused me to wonder about the shoes she'd worn as a girl. Her banker father would have bought her silk shoes with delicate heels. I swallowed the regret that she left that life to marry my father.

"Come along," she said. "We must be punctual."

The early autumn leaves had not yet turned color. The wind whipped, chilly against my face. Fresh, rich air moved around, making me feel alive. I breathed deeply of the freedom I found away from that house. I hadn't been for a walk in so long. The clean air, friendly sunshine, the music of singing birds. All birthed within me the desire to run away. To never return to the shack. I tucked the fantasy away, fully aware of the impossibility of such an escape.

"Listen, Cora, this is important," she said, her breathing labored. Each step in those heavy boots taxed what little energy she had. "We are going to the ladies' Bible study. We have to tell them what your father did to Marlowe. They will help us. I just know they will. They have to."

"Mother, why would they help us?" I put my arm through hers to keep her on her feet. We climbed higher up the steep mountain.

"I have faith that they will, darling, because that is what they are told to do by Jesus Himself." She stopped to reclaim her breath. "I have been committing this to prayer, Cora. They have to help us. We need them to."

She gazed at me, eyes wild with hope. Hope can be a terrible thing after you have lost everything else. It can trick you into thinking that something better is possible. But so often it is false. Only leading to more heartbreak, more disappointment.

After walking for nearly an hour, we reached the small church building. Tiny, sharp stones had worked their way into my shoes through the holes in the soles. My head ached from resisting the urge to fall into hope. Somewhere inside I knew those women would never help us.

The chattering, laughing, squawking voices of the women led us to where they gathered in the church basement. They stood together in little circles, filling the fellowship hall. My doubt grew stronger the closer we drew to them.

One voice carried above all the rest of the gossip in the room. My mother pulled me toward that woman.

"So, I says to her that she got to actually clean that house of hers to get that husband to stay happy," the woman said to her friend. "Ain't fittin' for a woman to expect her husband to keep true if she ain't doin' her duty by him."

The woman used her fingertips to pat the hair which sat like a dead raccoon atop her head. Her overly painted face moved with expression as she spoke.

"Mary Wheeler," my mother whispered to me. "You remember her, don't you?"

"Yes, Mother," I answered.

Mary Wheeler raised her voice even louder, hoping to garner more attention. "I says, 'Sister, ain't no doin' if you ain't doin' right by your man.'"

"Well, what did she say to that, sister?" her friend asked, a scandalized smirk on her lips.

"She says, 'Oh, Sister Wheeler, you's a fountain a wisdom.' I looks at her, right in her eyes and says, 'Lenore, I just been sayin' the very words of Jesus.' You should'a seen the look on her face."

The two women giggled in their self-righteousness.

My mother took one labored step toward the women. She dingy and thin. They clean and plump.

She cleared her throat loudly to gain their attention. The chatter continued to fill the room.

"Excuse me, sisters. Might I have your attention? I need to have a word with you." She stood straight, dignified and with some sort of authority. I tried to disappear into a corner.

"Oh, ma'am, this ain't the proper place for you to come and get no charity." Mary Wheeler said, voice snooty, merely glancing over her shoulder. "We got our food bank open on Fridays. You come back with your little girl then."

"I am not here for charity, sister, although I appreciate the sentiment," my mother said. "I am in need of another sort of help, however. And it is a desperate need. It must be addressed with the highest sense of urgency."

"What's your name? I ain't never seen y'all in church before," a woman from the other side of the room asked.

"My name is Thelma Yarborough. I have been a member in good standing in this church all my life. My maiden name was Levenson. I live on the ridge. I haven't been able to attend church in quite some time due to illness."

"Oh, Sister Yarborough. We ain't seen y'all 'round here in a coon's age. You look different. You say you been sick? You sure do look sick to me." Mary Wheeler's words bore an edge of bitterness. She crossed her arms, stretched her neck, and thrust out her chin.

"I have come today to ask for help."

"Surely the daughter of a rich banker wouldn't need no help from such poor women as ourselves."

"I have no need for money." The tendons in her slender neck tensed as she swallowed.

"Well, I'm right surprised y'all don't. Didn't your daddy disown you when you got yourself in the family way outta wedlock? 'Cause y'all wasn't married yet?" Mary pursed her lips and glanced around the room to make sure everyone heard of my mother's shame.

"Out of wedlock typically means before marriage." My mother shot her a piercing leer. "I am not ashamed of what occurred before my wedding. It is well known and I have been forgiven. I, at least, do not have to keep secrets about relations I had with men before marriage. Would you know anything about that, Sister Wheeler?"

"Well, I! What are you sayin'?" Mary Wheeler asked, scandalized.

"Oh, nothing, Mary. Nothing at all about why you hate me so much." She sighed. "But that is not why I have come here today. I need your help."

"Y'all got problems with Ducky? I heared your husband been workin' for him. Ducky is a vile sinner that the flames of hell are warmin' up just special for him."

"Amen," women from around the room chimed in agreement, nodding pious heads.

"Please, listen to me. You and I both know that we have made mistakes in the past. And I am sorry that I hurt you. Believe me, Mary, I wish I could take it all back, I would. I wish I'd never have spoken to Harold in the first place. But all of that is done. It can't be made untrue. But I am in need. And I need you to help me. All of you. Please, I am begging you to hear me."

"Beggin' ain't becomin' of a lady."

"Mary Wheeler, you listen to me!" my mother demanded, desperation creeping into her voice.

"You best not be speakin' to a pastor's wife like that," one of the ladies said.

"I will handle this, ladies," Mary said. She looked at my mother, conceding for a moment, nodding at her. "Go ahead, Thelma."

"It is dire that you ladies, my Christian sisters, help me. I am here to talk to you about my daughter Marlowe."

"Ah, yes, Marlowe. One of Jesus's precious angels. God rest her soul." Mary nodded her head, feigning compassion. "We been prayin' for y'all. Her death was a tragedy for us all. God must'a had a need for her in heaven."

"She is not dead." The color drained from my mother's face. Her shoulders slumped. "You have all been deceived."

"Oh, sister, she is dead, indeed. And you know it. We heared all about it from your husband. God bless that man." Her head continued to nod. "He come here tellin' us all 'bout the bills y'all got with the doctor. How he gotta slave away at Ducky's just to make ends meet so y'all don't lose the house. Such a sad history. We took up a offerin' for y'all to pay some of them bills. We sent him home with fifteen dollars."

"He lied. He's a liar!" My mother started to sway. I rushed to her, held her around the waist. "He drank up all our money. He gambled everything else off. He sold my daughter Marlowe to pay for his vices. He sold her to Ducky. He sold my daughter!"

"Thelma, I am shocked! The way you speak of your husband." Mary spoke as if breathless. "This ain't at all becomin' a Christian wife."

"Perhaps you would all benefit from taking a better look at your husbands. Where do they spend their evenings? What happened to their Christmas bonuses from the mine?" my mother asked, defiant. "I would wager that they have seen my daughter at Ducky's. And many of them may have raped her. Why don't you ask them about where my daughter is?"

The women in the room looked at my mother with wide, shocked eyes. Mouths dropped open. One woman gasped.

"This ain't at all fittin' for you to come in here and talk about that den of debauchery. And accusin' when you don't know nothin'. You ain't got no proof. We is a group of upright, Christ-fearin' ladies. And our husbands ain't never once stepped foot in that chamber of sin. I'm downright scandalized that you could even think that way. And to call your husband a liar, yet you turn around and lie yourself about your little girl not bein' dead. It just ain't right, and I ain't listenin' to one more word of it." Mary pointed at my mother. "Perhaps somethin' dark has took possession of your soul. We'll be sure to pray for you, ma'am."

"But, I..." my mother stammered.

"I said we'll pray for y'all," Mary interrupted. "We'll pray that y'all have plenty food to get you through the winter. That's all we gonna do for you."

"But my daughter is being raped. She is being forced." Her voice broke of all authority, all control, all power. "Not one of you cares?"

"Let's go home, Mother." I pulled on her arm. "They aren't going to help us. They never would have. They aren't the good Christian women that we hoped for."

"Whitewashed tombs," she muttered.

"What was that?" I asked, looking into Mother's eyes. Bright red blood vessels striped the white, making her glare fierce, wild.

Peeling my hands off her, she stood tall and straight once again. She screamed. A primal, terrifying scream. The women, including Mary Wheeler, turned back toward her. This time, in fear.

"You all look so pretty on the outside, don't you? So clean and dressed in your best clothes just to make everyone else think you're so good, so high and mighty! You all painted on fresh makeup from the five-and-dime and sprayed your hair in place. You just want to look so perfect to each other. Such a nice looking bunch of mean, angry, horrible people. You look okay, but you are all disgusting! All of your hearts are rotten. You are dead inside. All you are is a bunch of women trying to hide the decay of your souls."

Mary moved her mouth to speak. No words came.

"Not all who cry out 'Lord, Lord' belong to God." My mother beat the air with her hands. "Don't you know that? If you don't know that, then I suggest you start opening your Bibles and reading it for yourself. Pastor Wheeler isn't teaching you anything if you don't know that."

Her arms moved, out of control, over her head. I had to move back so she wouldn't hit me.

"Jesus tells us that if you didn't do for the least of these, you did not do it for Him. If you ignore those in need, then you are ignoring Jesus Himself! Well, get a good look. Look at my hair, the bones sticking out of my body, my worn clothes, these old work boots. Take a look, I tell you. You are looking right at the very least of these. I am beat up, poor, my daughter sold to a brothel. I am the least of all the world. Look at me! And you refuse to help me. You are looking right into the eyes of Jesus and telling him 'no!'" She spat in the direction of Mary Wheeler. "I pity you."

"Mother, we need to leave now," I whispered into her ear.

She followed me, muttering, out of the fellowship hall, up the stairs and out of the church building. We walked back down the mountain and to the ridge with much stumbling of steps. By the time we reached the shack, her arms around my neck, I carried her.

My father returned home that evening, furious at the news of her outburst.

"Ain't nobody gonna never believe a word outta you again," he yelled amid curses. His open hand made sharp noises against her face. Her back. Her arms. "This is our family business. Ain't no one else in the world gotta know nothin'. You think you so smart 'cause you got through high school? Well, how smart is you now?"

When he finished with her, he found me.

"You be still," he snarled at me. "Don't you think to make no sound. You hear?"

It was the first time a man ever touched me. And it was my father. After it was over, I rolled up tight, trembling.

"Now you're dirty like that whore sister of yours," he said, fixing his clothes. "But she do that fifteen, twenty times a day and makes me good money. You watch yourself or you gonna be movin' out to Ducky's too."

For all my tears and silent begging, Jesus slept the whole time.

Lisa wiped the tears from her face. Grabbing a napkin from the kitchen counter, she blew her nose.

"Oh, Cora," she said, shaking her head.

"Why are you crying?" I asked, putting the warm cookies on a plate.

"I am so sorry." She rubbed her eyes, smearing mascara and foundation across her face.

"It's okay," I said. My eyes remained dry.

"It's not. Not at all. They should have helped you."

"Oh, now that I think about it, there really wasn't much they could have done."

"It doesn't matter." She cleared her throat. "They should have done something for your family. They let you down."

"But they wouldn't have been able to do anything for Marlowe. Ducky was a very powerful man."

"If they had done the right thing, your father would never have raped you and beat your mother that night." She frowned. "That was something they could have protected you from."

"Well, I hate to mention this, but God didn't help us either." I handed her a cookie. "He could have saved us from my father. But He didn't do anything at all."

"He was trying to use those women to help you. I'm sure of it. They could have done His work. Instead, they just didn't do anything. Well, except insult your family. They failed."

"I suppose. But what really nags at me is this. Why didn't God stop it from happening? Why did He let my father do those things to me?"

"I don't know." She sighed. "But I can tell you this—God knew what was happening. And He was there with you. You just may not have known it."

He'd been there with me. But He hadn't stopped my pain. Doubt and faith both throbbed in my heart.

"Hold still, Dorothea!" Grace said, along with a few cuss words.

"Three dollars," I said.

"It's gonna be a whole bunch more if you don't stop goof-ballin' around."

"Isn't that better, Grace? Lola would be very impressed by your creative word choice."

"Oh, whatever." She rolled my hair with a curling iron. "So, you and Promise talking yet? You know, after your big fight."

"What?" I turned to look at her. "How did you know?"

"Hello. These walls are thin. We all hear each other's business. Quit moving." She held my head still and sprayed something in my hair. It smelled like flowers. "Well, are you guys talking again?"

"No. She hates me." I covered my face with my hands.

"Best find a way to bless her, Dorothea."

"What are you talking about?"

"Do you ever listen in Bible study? Yesterday, Lola talked about blessing those who hurt us. Remember?"

"Not really."

"Geesh, Dorothea." She stepped in front of me, moved my hands, put her face close to mine. "Promise hurt your feelings, right?"

"I guess so."

"Well, you gotta find a way to bless her. Do her chores one day. Or make her some brownies. I don't know. But find a way."

"To heap burning coals on her head?" I smirked.

"I don't know what that's all about, but it don't sound so nice to me."

"It's in the Bible."

"It still don't sound as nice as blessing her." She stepped behind me to fuss with the back of my hair.

"Whatever, Grace."

"So, where's Mr. Hotty taking you on your date?"

"It's not a date."

"Oh, give me a break."

"Seriously. He never used that word, if you really need to know. And don't call him 'Hotty.' His name is Paul."

"Did ya miss your nap, Miss Grumpy Pants?" she asked, pushing a pin into my hair.

"What the hee haw, Grace? I mean, really? You're going to be like this right now?" I said, irritable. "Listen, I can finish doing my hair if you're going to interrogate me."

"Shut up, Dorothea. You're acting like a baby."

I sighed. "You're right."

"Besides," she said. "Your hair would be a hot mess if you did it."

"Sorry," I said. "I'm really sorry. I'm just pretty nervous."

"I forgive you."

"Thanks a lot."

"You ever been on a real date?" she asked.

"No." I exhaled. "Only those kind of dates. You know?"

"Oh, yeah. I know those kind. The kind where they give you a few bucks extra to…"

"Right," I cut her off. "So, I kind of don't know what to expect."

"Well, I think it's sweet. Your childhood buddy's your first date."

"Hey, can I ask you something?"

"Yeah. You can wear my black shoes."

"Thanks. That wasn't my question, but I need them," I said. "Anyway, Promise said something to me the other day. I just need to know if it's true."

"What did she say?"

"She said I act like I'm better than everybody else." I tilted my head. "Do you think that's true?"

"Well, maybe she just feels like you had a better childhood. That might be it. But I never been mad at you for that." She pushed my head. "But I'll be mad if you don't stop moving all over the place. I swear, you're like a bobble head."

"Golly. So sorry."

She worked on my hair for a few more minutes.

"All set." She handed me a mirror. "So, what do you think?"

Grace stood in front of me with a huge smile. I moved the mirror around to get a look at her work. She'd made my flat hair billowy, flowing.

"Well, I think the cosmetology school is paying off," I said, beaming. "I've got the best roommate in the whole world."

"Dorothea, your boy's here!" Peace screamed up the stairs.

"You'd better get down there. Them girls are gonna scare the polar bear outta that boy." Grace pushed me out of our room.

"Polar bear? Good one."

When I got myself down the stairs I saw Lola and Paul on the porch through the wide open front door. I sat on the steps.

"Paul, I like you a whole lot," she said. "But I have to go over a few rules with you. Just the same as any other gentleman caller that graces the doorstep of my house." Her voice was formal, yet warm.

"Sounds fair," he answered.

"Dorothea may not drink anything with alcohol. She may not smoke or take any kind of drug. You must remain in a public place at all times. No going into a room alone with her. She needs to be home by one a.m. Otherwise, if you are certain that your tardy arrival is unavoidable, you must call me at least fifteen minutes before curfew. And you must at all times conduct yourself as a gentleman. Open doors for her, help her cross the street and so forth. No public displays of affection. No sitting in a car that isn't traveling down the road." She sighed. "I think that is all."

"Okay." He smiled at her.

"Any questions?"

"Yeah. How do I look?"

"Very handsome." She fixed the collar of his shirt. "Listen, I trust you, Paul. Please don't do anything to break that trust. Dorothea is like a daughter to me."

"Her big brother was my best friend. I won't do anything to break that trust either."

"Thank you." She turned toward me. "All right, Dorothea, he's ready."

I walked toward them, trying so hard not to trip over my own feet. I couldn't look at Paul. His smile would have made my stomach ache with the flight of a thousand butterflies.

"These are for you." Paul handed me a bunch of yellow roses. "I hope it's still your favorite color."

"Wow. Thanks." I looked at the blooms. "They're beautiful."

"Yellow roses are the flower of true friendship." He smiled.

"That's nice." A flush crept into my cheeks. I touched my face, trying to hide the pink. "Friendship is good."

"Yup, it's a good place to start." He scratched his head. "You know, I was hoping to make up for the time I cut the streamers off your bike handles."

"That was you?" I gaped at him.

"I needed to borrow it. I didn't want to look all girly."

"I blamed Pete!"

"I know. Sorry." He motioned to his car, smiling with his hazel eyes. "Would you still like to join me for dinner?"

"Well, I guess so," I said, walking down the path with him.

He drove me to a very nice restaurant. Held doors for me. He won me over little by little. I didn't mind.

"So, what have you been up to all these years?" I asked, sitting across the table from him. I picked at my salad, too nervous to eat.

"You don't want to hear about it. Nothing too exciting." He smiled, cutting a chunk off his steak. "You know, high school. That went by pretty fast. Football, proms, doing stupid things. Pretty typical. You know, right?"

I nodded. But I didn't know. I'd never been to a single day of normal high school.

I sipped my soda as he told me about trips he'd been on, girls he'd dated, jobs he'd had. Story after story of a good life. A life I didn't recognize. I sat, intrigued, eating my dinner.

"Wow," I said. "It sounds like you've had a pretty perfect life."

"Not really." He looked at the table. "I've had a few slip-ups. Nothing major. You know, girl stuff mostly. Nothing I'm proud of."

"Yeah, but still." I pushed my plate to one side. "You've had some great stuff happen for you."

The server brought the check for the meal.

"Well, I feel like a jerk. I just talked about myself the whole time. That's not right." He pulled his wallet out of his pocket. "I really hope you don't think I'm that self-centered."

"I already knew you were," I said, smiling at him. "Don't worry about it. I seriously liked hearing about you."

"Can we get some coffee or ice cream so we can talk about you?" He checked his watch. "We've got plenty of time before you turn into a pumpkin."

"Really, my life isn't that important."

"Yes it is. I want to know what's been going on for you."

We stood, walking together toward the exit.

"Okay. But you're going to have to get it in segments. I can't tell it all at once."

"So, did you just ask me out for a second date? And this one isn't even done yet."

"This was a date?"

"Of course it is," he said.

I looked at him out of the corner of my eye. A faint blush had rushed into his face.

He took me to a little coffee house downtown. We sat at a table right next to the window.

"Okay, so you already know some of this. But there's more to what happened than you all knew," I said, breathing deeply.

"Are you okay?"

"Yeah. I just haven't really talked about this in a while. I'm a little nervous."

"I understand that. You just take your time." He moved his hand across the table, stopping just short of touching my arm. "No matter what you have to tell me, I'll understand."

"Thanks." I glanced at his hand, wondering if he'd be so eager to touch me after he'd heard my story.

Not long after dad's funeral, people slowly tapered away from our lives. We stopped getting calls. The cards no longer overflowed the mailbox. Nobody brought meals. Even the preacher at church stayed away.

Everyone else moved on with life, leaving us behind. I wondered if they ever thought of us at all. And, if they did, was it in passing? Did they fear that what happened to us might happen to them? I wondered if we were a reminder of how quickly life could change for a family. And for the worst.

My mom withdrew from us, too. She'd stay in her room, the door locked, all the time. After school, I would climb the stairs and sit on the floor outside her door. Her moans and cries escaped through the door frame.

One day, I used an old, dried-up pen to carve into the paint on her door.

"I love you," I'd written.

As I sat on the floor, listening to my mom grieve, I'd run the tip of my finger over the letters. Repeating with my tracing, "I love you, I love you, I love you."

Just about every other day, she would come out of her room, convinced that she had strength enough to take care of us. After a shower, she'd come into the kitchen and start cooking something. Cookbook open, ingredients on the counter, oven preheated. Then something would snap. She'd see something in Dad's handwriting, a picture, the recipe of one of his favorite meals. The grief overtook her. Defeated her. Pete would help her back up to her room where she'd stay for another day.

One day, I noticed a row of small cuts on her arms. The most perfectly straight lines. She had tried to hide them under her clothes. But I saw them.

"Mom, what happened?" I asked, as she reached up in the cupboard for the flour. Her sleeve had fallen up her arm, revealing the red lines.

"What?" she asked, not looking at me.

"Those cuts on your arm. What are they from?"

"Nothing." She pulled down her sleeves and walked away, leaving me to clean up the kitchen.

I followed her. She'd retreated to her room. Shut the door. Locked it.

"Mommy," I cried. "I'm sorry."

I heard nothing.

"Please come back out here." I sat on the floor, traced the letters. "Don't be mad at me. Please, Mommy."

She didn't answer me. Just stayed in her room.

I used my fingernails to scratch out the "I love you," trying to dig through the door. All I needed was a hug from her. A kiss on the forehead. Some kind of reassurance. But all I got were tiny chips of paint jammed under my nails. It hurt.

I gave up. Walked away from the door.

After that, she didn't come down much anymore. She left Pete and me on our own.

Eventually the electricity was turned off. Then the gas. Next came a notice about the mortgage going unpaid. Pete wrote checks and mailed them out.

Then came the letters about the bounced checks.

We didn't know what to do. We didn't think we had anyone who could help us. Our grandparents lived in Oregon. We didn't want to worry them. If we told our teachers they would have us put in foster care. If we told our preacher, he'd do something to embarrass us. And the last thing we wanted was more pity.

We walked across the street and ask the Wests for help. We knew we could trust them. They were our only option.

Mrs. West welcomed us inside, had us sit at the kitchen table.

"Oh, guys. This just shouldn't be your problem," Mrs. West said, reheating the leftover chicken and dumplings she served her family an hour earlier. "Paying the bills just can't be your job. How many checks bounced?"

"Three." Pete held his head in his hands, rubbing his temples. "And they were really big checks. We're in so much trouble."

"Okay, Pete. Just relax a little. Mr. West will be back any minute from his meeting at the school." She winked at us. "Don't you worry. He'll know exactly what to do."

Within a few days, Mr. West had everything straight and fixed. We would be fine and together and taken care of.

We ate dinner with the Wests every night. They became our second family. Pete and I had a new home.

My mom stopped living for us. She just stayed in her room. And I no longer sat outside her door. I couldn't stand to listen to her cry anymore. The way she had closed herself off from us made me angry.

I hadn't just lost my dad. My mom was gone, too.

After the rejection of the church ladies, my mother took to sleeping in the bedroom. My father had left her there after beating her. She just hadn't gotten up for much after that night.

For seven days I scrubbed and cleaned. Floors, windows, walls. Nearly ridding the house of the acid, musty smell of him.

On that seventh day, I checked on my mother. Like all other days.

"Mother," I said, walking into her bedroom. "Do you need to get to the outhouse?"

She stirred, just a small movement. "Where's your father?" she asked, thin-voiced.

"At work," I answered, pulling the tattered blanket off her.

"He's at the mines?" she asked, letting me lift her to sit on the bed. Her skin-and-bones legs dangled over the side.

"No, Mother. He works at Ducky's now." I hefted her to her feet, my hands in her armpits.

"He must be watching over Marlowe. He would take care of her." She groaned, moving her legs for the first time that day. "Do you think she is still there?"

"Maybe," I answered. My arms around her tiny waist, I lifted her to carry her outside.

"Do you think she's okay?"

"Marlowe is alive," I whispered, shuffling my feet through the house and to the backyard. "She is alive."

While my mother sat inside the leaning outhouse, I collected wildflower petals. Filled my pockets until no more fit. Yellow primrose grew uncontested all along the old shack. The bright sunshine of flowers against the crumbling grime of our house.

"I'm finished, honey," my mother called. "Would you please come get me? I don't believe I can walk back to bed by myself."

Her sparse weight easy to bear, I carried her into the house, to her room. I laid her back in the bed and pulled the blanket back up to her chin. Her soft snoring began near instantly.

I fingered the flower petals in my pocket as I walked back into the living room. The light blue paint chipped in small flakes across the windowsill. Mold dotted the wood where moisture had soaked in.

Passing my hand over the surface, fragments of old, dried-up paint stuck to my skin. I rubbed the flower petals between my fingers as I sprinkled them across the windowsill. The bright yellow covered the decaying wood.

The sound of hard boot steps on the front porch broke my concentration. My heart pounding, I glanced out the window. Titus stood, wiping his feet on the door mat.

"How was work?" I asked, opening the door.

"Fine," he answered, pushing past me.

"I have a basin of water in the back. You can clean up there." I followed after him. "Are you hungry?"

"Yup," he burped, liquor on his breath.

"Once you're all cleaned up, I'll get you some dinner." I rushed into the kitchen.

"I'm goin' out tonight," Titus said, from the back porch.

"Where are you going?" I asked, pulling a casserole from the oven.

"Out. Ain't none of your concern," he said over the scrubbing of a brush across his nails. "Pa's pickin' me up in his new truck."

"He got a new truck?"

"Yeah. Says he done got it for a song 'cause of Ducky."

"Where'd he get the money for that?" I asked. "Seems he's been getting a lot of new things lately. But we're just about to run out of propane in the tank and I have to use our garden vegetables to trade for meat. We're going poor, but he's got enough to buy himself a new truck?"

"Cora," Titus said. "It's best ya don't ask no more questions like that. Gonna get yourself in trouble."

"I don't care."

"Well, you oughta."

"You aren't going to Ducky's tonight, are you?" A wave of nausea hit me as I looked out the back door at my brother. He looked like a man, and it frightened me.

"That's another thing you ain't gotta know," he said, his voice like a slap. "You gonna do a lot better if you don't stick your nose in it."

"I don't want you to turn out like him."

"Like who?"

"You can't be like Pa."

He walked past me into the kitchen. His skin and hair still stained black beyond scrubbing. He turned toward me, his muscles tensed. Patches of stubble grew along his jaw and upper lip.

"I ain't gonna be like that man." The lid over his eye twitched. "I ain't no good. But I'm gonna try not to be like him."

"You're a better person than him."

"I ain't." He looked at his fists. "If I was, I wouldn't let him hurt you and Ma."

"There isn't anything you can do about that. It's just the way life is."

"I'm gonna do somethin' about it, Cora." He set his jaw, determined. "I'm gonna find Marlowe first. Then I'm gonna get all of us away from Pa. Ain't right, all us sufferin' just 'cause of one man. I'm gonna fix it."

"You can't." A tear escaped, tumbling down my cheek.

He reached out his hand and touched my shoulder. Flinching, I cowered away from him. He stepped toward me and I raised up my arms to cover my face. All learned movements. All automatic. To shield myself.

"I ain't gonna hurt ya, Cora," he whispered. "What's that man done to you? You know I ain't like him."

"I know," I lied. I turned away before lowering my defenses.

"Listen, I can get us outta here. I got a plan. You just gotta trust me," he said.

"I don't trust anybody," I said, spooning the casserole onto a plate. "Here. Eat this."

"I gotta go to Ducky's," he said, taking the plate. He shoveled the steaming food into his mouth. "I'm gettin' a job there. Pa told me he wants me in the family business."

"Family business?" I cut two thick slices of bread from a loaf.

"I don't know. But he told me that today's my last day in the mine."

"I think working for Ducky'd be more dangerous than the mine."

"Yup. But it's gonna get me close enough to get Marlowe."

The tears fell, uncontrolled, from my eyes. I wobbled, knees weak at the thought of giving in to hope. My hands on the counter, I steadied my body. But my ideas got away, spinning wildly.

"I wish this wasn't my life," I whispered, closing my eyes.

"What's that?"

"Why do we have to live like this?"

"I don't know."

"It isn't fair." I opened my eyes and turned around, my back to the counter.

He sighed.

"What do we do if Marlowe's not there anymore?" I asked. "What if she's..." The word stuck in my throat like a lump, refusing to emerge.

Titus walked over to me, putting his plate on the counter.

"Marlowe isn't dead," he said. "I know she's there. A guy at the mine's been talkin' about a girl he seen there. He been real mean and dirty about her. I liked to have killed him. But he told me all about her. It sounded like Marlowe. I know it's her."

"You think you might see her?"

"I aim to."

"If you see her, tell her that I love her. And I miss her." I touched his arm. "Tell her that I haven't forgotten her."

"If I see her, I'm gettin' her outta there. Right then." The twitch of his eyelid jostled a tear loose.

The gravel of our driveway crunched under the weight of a truck.

"That's him," Titus said.

The truck's horn blared.

"You better go."

"Take care of Ma. I'll be back late." He kissed me on the forehead. This time I didn't flinch.

"Be careful," I begged. "You're all I have."

"Don't worry about me."

The door slammed behind him.

A small, blue paint chip remained on my hand, still attached to my skin.

"Here you are," Paul said, walking me up the porch steps.

"Yup, here I am," I said, turning to face him.

"Thanks for letting me hang out with you tonight." He put his hands in his pockets. "It was really great to talk and catch up a little."

"It was." I looked at my feet. I hated my ugly shoes. I'd forgotten to change into Grace's.

"This is always the weird part, right?"

"I know. Or, really, I don't." I looked up. "This was my first date."

"Really?" He smiled sweetly.

"I know. It's lame."

"Not lame at all." He hesitated. "You know, Pete told me that he wanted me to take you to prom when you got old enough. He didn't think he'd ever be able to trust any other guys with you."

"He was an awesome big brother. I miss him so much."

"Me too."

I turned, checking to see if any girls stared down at us from my window. The house was quiet.

"Well, listen, I need to get inside. It's close to time." I turned awkwardly. "Thanks for dinner and coffee."

"You're welcome."

I opened the door just as Lola walked into the entryway. She had on a jacket and her bag was slung across her shoulder.

"Hey, Lola, I'm back. You can call off the search party," I said. "I'm even a few minutes early."

"Oh, Dorothea," she said. "Promise is gone."

"Where did she go?"

"I'm not sure."

"What about the baby?"

"She left him here." She grabbed the van keys from her purse. "Let's go."

"Lola, the van's still in the college parking lot."

"You're right." She pointed at Paul. "Do you mind being our driver?"

"No problem," Paul said.

"The pastor's wife is here, Peace and Mercy are taking care of Nesto." She closed the door behind her, locking the deadbolt with her key. "We're all set. Let's go find Promise."

"Where should we go first?" Paul asked.

"The streets. I'll direct you." Lola looked into my face. "Did she say anything about where she would go?"

"Yeah. There was a club she wanted to work at in Muskegon. But she didn't have a ride. She was going to stay with somebody downtown."

"Well, that's a beginning, isn't it."

We walked to Paul's car. I grabbed Lola's arm and whispered in her ear, "He doesn't know."

"About you?"

I nodded.

"Right," she said. "I'll be careful."

Paul drove us all over the city. Lola directed him to the side streets where the dim lights made it the perfect place to hide what was going on. A few girls stood on a corner. They gawked into the cars driving past, waiting for one to stop.

A car idled on the side of the road. One of the girls climbed in. The car sped away.

"What would Promise be doing down here?" Paul asked.

"This was her track," Lola said.

"Her what?"

"This is where she worked. I apologize for being unable to sugar coat this for you, Paul. Promise was prostituted here."

Paul swallowed a few times before he was able to say anything. "Was she old enough for that?"

"Son, most of the girls out here start pretty young."

"How old?"

"Sixteen. Fourteen. Twelve."

"That's not even legal," he said. "Why doesn't anyone do anything about that?"

"We're trying, Paul. We truly are. It's a victory that must be achieved one person at a time." Lola patted him on the shoulder. "For the moment, that one person is Promise."

We searched for hours. Paul drove us up and down the streets. Lola went into strip clubs to ask about her. I asked a few of the girls standing on the corners. No one had seen her.

"It's four a.m.," Lola said. "We should head back to the house."

"Shouldn't we keep looking?" Paul asked.

"Paul, you are a dear, and I hope you don't think my heart calloused for saying this. But if Promise doesn't want to be found, we'll continue to search in vain. She will come home eventually."

Paul drove us home and then walked us to the front door.

"What's going to happen to her baby?" Paul asked.

"She left the adoption papers signed and on her bed. There is a family interested in bringing Nesto into their home." Lola unlocked the door. "I'll have to call Child Protective Services as soon as I get inside. Then his new family will be granted custody, I imagine."

"Hey, Lola," a man whispered from the hammock. "Don't get scared or nothin'."

"Antonio?" Lola asked. "What ever are you doing here?"

"Listen, I heard about Jenny. Can I talk to you without somebody shootin' me?"

Antonio sat up. Paul held the hammock to steady it.

"Thanks, man," he said. "So, Lola, you gotta believe I didn't have nothin' to do with Jenny leavin'."

"Do you have any idea where she went?"

"Yeah." He coughed. "She said she had to get outta here."

"You spoke with her?"

"Yup. She got a cell phone."

"Do you know how she came by one?"

"She got herself a new pimp. Outta Muskegon."

"Thank you very much for telling me."

"Whatcha gonna do now?"

"Pray that she contacts us."

"That's it? Why don't we go find her?" Antonio sounded scared.

"I truly appreciate your concern for her. Your compassion is moving. My fear is that if we continue to search, she'll be in even more danger. We don't know what this new pimp may do if he feels threatened." Lola sighed. "Our best chance is if she calls."

"What about the kid? You said you're callin' CPS on him."

"Yes. He'll be assigned to a social worker who will facilitate the adoption."

"That's it, then?"

"I don't suppose you are asking to take custody of him."

"No." Antonio stepped off the porch. "Just make sure that family gets him. It's better for him. I'm sure Jenny picked some good people."

He walked away, hands in his pockets, head down.

"You can't save everybody, Lola." I put my arm around her shoulders.

"I know." She hugged me. "I can't save anyone. That's Jesus's job. I just try to let the Holy Spirit do His work through me."

"What can I do?" Paul asked.

"Actually, not a whole lot right now." She looked at him. "Except, please pray for Promise."

"I can do that." He waited until we stepped inside. "Listen, I'll be at my parents' house tonight. Call if you need anything. Dot has the number."

"Thank you," I said, waving before I closed the door.

In my room, Grace snored loudly. I tossed, unable to sleep. I imagined Promise, unsafe and hiding her fear by getting high or drunk. Or both. I sat up in bed, giving up on sleep. I walked downstairs as quietly as I could. Entering the kitchen, I decided to get started making breakfast.

"I guess I just don't understand how Ducky's stayed open." Lisa sat, curled up on the couch, enthralled. "I mean, child prostitution, illegal moonshine, gambling. You'd think the police would have shut the place down."

"Oh, no. Ducky owned the town." I scratched my arm. The cuts I'd made after Stewart's suicide were healing and itchy. "Everyone claimed to hate him and what he did. But no one would have had anything without him. He owned the grocery store, the gas station, just about everything. If someone had a job on that mountain, they ultimately worked on his payroll. And he was dangerous. If he couldn't buy a person's silence, he found other means."

"How terrible," Lisa said. "Go on."

After Titus left, I kept myself busy, trying to keep the hope of escape out of my mind.

I made mush of a plateful of casserole and carried it to the bedroom.

"Mother," I said, turning on the lamp next to her bed. "Let's get some dinner into you."

She fluttered her eyes open and shut, shaking her head. I propped her up in the bed. Spooned food into her mouth. She pushed it with her tongue against the place her front teeth had been only a week before.

"No more," she said after only a few small bites. "It just hurts."

"Your teeth?" I asked.

"They aren't healed yet." She put her fingers to her lips. "Your father sure did hit me hard to knock them out like that."

"Should I see if the doctor can give you some medicine?"

"No," she shook her head. "Just the sleeping pills, darling."

She swallowed the medication, and I covered her up. Tucked her in.

I went to the living room. I pulled up one of the loose floor boards in the kitchen and retrieved my copy of Sense and Sensibility. I'd found it under my parent's bed. Just a plain blue cover with simple gold letters. A remnant of my mother's childhood possessions. Sitting in the rocking chair, I read about beauty, love, loyalty. I read until my eyes grew heavy. Until I fell asleep, slumped in the chair, the book open on my lap.

Pounding noises on the door woke me. Gasping, I opened my eyes wide. The book fell to the floor.

"It's the sheriff. Come, open the door, Ms. Yarborough," a voice called from the porch.

I went to the door and unlocked it. The sheriff stood on the porch, eyes tired.

"Young lady, I gotta talk to your mama," he said.

"She's sleeping." I peeked around the door. "She took her pills and she won't be up until morning."

"Well, I guess you're gonna be the one comin' with me to the station."

"Did something happen?"

"I can't tell ya a thing right now. You just have to come with me." He turned around. "Get in the car."

He let me sit in the front seat. We didn't talk on the drive to the station. I saw the trees blur as he drove faster and faster. When we arrived at the station, the lights blazed through all the windows. A small, cube building, it held only one cell.

"I got a fresh pot a' coffee on, if ya wanna drink some," he said, leading me to the door.

We walked into the building. It smelled like too-strong coffee and another odor. A horrible, thick, stomach-sickening stench. I'd never smelled anything like it before that day.

I looked in the prison cell. A sheet covered something on the floor. I knew that it covered a human.

"Is that person dead?" I asked, unable to take my eyes from the form.

"Sure is," he answered, slinging back a small cup of coffee. "I'm gonna need ya' to take a look at that there body. Need ya' to tell me if you know anything about this. And I expect the truth. Ya hear?"

"How did that body get in here?" I asked, whispering.

He hesitated. "Well, young lady. I don't know." He looked at me, ashamed. "I guess somebody dumped it on the front step out there."

"And you want me to look at it?"

"Yup. I gotta make sure it's who I think it is."

With a sinking, out of control, dizzying sensation, I moved toward the bars of the cell. I leaned against them to keep myself from collapsing. The shape of the body appeared to be tall, slender. The sheet soaked up the red that bled out of the chest.

Let it be my father, I prayed silently.

The sheriff stooped next to the body. He grabbed hold of one edge of the sheet and pulled it away from the face.

"No," I cried. "No. Jesus, no."

I stepped in the direction of the body, but stumbled, legs weak. I fell next to the edge of the sheet. Pushing myself up, I grabbed the sheet and ripped it off the rest of the way, revealing the whole body. I touched the sandy blond hair, full of coal dust.

Unbearable pain clenched my chest. Tears wouldn't come, no matter how I tried to release them. To scream and tear at the sheriff. To insist that justice be served for Titus. For Marlowe. For my family.

But, instead, I knelt quietly, touching my brother's face and hair. I couldn't do anything else.

"Can ya' tell me who this is?" the sheriff asked.

"My brother," I whispered.

"And what was his full name for the record, ma'am?"

"Titus Carlton Yarborough," I answered, weak and exhausted.

Large, jagged holes were torn into my brother's chest. I covered them with my hands, wishing I could push the life back into him. That I could scoop up all his lost blood and force it back into his veins.

"Ma'am, I'm gonna have to ask ya not to touch that body no more."

"How did this happen?" I asked, turning my eyes up to the sheriff.

"Oh. Well, I ain't got the right to tell ya that, little girl."

"My name is Cora. You know that, sheriff." My boldness surprised me.

"Cora, I can't tell ya what happened." He pushed me back and pulled the sheet back over Titus's body, leaving only his face uncovered. "You're just a little girl."

"Sheriff, I am far more grown-up than you think. You have no idea what life is like for me. So, please, just tell me what happened."

He told me that Titus was in a room with one of the girls at Ducky's. He broke out the window. They accused him of skipping out on paying. He slipped past the bouncer, holding the hand of the girl, pulling her with him. He meant to take her from Ducky. One of the men unloaded his gun into Titus' chest.

"Who was the girl?"

"I don't know nothin' about none of them girls. Ducky don't keep records. Ain't no business of mine."

"Who shot him?"

The sheriff shifted his weight, uncomfortable. He avoided my eyes.

"You tell me who shot my brother," I yelled.

"Well, I don't know for sure. You need to stop askin' questions, little girl. You don't know who you're talkin' 'bout right now." He stepped out of the cell. "You go ahead and say your last good-byes. I best be takin' you home real soon."

Disregarding the sheriff, I touched Titus's face one last time. The rough stubble on his chin. The strong cheek bones. His blood still wet on my hands, I marked his cheeks with my touch. I covered his face with the sheet. The only proper burial he would receive.

"Let's get ya home, missy." The sheriff pulled me up. "Don't want your mama to wake up without ya there."

That mountain held me captive. In that little shack. And the force that detained me was far stronger than my father. I resolved to turn my heart off to hope.

I had no one left to protect me from the dangers that surrounded me.

Or so I thought.

"How's the breakfast coming along?" Lola asked when she walked into the kitchen later that morning.

"Okay, so far." I checked the cinnamon rolls in the oven. The sweet fragrance of dough and cinnamon mingled with the rich aroma of coffee. My stomach grumbled with hunger. "I can't tell you how many times I've thanked God for coffee this morning."

"I'm sure I could guess." She poured herself a cup.

"How are you doing?" I asked, mixing the ingredients for some icing. "Losing Promise was a shock, huh?"

"Not really all that surprising." She sat in her seat at the table. "I saw a lot of warning signs. I was just praying that she'd let the Holy Spirit tug at her heart."

"How many girls have run away like that?"

"Well, in twenty years I've had fourteen go back to the streets." She frowned. "And each one breaks my heart all over again. It is a harsh life to which they return."

"I'm sorry, Lola."

"I know. Me, too." She paused. "I just have to trust that the Lord will have His will in her life. It's the same hope I have for all of you."

"Wouldn't it be nice if everything would just work the way we wanted it to?"

"Oh, no, Dorothea. I know my mind far too well to desire that." She looked at me. "I regret that we haven't been able to talk about your get-together with Paul."

"He was nice." I smiled. "He treated me very well."

"I'm glad. He's a good feller."

"He really is."

"I hope you don't mind me asking this, Dorothea. But do you think he has intentions of a relationship with you? Other than friendship, that is."

"I don't know, Lola. Part of me hopes so. But another part of me isn't sure I could handle that right now."

"Dorothea, if you end up in a relationship with him, you are going to have to disclose certain unpleasant information with him. You are aware of that, correct?"

"I know." I pulled the rolls out of the oven and instantly covered them with the thick, sticky icing. "Did you ever date anyone after you left the life?"

"I did have a few interested gentlemen."

"How did you tell them?"

"Well, the first one never knew." She sipped her coffee. "I told the other one after a year of dating. The next day he sold the engagement ring that he'd bought for me. I hadn't known he was about to propose."

"That stinks."

"It most certainly did." She grimaced. "He assumed I got into the business by my own choosing. He wouldn't hear contrary to that idea. Now I'm glad we never married. How could I do this ministry with a man would refuse to understand?"

"Do you think Paul would be mad at me?" I asked, small voiced.

"No I don't. He's a special guy. But I do think that you need to tell him before he gets intentions."

A flutter in my chest, a tightening in my throat. I gasped for breath. The bowl of icing fell out of my hand and to the floor.

"Dorothea?" Lola got up and poured me a glass of water. "One of your attacks?"

I nodded. She led me to a chair and made me sit.

"I can't tell him," I cried between sucking in air and breathing out wheezes. "I don't want to remember."

"Those days are over, sweetie. No one is going to hurt you like that again." She rubbed my back. "You are safe."

After a few minutes, I regained my calm. Breathed easier. Tinges of the anxiety still pulsed, but most of the fear was gone. Lola used a wash cloth to wipe the sweat from my brow. She let it rest on the back of my neck.

"Sometimes I get all those closed-in feelings. Like I'm still trapped."

"I know, Dorothea. But you aren't stuck anymore."

"Do the memories ever mess with you?"

"Yes. Often." She stooped to wipe the icing off the wood floor. "I think the nightmares are the worst."

"Yeah." I closed my eyes. "I just wish they would all go away. Like, that I'd grow out of them."

"Me, too. But I also dream often about the day I got away. And those are glorious, thankful dreams."

"Tell me the story, Lola."

"You've heard it before, Dorothea." She rinsed out the wash cloth.

"I know." I put my head on the table. "But I want to hear it again. It always makes me feel better. Please, Lola."

"Very well," Lola said.

She told about walking the streets in Grand Rapids. After years of working for the same pimp, she gained his trust. Instead of insisting that she check in every hour, she only had to report back each morning before returning to her motel.

One night, a man picked her up for a date. The customer asked very specific questions about what she would do and how much he would need to pay.

"Are you a cop?" she'd asked.

"No," he had answered.

"If you're a cop, I want you to arrest me right now. I promise that I'll tell you everything you want to know. I'll tell you about my pimp and who he works for. I'll tell you where his money is laundered and where he keeps us girls. I'll tell you about the drugs and the guns and the under aged girls. I will tell you everything. And I promise I won't fight you."

Lola was arrested that night. She said she slept better in that jail cell than ever before in her life. She tasted freedom for the very first time when locked up behind bars.

The next morning, after giving all the information she could, she entered a protection program and waited to testify.

Nobody cared to try that kind of case. So, the charges against the pimp were dropped. Her protective custody was lifted and she moved around for two years, hiding, trying to stay safe.

After those two years she purchased the house that would be a safe place for all of us girls. She'd somehow raised enough money from churches and fundraisers.

Lola's gentle voice lulled me to sleep that morning.

Later, I woke up to the sounds of family breakfast. Plates clinking, laughter, chairs scooting across the floor. I sat up slowly, trying to wipe the drool from my chin without anyone noticing.

"You're cute when you're drooling all over the table," Paul said, sitting in Lola's chair. He took a bite of cinnamon roll. "These are really good, Dot."

"Thanks," I said, too confused to be embarrassed. "Wait, you're not allowed in here."

"I know. But I brought Mom and Dad. They wanted to see how things work here. Lola said it was okay."

I nodded, pushing the hair off my face.

"And I wanted to see you. Drool and all." He smiled. "So, can we get burgers later? Pick up where you left off?"

"That would be great," I said. "Are you sure you can handle my story?"

"I think so. Why?"

"Because I can hardly stomach it." I smiled. "Speaking of stomach, I'm starving. You wanna share that cinnamon roll?"

"For you, anything," Paul said, pushing the plate to the middle of the table. "I mean that, you know. Right?"

"I think so," I said, stuffing a piece of roll into my mouth.

"Good morning, Cora," Lisa said.

"Hi," I said, scooting over on the couch to make room for her to sit. "I thought you had to go on a youth group trip today."

"Thank goodness, someone else volunteered to go. I'm just a little too old to hang out with twelve teenage girls all day. I'll gladly leave that to the twenty-something crowd."

"I can't even imagine. The world must be so different now. It's been so long since I've been out there."

"Yes. You'll have a lot of catching up to do when you get out of here."

"I don't think that's something I'll need to worry about for quite a while. I'm not nearly well enough for that."

"Actually, you do need to start thinking about it." She placed her hand on mine. "Cora, haven't they told you?"

"Told me what? Who?"

"Dr. Emmert said he was going to tell you the other day." Lisa sighed.

"What? What do they need to tell me?"

"The State is closing this facility. They don't have the money to keep it open. They've placed Edith and Wesley in other programs." She looked at me with a hopeful smile. "But they've determined that you're well enough to go home."

"I don't have a home," I said, nearly panicking. "Where am I supposed to go? I have no money. I have nothing."

"I know," Lisa said. "But you have me."

"Who?"

"You have me." She squeezed my hand. "Listen, first we're going to have to get a hold of Dot. We'll see what she thinks about everything."

"She won't be able to support me."

"I know. And that's why I was hoping you might just agree to come live with me."

"Why would you want that?"

"Because you're my friend." She pulled a picture out of her bag. It was of a house in the process of construction. "See this? I'm building a house. There are far too many rooms in it for just me. I thought I'd like to have you live with me."

"But I can't pay you anything."

"I know. Maybe you could help me learn how to cook. Teach me how to make cookies."

"Oh, I don't know, Lisa. I just don't know."

"Well, think about it. You have two weeks to decide."

"Two weeks isn't enough time."

"It's plenty of time." She smiled at me. "Now let's get back to your story."

Struggling to grasp the goodness of Lisa's offer, I looked at her hand on mine.

"Where did I stop last time?" I asked.

"You'd just identified Titus's body," she answered.

"Oh, yes." I cleared my throat. "And it must get far worse before it gets better."

The sheriff drove me home. By then, my mother had awakened. He told her about my brother's death. She took the news with closed eyes and streaming tears. Silent, shaking sobs that moved the whole bed. She covered her face with the blankets.

She mourned Titus without sound for weeks. Not eating, not getting up for the outhouse. She refused to speak. My life consisted of caring for her. Giving her pills to swallow. Changing the sheets when she messed the bed. Fretting over her.

One morning, after so many days of silence, I heard my name. A faint, fragile voice called for me.

"Cora," my mother called, standing in the doorway of her bedroom. "Honey, I'm ready to get up now."

I dropped my dust rag and rushed to her, gently wrapping my arms around her. So afraid that I would break her if I held too firmly.

"Be a dear," she said. "Help me to the rocking chair, please."

I helped her into the chair, stuffing pillows at her sides to keep her upright. An old, threadbare afghan tucked over and around her legs.

"Cora, honey," she said "Would you be willing to get me a glass of water, please?"

I brought her a small canning jar of water. She wrapped her bony fingers around it.

"Thank you." She lifted the jar, unable to get it to her lips. She lowered it into her lap. "This is a heavy glass."

"Would you like me to hold it for you?" I asked.

"Please, darling. That would be kind."

I tipped the glass to her mouth, gently pouring a thin stream of water into her mouth. She swallowed the small sips. Then put her hand up when she'd had enough.

The blue of her irises gleamed like jewels. She pulled her brow together. The slack skin of her cheeks was turned down in a pained frown.

"How about you sit with me for a minute, Cora?"

"I can't, Mother. I have so much to do." I took the jar into the kitchen and put it on the counter. "If my father comes home and sees this filthy floor, well, I shudder to think what he'd do."

"Your father has never cared about the condition of this house, dear."

I walked back into the living room. "But I—"

"But nothing. When he walks into this house all he is interested in is getting sleep." She flashed a shamed look at me and then turned her eyes to the floor.

She massaged the center of her forehead. "Just sit with me, please. I would like to talk to you. It isn't asking too much."

I sat on a stool by the window. The chilled air seeped in through the cracks around the glass. The yellow flowers from weeks ago had fallen to the floor, exposing the windowsill once again.

"You know where your father works now, don't you?" She looked directly at me again.

"Yes, ma'am." I turned my face away from her.

"Do you know what he does there?"

"No, ma'am."

"Well, what he does is not good. Not even a little. But I think that you're old enough to know about it. Do you think you will be able to handle knowing such a harsh truth about him?"

I had watched my sister taken to be sold. I had been the one to identify my brother's bullet-torn body. My own father raped me. My life was nothing if not completely consumed by harsh truth.

My heart raged against her. I kept us alive and took care of everything. She had given up, incapable of helping me. A few pills down her throat and she could escape into sleep. I held such resentment in my soul against her. She had been the mother. I was the child. And, yet, I mothered her.

But, instead of screaming and yelling and slapping, I answered her in a weak voice.

"Yes, ma'am. I believe I am ready to hear about what he does."

"See, your father…" She spoke slowly, with intent, her hands folded in her lap. Her calm defused me.

"Yes?" I asked, leading her.

"Well, allow me to start this way. What happens at Ducky's is far beyond the law. Do you know what they do there?"

"I do. Yes. The men go there to drink and gamble. There are women there for the men to fornicate with." I blushed on account of the word.

"Correct. And all that money goes to Ducky. Men are willing to pay a lot of money to have their way with women."

"I know."

"Well, it is your father's job to make sure that the men pay. He also keeps the women in line."

"Do you think he hurts the girls?"

"I don't know, Cora."

"Marlowe is one of those girls."

"Yes, Cora. She is."

"But she wouldn't want to let them do that to her. I just know she wouldn't. So, how can they force her to do those things?"

"Oh, Cora, what they do to those girls is very wrong." She sighed. "But Ducky is a dangerous and powerful man. I have no idea how he came about such influence, but he certainly is in control. People are afraid of him. Even the sheriff seems to be under his thumb. No sheriff I have ever heard of is able to afford a new car every year."

"The sheriff works for Ducky?"

"Yes, he most certainly does." She paused. "Cora, your father is stuck. He's gotten himself into a bad situation and he doesn't know how to get himself out."

I looked at her. She'd buried her hands under the afghan.

"Your father has many problems, Cora. He drinks too much and is no good at playing cards. Both of those things have gotten him into a lot of trouble."

"So he had to work at Ducky's to pay off his debts."

She nodded slowly, solemnly.

"I hate him," I whispered. The raw emotion pounded in my heart. "I wish he would just drop dead. I pray that someday he will be killed. I want him to die and I want it to hurt him real bad. If I could kill him myself, I would be glad."

"Oh, Cora," she said, pulling her hands up to her chest. She shook her head. "Don't say such things, honey."

"Why shouldn't I?" Anger burned in my quiet voice. "And how can you stand up for him? He hurts you, too."

"He is not a bad man, Cora. He has been hurt in his life, too. And he has made some terrible choices. But you can't hate him. You must never allow yourself to hate him." She sighed, letting her head drop slightly. "We have to love our enemies. As impossible as that seems, it is what Jesus calls us to do."

"I don't care what Jesus says. I will love everyone else in the entire world, but I will never love that man. That's a promise. And I will never forgive him. Never." The force of the words punched through my voice. "I would rather die than love him."

She looked down. Her shoulders shook with a sob. She raised one of her skeletal hands to wipe the tears from her face.

"I know what he has done to you," she wept. "Oh, God, help me. I know what he has done."

My stomach turned, for fear that she would be angry at me. "I'm so sorry, Mother."

"It isn't right for a man to take advantage of his own daughter that way." She dropped her face into her hands. "It is an evil thing to do."

"I hate him," I said again.

"I know, honey. I know."

Suddenly, her arms encircled me. How she got from her chair to me, I didn't know. But her arms held me tighter than I would have expected. Each wave of my weeping nearly broke her brittle body. She held on to me through it all. When the storm of grief passed, she sat me up and wiped my face with the heel of her hand.

"I am sorry that I have never been the mother you needed. I am sorry that I have failed to protect you. I just didn't know what to do."

"It's okay, Mother." I forced a smile.

"No, it is not okay," she said, her energy drained. She leaned against me. I could tell her head felt heavy on her neck. "I need to go to bed."

"Would you like something to eat?" I stood to help her to her feet.

"I don't have a stomach for anything."

I lifted her body into bed once our shuffling feet got us into her room. She felt lighter than ever before.

"Dear, I'll need my sleeping pills." She held out her hand as I grabbed the bottle of medication. "Leave the bottle on the bedside table, dear."

I gathered the dirty laundry from the basket in the corner of the room. As I walked out, I heard her small, fading voice.

"I'm so sorry, Cora." She reached her stick arm toward me. "Promise me something, will you? Promise me that if anything happens to me, you will leave this mountain."

"Nothing is going to happen to you, Mother."

"Just promise." Her arm fell, too heavy to hold up. "Whatever it takes, you must get away from here. You'll never have more than this if you stay. It will only get worse. Just promise me."

"Okay, Mother. I promise."

"I love you."

"I love you, too."

"Now go so I can get some rest."

I felt her eyes on me as I walked out of the room.

"So, how many yellow roses can one guy buy?" I asked, inspecting my second bouquet from Paul.

"As many as it takes." He smiled at me. "Hey, somebody like me getting another date with somebody like you. That's worth celebrating."

"Oh, Paul," I giggled. "Wait on the porch. I've got to put these in some water."

The kitchen still smelled like bacon from the morning's breakfast. I reached under the sink for a vase. Lola walked in behind me, talking on her cell phone.

"Please listen to me, dear." She paused.

I looked at her. She mouthed "Promise" and pointed at the phone. I stood and turned on the water to fill the vase I'd found.

"Yes, I do understand that living here was difficult for you, Jenny. Believe me, I understand that more than you know. But running away was not the best solution to the problem."

She listened to Promise's voice on the other end of the line.

"No, Nesto isn't here. He was picked up by child services this afternoon. He'll be going to live with the family you met with last week." She dabbed a tear from the corner of her eye. "You're working tonight?"

I put the flowers into the water.

"Well, I'm concerned about you dancing for that man. If you would just please tell me where you are, I'll come get you." She grabbed a piece of paper and a pen. But she didn't write anything. "No, I won't call the cops on you. I just want you to be safe."

Lola pushed the paper to the back of the counter. "Just please be safe, Jenny. And no matter what, you are always welcome to come back here. Even if it's just for a visit." She frowned. "Please be careful."

She closed the phone and put it in her pocket.

"Have a nice evening, dear," she said, patting my shoulder. "I'm going to bed. Please don't be late."

"Lola, if you want, I could stick around tonight," I said, putting the last rose in the vase. "Paul and I could play cards with you on the porch or something."

She turned toward me and smiled.

"Dorothea, your kindness is beautiful. I shall be fine. I just need to spend some time praying for our sister Promise."

"Okay." I picked up the vase of flowers and handed it to her. "Take these. You need something to brighten that teeny tiny closet while you pray."

She took the vase.

"Thank you." She winked at me. "Now, go be wooed."

Paul sat on the steps, his back toward me. When he heard my footsteps, he turned and smiled at me. It was a smile that took up his whole face. And it was for me.

"Ready?" I asked, my heart pounding.

We rode in his car. When he reached for the gear shift, I wanted to hold his hand. Just for a little contact. Some connection. But touching him seemed impossible, terrifying.

"Do you think Promise will come back?" he asked.

"I don't know," I said, glad for the break in tension. "I just hope she stays safe."

"I guess that would be a pretty dangerous lifestyle." He glanced at me. "Aren't you glad you've never been in that situation?"

I didn't answer him. We rode the rest of the way in silence. After a few minutes, he pulled into the parking lot of a restaurant.

"So, last time we talked about my parents saving the day. What's next in the life of Dot?" he asked after we slid into a booth.

"Oh, gosh. I seriously don't know why you have to hear about all this."

"Because I want to know. And you're a good storyteller."

The waiter stopped by our table. Took our food order.

"What if I don't want to tell you?" I asked.

"You do. I know you do." He looked at me, his face was serious. "Dot, you've had the roughest life of anyone I have ever known. I want to be part of your life. You know, I want to try and make things better for you."

"Well, sometimes it's just not very fun to talk about all that stuff."

"I bet. But you know I'm not going to sit here and judge you. It's not like you have some huge issue that you're so ashamed of or anything."

"Maybe I do. And maybe I have a hard time trusting people."

"That's okay." He took a napkin from under his silverware and wrote on it. "This is my contract to you. If you're worried about being judged, then I promise that I'm not going to judge you. If you're worried that I'll tell other people, I promise that this conversation will go nowhere outside the two of us. If you're worried I'll run away from you because of how terrible things were, I promise that I'll stick around at the very least to be your friend."

He signed the napkin and passed it across the table to me.

"Paul, you didn't have to do that."

"Yes, I did. If I break any of those promises, I will personally give you all the money in my savings."

"Yeah, I bet you have twenty bucks in there."

"Dot, do you happen to remember that my father is a money manager?"

"Oh, yeah."

"Dorothea, this is important."

I knew that I had a choice. I could have clammed up and kept everything to myself. Or I could trust him and share my burden. But that would require so much more from me than I thought I was able to give.

"Trusting you is scary, Paul," I whispered, twisting the napkin in my hand.

Our waiter brought our plates of steaming food.

"Why?" Paul asked after we were alone. He sat forward, looked concerned. "What's so scary about trust?"

"I don't want to be exposed. I'm not so sure I'm ready for you to see all of my heart."

"Then take it slow. I've got time."

Christmas came the year my dad died. For some reason my nine-year-old brain assumed that life wouldn't keep moving. But it had. And we were without a tree or presents or a big meal when the day arrived. It was just like any other day.

The Wests went on a vacation to Florida. They made sure we had plenty of food to get us through the week. We had the number to their condo in case of an emergency.

Pete and I sat, watching a football game that neither or us cared about and eating Ramen noodles from little foam cups.

"I hate football," I said, my mouth full of the salty, gummy noodles.

"I hate these noodles," Pete said, spitting them back into the cup and tossing it on the coffee table. "Merry Christmas, huh?"

There we stayed for hours. Every once in a while one of us would go to the kitchen for a cookie or a glass of milk. Before we realized that the day was half gone, the sun set. We turned on the lights.

We barely heard the soft footsteps on the stairs. Not until I caught the movement of her slippers did I realize that my mom had emerged from her room.

"Pete," I said, pointing to her. "It's Mom."

Pete stood up. He walked to her and held her hand, steadying her as she made the last few steps. He helped her into a chair. She had become so thin. Thinner than anyone I'd ever seen.

"Thanks, Pete," she whispered.

"Do you want something to eat?" he asked, his voice so gentle.

"I don't know," she answered. "I just don't have the stomach for anything."

She sighed, rubbed the center of her forehead with her fingers.

"Mrs. West made us a giant tub of cookies," I said, crumbs falling from my mouth and melted chocolate in the corners of my lips. "They're super good."

"I can see that." She looked at me. "How many of those cookies have you had?"

"I have no idea." The sugar made my body jittery.

"Well, I suppose I could use a little of that energy."

Pete went to the kitchen to get her a cookie.

"Merry Christmas, Mommy," I said.

Her whole face winced. Pete handed her the cookie.

"Is it really Christmas?" she asked.

"Yes," I answered.

"How did I lose track of all this time?" She rolled her eyes. "I'm becoming just like her."

"Like who?" Pete asked.

"Nobody. I just feel like the worst mom in the entire world. How does a mother forget all about Christmas?" She took a bite of her cookie. "And I used to be the one to make all the cookies around here."

She scanned the living room, seeing the mess created over months. Dishes were stacked on the coffee table, school books scattered across the carpet, a thin layer of dust covered everything.

"And I would never have let this house get so filthy." She sat up straighter. "I can't do this anymore. What would your daddy have thought of me?"

"I don't know," I answered.

"Well, I'll tell you. He would have told me to stop moping and take care of you." She scratched her scalp. "Dot, how long have you been wearing those pajamas?"

"I don't know." I looked down and saw the stain from a sloppy joe. "Four days. We had sloppy joes four days ago. But I think I put them on the day before that."

"That is just horrible. Oh my goodness." She sighed again. "I want the two of you to go get dressed. You do have clean clothes, right?"

"Yeah. Mrs. West did all the laundry before they left," Pete said.

"Well, that was very nice of her." She stood, wobbly. "Get something on. We're going out to eat."

"But it's Christmas," Pete said. "Nothing will be open."

"Haven't you ever watched any Christmas movies? Chinese restaurants are always open on Christmas."

"Why?" I asked.

"Well, I don't know. But they always are."

She struggled to walk to the staircase. The sadness wasn't gone from her. I could still see it in her eyes. But I also saw some determination. She was getting up and out for us. It felt like things might get better.

After we all got into clean clothes we piled into our car and she drove us to a Chinese place in a strip mall. We filled up on sweet and sour chicken and egg rolls.

"This tastes so good," Pete said, mouth full.

"It sure does," my mom said, taking a small bite. "Your Dad would have loved this. I think this might have to be a new Christmas tradition."

"Sounds good to me." Pete shoved a crab Rangoon into his mouth.

A large, scruffy man walked past us. The smell of sour booze and cigarette smoke lingered behind him. My mom looked up just as he past her. She cleared her throat and took a drink of water.   .

"Hey, Mom, do you think that guy was homeless?" I asked.

"What?" She seemed back to that far away place where she'd been after my Dad died. "Oh, that man? I don't know."

"Excuse me, ma'am," the waiter said. He carried a plate of orange slices. "The man that just left ordered these for you and your children. Merry Christmas."

"Thank you, but we're fine." She looked at the two of us. "I don't think any of us could eat another bite, could we?"

"He said it was a peace offering."

"A peace offering?" she asked. "Well, you eat them. Or just throw them out. We don't want them."

"He said he'd be seeing you around." The waiter put the plate on the table. "He told me to say that you don't look so much like 'her' anymore."

"We've got to go." She pulled money from her purse and left it on the table. "That should cover the bill. Pete, Dot. We need to go now."

We left so quickly that we didn't have time to get our coats on.

"Get in," she said, turning on the ignition.

She put the car into reverse. The scruffy man stepped right up to her window and knocked.

"Found ya," he said.

My mom made whimpering noises as she struggled to move the car away from the man. The wheels spun on the ice, unable to gain traction. The man reached for the door handle. Pete leaned over the seat and hit the electric locks.

"Mom," he yelled. "Drive."

"I can't," she cried. "He's going to get us."

The man doubled over, suddenly and surprisingly. He coughed violently. His entire body heaved with the hacking. Somehow, while he was bent over, the wheels caught a bit of dry pavement, moving us backwards. Suddenly. Out of control.

Recovering from his fit, the man walked toward us, his hand inside his jacket. My mom struggled to put the car into gear. Panicking, she screamed, pulled on the gear shift. As soon as the car went into drive, she sped away, leaving the man behind us.

"I brought you a chai latte today, Cora," Lisa said. "It tastes like pumpkin pie."

"Just in time for Thanksgiving," I said, tasting the warm, creamy spiced tea. "Oh, that's good. I didn't expect you this evening."

"I know. But my day just isn't the same without my Cora time. Even if it is later than usual." Lisa handed me a bag. "I brought you a pumpkin bar."

"You're spoiling me." I patted my stomach. "You know, I am getting a little soft around the middle."

"I think you look good. Healthier."

"Did you know that there's an island somewhere in the Pacific where they try to get their women as big as possible? They think it's attractive."

"Where did you hear that?"

"Some afternoon talk show. I watched it with Edith." I smiled. "Edith even swayed her head a little while we watched it."

"Maybe Dr. Emmert should use that in therapy." Lisa sat next to me. "How did it feel to spend time with her?"

"It was pretty nice to take a little time to think about someone other than myself for a change. Goodness. I have been so self-centered for the past decade."

"I'm proud of you for thinking that way." Lisa took a bite of her bar. "But I am going to ask you to keep talking about yourself."

"That's okay. The sooner I'm done telling you all this, the sooner I can move on to something new."

"It's exciting isn't it?" She sipped her tea. "We left off with your mother making you promise to leave."

"Right."

"How did it make you feel to make that promise? You were just a teen."

"Barely even that." I inhaled deeply. "I guess it made me feel like I had permission to go. That she didn't want to be what held me back."

"Okay. So what happened next?"

"Later that night, there was a storm...."

The wind that night shook against the shack, whipping it with such force, I expected to be blown away. Thunder growled, echoing off the mountains. With each slap of lightning, I cowered, flinching in anticipation of something, anything to crash into the trembling building. Rain poured in through the rusty holes of the roof, running down the walls, making puddles on the floor. I moved around the living room, placing buckets and pots and pans under leaks.

I hurried to the bedroom to make sure my mother wasn't drenched in her sleep. The lamp next to her bed flickered as I turned the switch. My mother didn't move or squint at the light. She remained still. And dry.

Opening a drawer in her dresser, I found the shard of glass from a broken mirror. I looked at the fragment of my reflection. One eye. A wisp of auburn hair. I couldn't see much of me. I drew it closer to my face. Beneath my nose, air steamed on the mirror. I wiped it clean on my shirt.

"Check Mother's breathing," I told myself. "Just in case."

My bare foot landed in a cold puddle of rain as I walked to her bed. I held the glass under her nose. Nothing. No breath. No steam. No evidence of life. My own breathing became shallow, quick. I put my fingers on her wrist to feel for the blood coursing through her veins. Nothing. I touched her neck. Nothing.

"Oh, Lord! I can't feel her life! Help me!" I screamed. I grabbed her head, made it to rest in the crook of my elbow. I pulled her face into my chest. Cradling her. Her head, so heavy, fell backward over my arm. Her mouth fell open. I pushed her hair back with the palm of my hand. It was soft.

"I should have checked on you earlier. I didn't know this would happen. Why didn't I just come check on you?" I whispered, my voice trembling. "What am I going to do now?"

Lightning flashed, killing the power. I held my mother's motionless, cold body closer to me. As tight as I could.

I was trapped in the valley of the shadow of death and I feared evil because I was completely alone. I laid her head down, not in a place of comfort. Not in tranquility. But in the bed that she'd devoted her life to for so long.

Stumbling through the dark house, feeling my way through the kitchen drawers, I searched for candles and matches. My hands shook, fingers unable to hold the small match sticks. They dropped to the floor before I could light them. Only one match remained in the box.

"Please," I screamed. "Make this one light."

I pinched it between my finger and thumb and dragged it across the rough side of the box. The smell of sulfur as it lit inspired relief.

Touching the flame to the wick of a candle, I let the glow warm me. I cupped my hand around the tiny light, protecting it from any breeze as I returned to the bedroom. Stood at the doorway. Looked at her body in the bed.

On the bedside table, a paper propped up against the lamp, folded in half. I stepped into the room and picked up the paper. A page from one of her ancient books. Torn out, raggedy edges. I unfolded it. Her penmanship scrawled across the page.

My dearest Cora,

I cannot tell you how terribly sorry I am. I would never,

in life, have been able to make up for all that you have endured. I did know that my death would be freedom for us. My living kept you tied to this house. You are freed from this prison now. You must go. Maybe God can forgive me. And I hope that you will, too. For all of it.

Don't forget your promise to me. Leave the mountain. Go tonight.

Look in the bedside table. There is an envelope for you. It's what my mother handed to me before I ran off to marry your father. I hid it and saved it for something like this. Use it to get away. Leave tonight.

All of my love,
Mama

I shuffled around her room, quickly gathering things to take with me. Slipping my feet into my worn shoes. I didn't allow myself to cry. Refused to let any thought dizzy my mind. There would be plenty of time for that later. I had to move fast.

In the drawer of her bedside table, I found the envelope. How it had escaped my father's searches, I couldn't surmise. But it sat in the drawer, fat, and leaned up against a small box. I grabbed the envelope and the box and shoved them into a bag I found in the closet.

Carrying the candle, I went to the front door. The doorknob was cool on my fingertips.

"You've got to help me get off this mountain," I prayed, turning the knob. "You owe me that much."

Headlights flashed through the window.

My father was home.

The motion of the car caused my stomach to flip flop. I feared that I'd get sick. She drove around as if she forgot where we lived.

"Mom," Pete asked. "Where are we going?"

"I just need to think," she answered. "What are we going to do?"

Eventually, she drove the car up our driveway and into the garage. Without a sound, the three of us rushed into the house.

She ran from room to room locking doors, checking windows, securing us from a danger that Pete and I didn't understand.

A vehicle rumbled down the road. Pete looked out the window.

"No! Don't look out the windows. Don't turn on any lights or the TV," she whispered, panicking. "Just go to your rooms and grab a few changes of clothes."

"Why?" I asked.

"We have to go somewhere else for a few days." She looked in my direction without really seeing me. "Just hurry. Warm clothes. Underwear. Toothbrush."

"I don't know what to do," I said, confused. "You're scaring me."

"You know what, don't worry about it. Let's just go. We'll get new stuff later."

I followed her up the stairs and into her bedroom. She opened her closet and spun the combination lock on the safe. Grabbed something and put it in her coat pocket.

"What's that?" I asked.

"Nothing. Don't worry about it, okay, Dot," she said. She stood and rushed back down the steps. "Get back into the car. I want the two of you to lie down on the seat until I tell you it's okay to sit up."

"What's going on, Mom?" Pete asked, following her. "Is this about the man at the restaurant?"

"Yes." She guided us out to the car. "He's very bad."

"Who is he?"

She didn't answer.

"Why don't we call the police?" Pete asked, closing the car door behind him.

"They won't help us," she answered, backing out of the driveway.

Pete and I put our heads down as soon as we got into the car. I could see the side of my mom's face. She checked the rearview mirror every few seconds. The reflection of her eyes in the mirror allowed me to see her fear. I looked away.

"We're going to have to stay here tonight," she said, bringing the car to a stop after what seemed like hours of driving. "Hopefully tomorrow we can find some help."

"Help for what?" Pete asked. "What is going on, Mom?"

She ignored his questions.

When we got out of the car, we saw a broken down motel.

"It looks like nobody's here," I said.

"Well, maybe that's good." Pete grabbed my hand as we followed our mom into the office. "Maybe that's the best thing if we have to hide."

The man at the front desk gave us a key. He ogled my mom, smirking.

"You'll be in room A-7," he said. When he spoke I saw his black teeth. "That's on the bottom floor."

We found our room. My mom opened the door. Pushing us inside, she closed and locked the door, securing the chain.

"It smells funny in here," I said, looking at the small bed. The stained, torn comforter hung off-centered on the bed. "I don't want to stay here."

Taking off her coat, my mom spread it on the bed and sat down.

She motioned for me to sit next to her.

"Put you head on my lap." She patted her thighs.

When I laid down, she ran her fingers through my hair. I feel asleep quickly. Something woke me with a start. Voices outside the door. My mom's icy fingers holding my shoulders so tight.

"Is it him?" Pete asked, whispering. "Is it the man from the restaurant?"

I looked up to see her nodding.

"This the room?" the gruff man asked, his voice muffled behind the door.

"It is." I recognized the voice of the man from the front desk.

"Skinny woman and two kids?"

"Yes, sir."

"How long they been in there?"

"A couple hours, sir."

"They bring anything with 'em?"

"Just their coats."

"Good. Unlock the door."

"Yes, sir."

The key made a grinding noise as it turned in the lock.

My mom gasped. Grabbing us she backed into a corner. She reached up and pulled her coat off the bed and onto her lap. She shielded us with her body and put her hand into her coat pocket.

The door didn't open. The chain only allowed it to move a few inches.

The gruff man used harsh words.

"Not a problem, sir. The chain's broke. It's held together by a paper clip. You just gotta push a little harder," the front desk man said.

The door flung open wide.

We couldn't move, couldn't scream. My whole body tensed.

"Here you go." The gruff man handed the other a wad of money.

"Thank you, sir. Merry Christmas."

The man from the restaurant parking lot stood in our motel room.

He shut the door.

"Cora, ain't ya gonna wish your pa a Merry Christmas?" he asked, his voice gravelly.

"How did you find us?" my mom asked.

"Where'd all your manners go, girl? Ain't ya gonna introduce me to my own grandkids?"

"No." Her voice had an edge I'd never heard before. "You need to leave."

The man sat on the end of the bed. He lit a cigarette and inhaled the smoke. He stifled a cough.

"Peter and Dorothea. Am I right?" he asked, pointing the burning end at us.

Pete grabbed my hand.

When I saw my father's truck in the driveway I rushed back to the kitchen, stowing my bag under the sink. I cut bread to make him a sandwich, knowing he would be hungry. If I didn't have food for him, he'd beat me.

"Get in here," he yelled, flinging the door open.

Two sets of wet feet sloshed into the house. I stayed put, waiting for him to call me when he wanted something.

"There. On the couch."

I heard a body fall into the old cushions. The springs creaked.

The sounds of his fists pounding the person were awful. He screamed horrible words.

"You're gonna do as you're told or you'll get more of that."

His belt clicked as he unfastened it. Then the zipper being pulled down. The couch moved more and more.

It wasn't unusual for him to bring one of Ducky's girls home with him. On those nights I was relieved that it wasn't me for once. Guilt and shame stabbed me at those thoughts.

The sounds of the couch stopped shortly after they began.

"Hey, girl," he hollered at me. "Get me somethin' to eat."

I picked up the sandwich and walked with it to the living room. He sat in the rocking chair, his pants still undone. He motioned for me to bring the food to him. I stood as far back from him as I could. His foul odor clouded around him. I wished I'd had the thought to poison him before that moment.

"Get yourself around. You gotta drive that back to Ducky's." He indicated the curled up body on the couch. "I gotta get some sleep. The key's in the ignition. You know the way, right, girl?"

"Just down the mountain a couple miles," I whispered.

"And if she don't make it back there, I'll make sure you take her place," he said, mouth ful of sandwich. "Ya hear?"

"Yes, sir," I answered.

I grabbed my bag from the kitchen and walked out in the rain to the truck. I could never have planned a better escape. I had a vehicle.

Paul sat across from me, elbows on the table, his eyes large.

"I think they're about to close the place," I said, nodding at the employee as he vacuumed around our feet.

"Yeah. I guess we should get going." He looked at me. "This is pretty intense. I guess I never knew it happened this way."

"I know. The reporters changed it up a bit in the paper." I turned my head, trying to figure out how to get outside. "And there's a whole lot more, too. I really don't know if you want to hear about all of it."

"Like you could just stop right there. You have me terrified." He took one last sip of his soda. "Was that guy really your grandfather?"

"Yup." I sucked in a gulp of air. "Just so you know, I'm about to have a panic attack."

"You need some fresh air?"

"That would be great." We walked outside. "I'm trying to keep myself together. Retelling it brings up all these emotions. Like it's all happening again."

"Are you going to be okay?" He touched the center of my back.

"Yeah. I just need a break." I turned, letting his hand fall off my back. "How about we just go back to Lola's and have some coffee on the porch?"

"That would be great."

"Besides, I really don't want to be in public for the rest of this story."

"I understand."

Less than half an hour later, we sat on the steps at Lola's, sipping hot coffee. In that safe place, I could breathe again.

The gruff man, my grandfather, sat on the edge of the bed, speaking inches from my mom's face.

"When I seen your picture in the paper, I knowed it was one of you," he said. "Somethin' about your husband gettin' hisself killed in the war."

Someone walked past the motel door, laughing. Or crying. I couldn't tell. I looked at the man. He shook his head, smile full of broken teeth.

"Don't you even think 'bout calling out for help. Ain't nobody 'round here gonna help ya." He sat up straighter, shifted himself further up on the bed.

"When did you come to Michigan?" my mom asked. She didn't take her eyes off the man.

"Ducky got hisself a strip joint up here. Got a couple motels, too. This just happens to be one of his." He scratched himself obscenely. "He got me a transfer deal. Then, when Ducky come on hard times I bought him out."

"Did you bring Marlowe with you?"

"Nope. She runned away long before that." He looked at me. The way he moved his eyes over me, where he held his gaze on my body, made me nervous. "That little girl of yours sure is a pretty little thing, ain't she. Looks better than you ever did."

"If you touch her I will kill you," my mom said, her voice savage. "I will do whatever I must to keep you away from her."

"You doin' what you wish your mama woulda did?" he asked, snarling. "She just sat back and let me do whatever I wanted. Didn't she?"

"She wasn't strong."

"Maybe she just didn't care." He lit another cigarette.

"I will not let you hurt my daughter," my mom said.

"You got real tough, didn't ya'?"
His laugh made goose bumps rise on my skin.

CORA

43

I sat in the truck, the rain pouring on the hood, lightning strikes illuminating the whole yard. I watched the shack. Candlelight flickered as a shadow crossed the window.

"I will never see this house again," I whispered. A wave of nausea flooded over me.

The girl walked down the porch step. She held her arms around her ribs as she stepped down. She moved closer to the truck and collapsed.

"Come on. Come on," I whispered to myself. "Just start the truck and go. Don't wait for her. She could ruin this."

I slid the key into the ignition, just about to turn the engine over. I looked at the girl, in a heap on the ground.

Something in my heart broke for her. If I left her, she would die. Or worse, be stuck in my place with my father. I climbed out of the truck.

"Hey, we have to get into the truck," I said, kneeling next to her. "We have to get out of here before he gets angry. Please, come on."

The girl rolled over and looked at me. Her face swollen and covered with blood.

"Just leave me," she said, her voice raspy.

"I can't do that. Now, come on." I tugged her arm. "Seriously, you don't want me to leave you here. Not with him. He's crazy. I'll carry you."

She stood slowly with some help. I helped her to the passenger side of the truck.

"Cora," she said. "Cora, it's me."

That voice. Just like mine. The hair, her hands. Just like me. I tried to look into her eyes. They were so swollen over.

"Marlowe?" I asked, my heart dropping.

"Cora," she said.

The other half of me, in my arms, bleeding. "Marlowe is alive," I said.

44

We sat in the corner of the motel room for hours. I put my head on Pete's shoulder, never moving my eyes away from the man's face.

"Hey, I need somethin' to drink," he said to my mom, trying to get his coat off. He shook so hard, he could barely control his arms. Sweat beaded on his forehead. "Go get me somethin'."

"Get it yourself," she said. "You know where the liquor store is, I'm sure."

He stood. The tremors caused him to stumble. Catching himself on the dresser, he cursed. Then punched the wall. His fist didn't even make a dent. He lacked the force to even break loose the peeling orange paint.

"You think you're so smart, do ya? Think ya gonna get rid of me just like that." He turned to us, hands on the dresser. "You gonna take that boy with you down and get me a bottle of somethin' strong. My girl Dorothea and me is gonna get acquainted. Now get."

He peeked out the curtains, letting a thin stream of light into the room. My mother pulled something from her coat pocket. She glanced at Pete and me, putting a finger to her lips to quiet us. She stood and pointed the object at the man's back.

"You are going to let us go now. And you aren't going to follow us," she said with authority.

Pete and I stood up. The man turned around. He bared his black, stinking teeth.

"Now, lookie here at that big old gun. Where'd a girl like you get that?" He laughed. "Ya know I'm gonna make you pay for this. Just like

I made your idiot brother and sister pay."

He reached into his pocket. The gun in my mom's hand made an earsplitting boom. I screamed. Grabbed hold of Pete.

The man fell to the ground. She shot him until the bullets in her gun were gone.

"Let's go," she said, calmly. She picked me up with strength that I couldn't understand. She couldn't have weighed much more than I did. "We need to go home."

As she carried me past the man, I saw a gun in his hand. I held tighter around her neck. She turned, looking at my brother. He stayed in the corner, eyes on the man, paralyzed.

"Come on, Pete," she said. "We need to go."

"I can't," he whispered.

"Everything's going to be okay," she said, reaching for his hand. "We just have to get away from him."

Pete looked from the body to my mom. He sprinted past the man. My mom put me down.

"Now we really need to get away from here." She grabbed our hands and rushed us to the car.

I climbed in behind my mom, still shaking and sobbing. Pete sat next to me, his arms around me.

My mom drove the car out of the parking lot. She made a turn, not looking.

Just then a horn sounded. The semi-truck's light shone alarmingly close to the passenger side windows.

We didn't have time to scream before the truck crashed into us.

45

"It was Marlowe?" Lisa asked, her voice quiet and cautious. "It really was?"

"Yes." I nodded. "My father brought her to the shack that night because she failed to please a customer. He had to refund that man's cash. He was punishing her for losing money."

"Oh, Cora. What a strange thing that must have been for you. One minute hearing him abuse her and then being reunited." She held her face in her hands. "And to know that God brought her back to you, just in time to escape."

"I wish it would have worked out that way." I rubbed my eyes.

"You must have had so many conflicting feelings. And with your mother dead I just can't get over the gamut of emotions for such a young girl to experience."

"I'm so tired. Do you mind if we finish this up tomorrow?" I yawned. "I really need to get some sleep. I'm not as young as I used to be."

"That's fine, Cora. I want you to pace yourself." She stood. "I'm thinking that tomorrow might be a good day for brownies."

"Isn't every day a good day for brownies?"

"So true, my friend."

"Lisa, you are making me fat."

"Eh. I think you look more beautiful than ever."

"Speaking of beauty, could you do something for me?"

"Anything."

"Would you be able to find a bottle of hair dye for me? Auburn? I'm so sick of looking sixty."

"You don't look sixty. But I think I can find some for you."
She winked at me.

I couldn't help myself. I smiled.

From the floor of the backseat, all I could see were the red and blue flashing lights of the emergency vehicles. I couldn't figure out how I'd gotten on the floor. Had I even buckled my seat belt?

"Dot! Get out!" My mom's screams broke through my muted, numb trance.

I looked up. The car wrapped around the front of a semi-truck, crushed. Sitting up, I saw Pete's head. It leaned awkwardly on his neck.

"Pete?" I said. "Pete, you okay?"

He didn't answer.

My mom reached in and pulled me by the arm. I followed the tug, crawling to the icy pavement. She held me, once again, lifting me in her arms.

The rescue workers moved quickly to remove Pete from the car. They had to tear the metal back to get him out in one piece.

A helicopter landed on the road, waiting to rush Pete to a Grand Rapids hospital.

"You have to let us go with him," my mom cried as they carried him on the backboard.

"There's no room," the pilot said. "You'll have to ride in the ambulance."

"I need to be with him," she screamed. "He can't die all by himself! Not him, too!"

"You've got to back up," the man said.

A police officer helped us into her squad car. She drove, siren blaring, to the hospital.

Pete lived in the Intensive Care Unit. My mom spent every day there, arriving at six in the morning and staying until eleven in the evening when they forced her to leave.

The doctors advised her to take Pete off life support. They didn't believe he would ever wake up. A spinal cord injury left him empty. Living dead. His organs could be used to save several other lives.

She refused. She couldn't let him go. She had already lost far too much.

Again, I relied on the West family. But this time, I was even more alone.

"You know we always loved having you at our house, right?" Paul reached over and held my hand.

I liked the way his hand felt on mine. But I couldn't let him touch me. I still had so much to tell him about my life. I pulled my hand back.

"Sorry. Lola's rules. No hand-holding," I said.

"I totally forgot." He crossed his arms. "Sorry, but I hate that rule."

"It's okay. We're just kind of close to breaking rules now anyway. You know, being alone."

"So, what happened with your grandfather?" Paul asked. "Was he really dead?"

"Yes. My mom told the police what happened. They believed her and didn't press charges." I stood. "Listen, I need more coffee. You want some?"

Without waiting for his answer, I grabbed his mug and went to the kitchen.

"Okay, God, I'm really nervous. I just need to know if I'm supposed to tell him all this stuff." I prayed out loud as I poured the coffee. "I just don't want him to think I'm terrible."

"If he thinks you're terrible then he ain't worth keepin' around," Peace said from the kitchen table.

"I didn't know anybody was up," I said, turning around, surprised.

"But, you know, I think he's gonna understand. You just gotta trust that he ain't like the other guys."

"Yeah. It's just scary."

"I know. Just trust." She stood. "I'm gonna be prayin' for you, Dorothea. You ain't got nothin' to worry about."

"Thank you."

She came near to me, put her hand on my forearm, over the black scar. The reminder of the old life. "All what happened to you, that ain't who you are. You just gotta remember that."

I watched her walk out of the room before grabbing the coffee and stepping back out to Paul.

"Here you go," I said, handing him a mug.

"Thanks." He looked up at me. "Dot, is this getting too hard for you to talk about? If it is, then I really don't need to know. I want you to feel comfortable."

"Listen, you have to understand something; this gets way worse. And some of it might make you see me differently."

"Remember the contract?"

"Yeah. But, Paul, you don't know what happened to me. There are things I did that will change what you think of me. You might not be able to handle it."

Paul looked at me and sipped his coffee. "I want you to know that you can trust me."

"I'm trying." I sat down. "Let's just get through Pete's funeral. Then I'll need a break."

"That's fine. Take your time."

Pete died almost a year after the accident. He got some kind of infection that his body couldn't fight off. My mom sat with him until the end. She called the Wests to have them tell me. Mrs. West held me until I stopped crying.

The visitation was the night before the funeral. I came with the Wests. By then people already filled the funeral home, standing in silent circles in the stuffy room.

Flower arrangements lined the walls and framed the casket. The dull smell of carnations thickened the air.

What I remember about that day is gray, black, and white. As I walked in, hushed whispers roamed around the room amongst the mourners.

"That's his sister."

"Poor girl."

"They lost their father not long ago."

"Her mother isn't well."

I walked between the circles. No one stopped me. They all parted to one side or the other. They didn't want to touch me. Tragedy might rub off on them. My feet seemed to glide across the floor in my black patent leather shoes. The people followed me, but only with their eyes.

I stood at the coffin, looked at Pete. He was alone.

I touched the smooth, gray outside of the casket. Traced a trail in the soft, blue velvet lining.

Pete's face looked calm. Makeup caked his skin. His eyes were sealed shut. Lips were pulled into a straight line. They'd parted his hair on the wrong side. I wanted to fix it, but couldn't reach up that far.

Instead, I put my small hand on his. He would have grown to have large hands. Like our dad's. I imagined him using those hands to help other people. Holding his wife's hand on their wedding day. He would have cradled his babies with those hands.

But all of that wouldn't happen. I'd known that for a year. He hadn't moved on his own since before the accident. When he hugged me to comfort me. Machines did all the breathing for his lungs and the beating for his heart. A tube in his side had pushed food into his stomach. A needle in his arm gave him water. He hadn't lived for a year. My mom just couldn't understand that.

I rubbed his stiff, cold hand with my warm fingers. I didn't know what I should feel. Sadness or joy or relief? I couldn't understand the grief.

I moved my face inches from his ear. The boy smell of dirt and sweat and warmth was gone. I whispered to him, knowing that he didn't hear me. But I needed to say it all the same.

"Pete, I love you. I'll miss you every day."

I walked away, my hand cold and smelling like death. My heart raw.

"How did you sleep last night?" Lisa asked, handing me a coffee and brownie.

"Thank you." I smiled. "Actually, I slept great. I didn't even take a sleeping pill."

She sat next to me. "I'm so glad."

"How about you?"

"Well, not so well," she said. "I was up all night thinking about you and Marlowe."

The end of the driveway had a dip in it before it exited to the dirt road. After all the rain, it had turned into a trench of mud. The truck got stuck as I tried to pull out. Neither Marlowe nor I were strong enough to push the large hunk of metal through the muck.

"Are you strong enough to walk?" I asked my sister.

"I don't think so." She held her sides. "I think I might have a few broken ribs."

"He'd catch us anyway." I turned to her. "We have to kill him."

"No, Cora. We can't do that." She spoke through a fat lip and missing tooth.

"You really think he should live? Look at what he did to you. He's done nothing but try to destroy us."

"Let God take care of that, Cora."

"God? As if He really cares."

"He does," Marlowe said, quietly. "God is going to get us both out of here somehow. We just have to trust Him."

A flashlight jerked around in the darkness. I saw it in the rearview mirror.

"Father's coming," I said.

A string of acid words flew from his mouth. He shoved his weight at the truck. Unsuccessful, he trudged around to the driver side door and opened it.

"You." He pointed to Marlowe. "Get out here and help me push."

"She's too hurt," I cried.

"Are you back-talkin'?"The whiskey on his breath burned my eyes.

"Let me do it." I tried to climb out past him.

Marlowe grabbed my hand.

"I'm coming," she called to our father. He went to the back of the truck. She whispered to me, "Cora, when we get you unstuck, you just drive away. Leave me here to deal with him. If you take me with you, Ducky will find us and kill us. I'm serious."

"Girl, where is ya?" my father bellowed.

"I don't want to lose you again, Marlowe," I said.

"Then let's pray that God brings us back together." She smiled at me. "Just do as I say."

"But you aren't strong enough."

"No. But the Lord is."

I nodded in agreement, incapable of winning that argument.

She climbed slowly from the cab and walked to the back of the truck. She leaned her small, thin, battered body into the hard metal and pushed alongside my father. Somehow, the truck started to move.

I hesitated. The beating of my heart sounded in my ears.

"Do what I told you, Cora! Go!" Marlowe screamed, standing in front of our father, protecting me yet again.

As I drove away, I looked in my side mirror. I watched him punch her in the back of the head. I knew that he would kill her.

It took me the rest of the night to drive down the mountain. Terror struck me whenever I saw headlights, sure that the sheriff or Ducky came to take me away. But no one came after me.

I followed signs that pointed north, driving until I ran out of gas. The sun crested the horizon. I walked to a gas station. Sold the truck to a man for seven-hundred dollars cash. He thought he got a great deal. But what he got was part of a dirty secret, a portion of a ruined family.

The man gave me a ride to the bus station.

"I need a ticket," I said, to the lady at the counter.

"Where you wanna go?" she asked before looking up.

"How far can I get?"

"Furthest ride tonight is goin' to Michigan."

"Then that's where I want to go." I pulled cash from my bag. "How much is it?"

She looked at me. A long scar went from her left temple all the way to the corner of her mouth.

"You know it's gonna be cold there. Probably snow up to your belly button by now."

"I don't care," I said.

"And ain't ya' too young to be goin' all that way by your lonesome?"

"Do you get paid to ask questions or sell tickets?" I asked, covering my fear with attitude.

She rolled her eyes and passed a ticket under the glass. I slipped my money to her.

"If you don't mind me sayin', you need to eat somethin'. You're too skinny around the face. You gotta have a little more meat on your bones to make it through northern winters." She pointed to a sandwich truck. "Go on and get yourself somethin' to eat there. Put it on my tab. Just tell 'em I sent you over."

"Thank you, ma'am." I looked at my feet. "I'm sorry I was so rude."

"Oh, it ain't no thing, darlin'." She laughed. "Ain't nothin' I never heared before. You gotta be strong sometime. Don't always know who you can trust."

She looked me over.

"You okay, honey?" she asked.

"No. But once I get a little farther away I will be."

"What ya' runnin' away from, sugar?"

I looked toward the mountain.

She nodded.

"You from up there, ain't ya?"

"Yes, ma'am. I've never been this far away from home."

"I know what you're runnin' from. Used to live up there myself. Got myself a job servin' drinks, but it turned up bein' different. Had to let men 'visit' me and do all kind of stuff to me." She pointed to the pink scar on her face. "See that? Ducky had his man do that to me."

"Why would he have done that?"

"I runned away." She felt it with her fingertips. "That's what he done when he catched me."

"How did you get away?"

"Got sick. They kicked me out. Best thing ever happened to me." She smiled. "Darlin', you're gonna get froze up north without a proper coat."

"I'll figure something out."

"Nah. There's a church in Johnson City collects coats." She turned and pulled a large coat from a box behind her. "This here's one of them. Take it."

She stepped out from behind the counter and handed me the coat. She walked with a limp.

"What happened to your leg?" I asked.

"Well, before Ducky cut me loose, his man broke my leg so I'd never forget him."

"I am so sorry."

"Well, weren't none of your doin'."

"If you see a girl come through that looks like me, will you give her a ticket to Michigan?"

"Sure will," she answered.

I handed her more money for Marlowe's ticket.

"When you get up north, give my cousin a call. She needs a babysitter." Her thick fingers worked writing on a piece of paper. "This here's her name and number. She done married herself a preacher man. They got ten kids. She needs a little help."

"Thank you."

"God bless you, honey. I'll be prayin' for you."

I got a sandwich and some milk and put them in my bag. When I climbed on the bus, I found a seat closest to the back. Watching all the others board the bus, I scanned the faces, fearing that someone would come looking for me.

After the bus started moving, I felt around my bag for the milk and food. My hand touched the small box. I'd forgotten taking it from my mother's bedside table. Pulling it from the bag, I smelled the cedar wood. The box was made simply. Just wood and a small, brass clasp. I opened it. The bus hit a bump and I dropped the box. The contents spilled out. Tiny blue paint chips littered the floor.

"Dorothea," Lola called from the kitchen, with an off pitch song in her voice. It made me nervous.

I walked down the steps and into the kitchen. Right to the coffee maker. I didn't want to make eye contact with her. She was sure to be upset about how late Paul and I were up talking the night before.

"You got a few pieces of mail yesterday," she said, pushing two envelopes toward me.

"What are they?" I asked, sipping my coffee.

"One is from the college. The other is from the state hospital."

"The mental hospital?" My stomach turned. I set my mug down. "Why didn't you tell me about these yesterday?"

"I'm sorry, dear. I was just a little distracted by the phone call with Promise." She winked at me. "And I didn't want to bother you at half past two this morning when you finally came inside from talking with Paul."

"Oh, about that. I'm sorry."

"Just be more mindful next time." She touched the envelopes. "Why don't you open them?"

I tore into the college letter first.

"Dear Ms. Dorothea Schmidt," I read out loud, skimming the words. "Accepted. I was accepted into college!"

Lola nearly jumped over the table to pull me into a tight hug. She held me tight, crying and laughing all at the same time. The other girls came into the kitchen, dressed and ready for church.

"Who's filming a flip-flopping Lifetime movie in here?" Grace asked, helping herself to my coffee.

"Man, it's so cheesy in here I gotta get me some chips," Faith said.

"Dorothea was accepted into college," Lola told them.

Grace joined our hug. Then Peace and Faith and Mercy. They crushed me.

"I knew you'd make it," Grace said. She cussed when she realized that her mascara got smudged. "Do you even know how hard it is to get these lashes right? Shoot."

After our hug, Lola looked at me.

"And the other letter?"

"Later," I said. "Maybe after church. I need to be alone for that one."

After church, Paul picked me up for lunch at his house. While we ate, I couldn't take my mind off the letter I had stuffed in my jacket pocket. The words could say that my mom was getting worse again. That the woman she'd once been disappeared. That she would never recover. I worried about her wasting the rest of her life in that institution without allowing me to see her again.

I made it through lunch and helped Kristi with the dishes. But that letter nagged at my mind constantly.

"Hey, Dot," Paul whispered into my ear as I dried the dinner plates. "You okay?"

"Sure," I answered, not looking at him.

"Good. I have something to show you." He turned me toward him, his hands on my shoulders. "It's a surprise. You have to close your eyes and promise not to look."

"You're a crazy person."

"I know. It's great." He grinned as he led me outside.

I closed my eyes, and he spun me around until I got dizzy. He pulled me by the hand, steadying me as I stumbled. I heard the click of a doorknob turning, the creak of an opening door.

"Step up," he said. "Ten steps up."

I followed his instructions, holding on to him for fear of falling.

After a few more turns, he stopped me.

"You didn't open your eyes, did you?" he asked.

"No. I love surprises."

"Okay." His voice filled with excitement. "Open your eyes."

The color yellow surrounded me. Yellow walls, yellow carpet.

"This was my bedroom," I whispered, putting my hands on my cheeks.

The room was empty of all my old things. But my memory filled in the space. I imagined my bed against the wall, my stuffed animals lined up on the pillow. The posters and pictures that hung above my dresser.

"Are you surprised?"

"How did you get me in here?"

"We bought the house."

"You what?"

"The people who lived here were about to go into foreclosure. We bought it so that wouldn't happen."

I looked around. Just being in that room made me feel eight years old again. I remembered my dad waking me up for school in the morning and praying with me at bedtime. I pictured my mom snuggling in bed with me to read a book before nap. Pete, playing games with me for hours until I finally won. I breathed in the air of that room. The smells of my family were gone.

Paul's arm around my shoulder snapped me back to reality.

"Hold on. What about Lola's rules? I can't be in here with you." I stepped out from under his arm.

"I already talked to her. She's cool with it."

"Good. Now, what are you going to do with this house?"

"We actually have a plan." Paul watched my face. "But when we walked through here, I just knew you'd want to see it right away."

"You're right." I sat on the floor. "Thank you."

"Just wait till you hear what we're thinking," he said, sitting next to me. "What do you think about an extension of Lola's House? Right here?"

"I've never heard a better idea in all my life," I said. "Who thought of it?"

"My mom."

"Of course. She's great."

"Well, there's one more thing." He breathed deeply. "Gosh, I feel so weird. It's like I'm back in high school."

I raised my eyebrows.

"Well, Dot, I wanted to ask you something. You know, I really like spending time with you. And I thought that with you coming to college next year we'd have more time to hang out."

I nodded, waiting for him to finish.

"And I guess I wanted to know if…man, this is so awkward." He wiped a trickle of sweat off his forehead. "Well, I guess I wanted to know if I can be your boyfriend."

A lump formed in my throat. Paul sighed, scratched his neck.

"You are very sweet, Paul," I said. "But I can't."

His eyes shot up to mine. His face sunk. "Really?"

"I'm not ready."

"Oh. Okay." He stood. "Maybe it was wrong of me to expect. I'm sorry."

"Wait. I'm not saying no. Not at all. I really want to say yes. Trust me. I'm just asking you to give me a little time." I smiled. "There are a few more things you need to know about me first. How about we save this talk for a few months from now?"

He exhaled. Smiled. Relaxed his shoulders.

"I can wait for you. We're young. What do we have to rush for?" He crouched next to me and put his hand on my cheek. "I just want to be a part of your life."

"Thank you." I pulled the crumpled envelope from my pocket. "Do you mind if I have some time alone to read this? It's kind of important that I can cry or scream or whatever when I read it. I can't do that if you're here."

"Sure. You stay in here as long as you want. I guess it's kind of your room again." He got back to his feet and walked to the door. "I'll just be at my house. Come on over when you're done."

I inhaled, waved the envelope in the air. As soon as I heard him close the front door, I held the letter close to my face.

"It can't be anything worse than you've already been through," I said to myself.

I slowly, carefully slid my finger under the flap, ripping the paper and pulled out the letter. Unfolded it. A floral design trimmed the paper.

"This isn't like the others," I thought.

The black words were written across the page in a flowing penmanship.

> *My Dear Dot,*
>
> *I don't know what to say to you other than I am so sorry that I haven't written you before this.*
>
> *Would you be willing to come see me? Visiting days are on Thursdays and I would love for you to come. My friend offered to drive you. I wrote all her information on the bottom of this letter.*
>
> *I understand, however, if you decided not to come. Just please write and let me know that you're okay.*
>
> *I really love you so much, Dot.*
>
> *Mom*

I ran through my old house and to the front door, my heart about to burst for joy.

Paul sat on his porch. He watched as I came toward him. I couldn't speak. Handing him the letter, I read over his shoulder.

"Wow, Dot. That's an answer to prayer," he said.

"I'm getting my family back."

My hug nearly knocked him over.

"I mailed your letter to Dot the other day," Lisa said as she placed a scone in front of me. "She should have gotten it by now."

"Thank you. What a nice Sunday treat." I broke a small crumble off the pastry and ate it. "Blueberry? My favorite. You know, I'm going to have to take up jogging again."

"Don't I know it." She patted her behind. "Sitting has never been so comfortable."

I laughed. I'd been letting the bubbling, ticklish laughter take over me more. I remembered the calm of happiness.

"Thank you for mailing that letter." I took another sugary bite. "I'm nervous, however, that Dot isn't going to want to see me."

"I know she will, Cora. I've never doubted that. She still loves you."

"How could you possibly know that? You've never met her, have you?"

"Well, I didn't tell you about this at the time; I wasn't sure how you'd handle it." Lisa sat next to me. "Cora, she's the one who sent the pictures."

"Really?" My heart throbbed. My entire face lifted for joy.

Joy. I remembered the feeling. Warm and satisfying. I welcomed it back.

I stepped off the bus in Lansing, Michigan. My ticket would have taken me all the way to Grand Rapids, but the family that needed a babysitter lived in Lansing. And I needed to go where I could find work.

I rented a room above an old lady's garage. Mostly blind, she couldn't see how young I was. I kept very little in my apartment. My few possessions could easily fit into a few bags, should I need to run again. I spent most of my time watching out for Ducky and my father, worried that they would come after me.

A few days after I arrived I used a pay phone to call the pastor's wife. They'd had three more since she last spoke with her cousin. And, yes, she needed the help of a young girl. I lied and told her that I'd just graduated from high school, telling her that I just looked very young for my age. She hired me to watch her kids, clean the house and help put together the church bulletin each week.

I delivered newspapers every morning before the sun came up. During the winter I shoveled driveways. Any kind of honest work I could find, I did. Hard work had been part of my life for so long, sitting still just made me anxious. So, I kept myself busy. Eventually, I saved up enough for a used car. That vehicle made my various escape plans more feasible.

Then I met Steven and life went in a completely different direction.

No longer did I look out for dangerous men. I didn't allow myself to think about what happened to my mother's body or whether or not Marlowe got away. All of my efforts went to covering up that part of my life, even from myself. No one really asked about my family. No one seemed to wonder about my past. I simply pretended that my life before Steven hadn't existed at all.

That was the lie I lived so well. I tucked all thought of my mother, Marlowe, and Titus away in an unreachable part of my mind. I willed myself to forget the shack with its falling apart windows, the loose floorboards, the leaky roof. The peeling paint chips on the wall.

"Have you ever thought about trying to find Marlowe?" Lisa asked.

"Oh, well, I haven't really given it much thought," I said. "I guess I didn't think I could. To be honest, I'm afraid to find out that she's dead. You know, she saved my life that night and I just drove away. I don't believe I could live with myself if he killed her because of me."

"I think I understand what you're saying," Lisa said, nodding. "But if she died that night, it would have been because of her love for you. You can't blame yourself for that. She was taking care of you. Sacrificing herself so that you could be safe."

"She did that our whole childhood." I hugged my arms around my chest. "Abandoning her wasn't the right thing to do."

"Well, Cora, you were doing what she told you to." She stood. "Let me do a little digging. I'll see if I can find out anything about her. Who knows, we might just find her. We'll pray for happy news. How does that sound?"

"That sounds great, thank you." I stood up next to her. "You have been a great friend."

I embraced her tightly.

"I'm thankful for your friendship, too." She rubbed a circle between my shoulder blades.

"I've never had a friend like you." I let go of her. "God has blessed me with you."

She held my hand. "I'm so proud of you, Cora."

"I'm getting excited about leaving this place."

"That's great." She let go of my hand and grabbed her purse. "I'm going to do some research. And then I'm going to pick out some paint colors for the house. What's your favorite color?"

"Oh, goodness. I have no idea." The excitement overwhelmed me. "I can't think of a single color right now. How about you choose for me? I'm sure I'll love whatever you pick out."

"I'm thinking something tranquil."

"Yes," I exhaled. "Perfect."

"I'll see you in the morning."

I waved before she turned to walk away. It felt as if the storm that raged through my whole life had finally been calmed. And I stood in wonder of this Man who could command the wind and the waves and the hearts of His children to have peace and be still.

After the excitement of my mom's letter, Paul and I sat in the dining room at his parents' house. Kristi made us cookies and brewed some strong coffee. She left the two of us alone to talk.

Barely able to sit still, I fidgeted and chewed on my nails.

"This is the bad part, Paul," I said.

"Okay. Take your time."

I had this memory of Pete's funeral. I remembered sitting next to my mom in a pew at the front of a sanctuary. We held hands. I traced the raised, purple veins in her thin hands.

After the service and the luncheon, we went home. Just the two of us. My mom and me. We sank into the comfort of the loveseat, still wearing our black funeral clothes. I put my head on her shoulder. The bumpy bones jutted out, hard against the side of my face. We sat like that for so long, I wondered if my cheek would bruise from resting on her sharp angles.

"I can't figure out what to do with myself now, Dot," she said. "What did we do with our lives before Pete got hurt?"

"I can't remember," I answered, staring at the coffee table.

"I guess before he was in the hospital I just spent a lot of time sleeping, right?"

I lifted my head and nodded.

"And before that your dad went to war and I cooked a lot."

"Right. You made a lot of cookies."

"And before that." She scratched her scalp. "What did I do before your dad went away?"

"I don't know."

Everything before my dad left seemed to be nothing more than a dream. A far away, long ago dream.

"Your daddy died a year and a half ago," she said. "I'm just so tired. I don't think I've slept all year long."

"Me either," I said.

"I don't want to sleep in my room, though. It's just far too lonely."

"You can sleep in my room. I have a trundle bed," I said, trying to cheer her. "We could pull that out. I'll let you sleep in my bed and I'll sleep on the pull-out part."

"I like that idea. Kind of like a slumber party?" she asked, her voice flat. "I never got to have a slumber party when I was a girl. I never got to have any fun."

I rushed to my room and got it ready for our sleep-over. Fluffing my best pillow, I set it on my bed, just for her. I turned down the sheet and blanket.

She came into my room slowly. I tucked her into my bed. The yellow blanket contrasted beautifully against her rich auburn hair.

"You can snuggle my bear," I said.

"Thank you, honey," she said, holding the bear to her chest.

"I love you, Mom."

"I love you, too." She touched my hair with her thin hand and looked right into my eyes. "Promise me something, will you?"

"Sure."

"If anything happens to me, promise you'll get off this mountain." She closed her eyes. "Just promise."

The way she said the words scared me. Confused, I pulled away from her.

Lowering myself onto the pulled-out bed, I tried to stay awake to watch her. She fell asleep so quickly, so deeply. Her breathing, heavy. My eyes rested under closed lids. I sank into sleep.

In the middle of the night, I sat straight up in the bed. Something crashed in the kitchen. Then a thud. My eyes darted around the room. My mom wasn't in the bed. She wasn't anywhere in the room. I got up, stumbling down the steps and into the kitchen.

That's where I found her, on the floor in a pile.

"Mom," I said, quietly at first. Then louder. "Mom? Mommy. Are you okay?"

I patted her hip. She didn't move. Shaking her, I screamed. Trying to wake her, get some kind of response. Anything. I panicked. Laid my body on top of hers.

"Not my mommy, too!" I begged God. "Please, don't take her, too!"

Mr. West heard me somehow and rushed over, letting himself in with a spare key. He tried to pull me off of her. I wouldn't let go. He reached around me to feel her neck.

"She's still alive, Dot," he reassured me. Patted my back. "Everything's going to be okay."

Mrs. West followed close behind him. "Come on, Dot. I'll make up a bed for you at our house."

"No," I screamed, clinging to my mom. "I have to stay here with her."

By the time the ambulance came, my mom yelled about people whose names I had never heard. She called out for Titus and Marlowe and her mother. She screamed that she'd killed her father in cold blood. That she had planned it. She'd been planning it since her childhood.

The paramedics strapped her to the gurney just so they could put a needle into her arm. After a shot of medicine, she fell back to sleep.

They loaded her into the ambulance and took her to the hospital. After a few days, they determined that she was mentally unfit to return home. She was too ill to care for me. They found the cut marks all over her body. She couldn't remember what year it was. Reality had been completely blocked out of her brain. They admitted her to the state mental hospital.

A case worker came to my house early in the morning and watched me pack my things. Only enough to fill two duffle bags.

The Wests stood on the sidewalk.

"Is there any way that she can be placed with us?" Mr. West asked, following the caseworker to the state-owned car. "We're willing to take custody."

"No, sir." She sighed impatiently and put her hand on my shoulder. "I have to take Dorothy with me."

"Her name is Dorothea."

"Right." The woman opened the car door for me. "Sorry, sir. I don't know anything about you. Until you're registered to be a foster family, you can't keep her."

"What does it take to be registered?" Mrs. West asked.

"Ma'am, I'm not the one to ask. I'm just doing my job."

"But she's been with us. She knows us. We'll take care of her," Mrs. West pleaded.

"I'm going to have to ask you to step back from the car now."

The case worker took my bags, placed them in the backseat. I climbed in, carrying my coat.

"Don't worry, Dot. We'll get you back here real soon," Mrs. West said as the car pulled away.

For the next few years I bounced around from foster home to foster home. I caused problems for the families that housed me. Punched holes in walls, stole money, lied about the families to my case worker.

At twelve years old I decided I was done living in the system. I figured I could make my way back home. To live with the Wests. So I ran away. Just took my things and walked out the door.

I traveled around the city, trying to build up the courage to call Mrs. West. I hoped that they would come get me. But I couldn't remember their phone number. I figured they would be disappointed in me. That they must have heard how bad I was for the foster families and decided that they didn't want me. After all, they hadn't come to get me.

All I could think to do was wander the streets.

That night seemed darker than any other I'd ever experienced. I walked for miles and miles, getting turned around and disoriented. I didn't recognize the street names or the buildings. I didn't dare ask for help.

When the rain began to pour, I found a covered doorway. I stood against the old, falling apart door, trying to make myself look tough. But I shook in the cold, drenched clothes. Fear kept me from falling asleep, despite my exhaustion.

The next morning, I found a small diner. Bought a bagel with some of the money I stole from the last foster family.

"You okay?" a man asked, approaching my table.

"I'm fine," I answered. "Leave me alone."

"Let me get you some coffee. You look so cold."

"I'm not. Go away." I tried to sound tough. But the words came out as a pathetic squeak.

He walked to the counter and got two cups of coffee. He set one of them down next to me.

"You don't have to talk to me. I'm just being a good guy." He looked at me. "I swear, I didn't drug it or nothing."

The steaming coffee made me realize how cold I was. I wrapped my fingers around the mug.

"So can I sit with you for a minute?" he asked.

I nodded.

"What's your name?"

"Veronica."

"That's a nice name, girl. I'm Jimmy. But folks call me Jinx."

"Why would they call you that?"

"Oh, it's kind of a joke. My friends tell me I'm bad luck."

I looked at his face. Acne covered his pale skin. I couldn't tell if his hair grew that shade of black or if he'd dyed it. He wore a jean jacket over a flannel shirt.

"Why are you bad luck?" I asked.

"You'd have to ask that, right? Man, I hate to be embarrassed in front of such a pretty girl." He laughed, flirted with his eyes. "Something to do with me being a klutz. You know. I fall down a lot. Knock stuff over."

"Oh." I drank the coffee black. No sugar. I wanted him to see how strong and grown-up I was. I wouldn't allow my face to pucker from the bitterness.

"You want some milk for that?"

"Nope. I like it this way."

"That's my girl." He reached across the table and touched my hand. "I like you, Veronica. I can tell you're a pretty special girl."

"I'm not," I said, pulling my hand away.

"Sure you are. How old are you? Fifteen? Sixteen?"

"I'm twelve."

"No way. You look way older than that." He looked at his hands, then back up at me. "You're really pretty. As soon as I walked into this place, I noticed you."

"Thanks," I said. His face looked so sincere. No one had said anything nice to me in so long. But I felt in my gut that I shouldn't trust that guy.

"So, tell me a little about you. Where do you live?" he asked.

"I don't really have a place right now."

"You get kicked out or something?"

"Kind of like that." I drank deeply of the coffee.

"You could come stay at my house. Sleep on my couch."

"No." I shook my head. "I don't even know you."

"Oh, come on Veronica." He reached for my hand again. I flinched, put my hand on my lap under the table. "Are you really scared of me?"

"I'm not going to live with somebody I don't know. I've done too much of that the past couple years."

"Ah, I see." He leaned back in the booth. "You been in the system, right? Foster care kid?"

I nodded and looked down, ashamed.

"I been there, Veronica. I got moved around every couple weeks or so. It's tough."

"Yeah. It is," I said. "How'd you get out?"

"I ran away. Stayed with my friends for a while. They got me work."

"How old were you?"

"Thirteen." He drank from his cup. "The streets are scary, ain't they?"

"I didn't know it was going to be so bad." I cried, even though I tried so hard to be strong. "I wanted to find a nice place. I just didn't think it through."

"How long you been out here?"

"Just last night."

"Aw, honey," he said, his voice deep and soft. "And it was so cold last night."

"Yeah. I was so scared."

"I know, babe." He leaned in closer and whispered. "I'm not trying to scare you or nothing, but a beautiful girl like you got to be careful. You don't know how many guys out there wouldn't think twice about snatching you up. Using and abusing you."

"Maybe I should just go back to my case worker."

"No. You can't do that. You know what they'd do? Put you straight in juvy until you're eighteen." He looked at me. "You think I'm kidding? I'm dead serious. I can't tell you how many of my friends done that."

"What am I supposed to do?"

"Let me help you out, Veronica. I swear I won't let anything bad happen to you. My friend Rhonda's got an extra room. I'm sure she'd love to have another girl around the house."

"I don't have any money."

"Don't worry about that. We'll talk about that later." He pushed himself out of his seat and stood. "Come on. Let's get you outta here."

He extended his hand. Dirty fingernails, scarred knuckles. I reached out and put my hand in his. He held mine in his firm grip. We walked for a few blocks, not talking. Some kind of nagging tugged at me. A warning.

"Get away," a voice seemed to say. "Run as fast as you can."

But then Jinx put his arm around my waist. Almost a hug. I let him guide me.

He took me to a small, dingy house, the yard full of junk.

"Ready to meet Rhonda?" he asked. "She's gonna love you."

"I'm nervous."

"Don't worry. She's cool."

We walked up the steps to the front door. Dense stench from the house hit me before it opened. It smelled like animals lived there and that they'd taken over the house.

"I don't know, Jinx. Maybe I should just go back."

"You don't want to do that, babe. Do you trust me?" He put his hand on my back, almost pushing me forward.

"Sure," I said, but my instincts told me otherwise.

He pushed the doorbell a couple times. "I forgot my key."

A large woman opened the door. She looked me up and down.

"Who's this?" she asked.

"This is my new friend," Jinx said, smirking. "Her name's Veronica."

"Nice name, sweetie."

"Thanks," I said, eyes on my feet.

"She needs a place to stay for a while," Jinx said. "You mind letting us in? It's kind of cold out here."

"Yeah. Come on," Rhonda said.

We walked in, and she closed the door behind us. My eyes stung from the thick, earthy smelling smoke. Like cigarettes with something else blended in. Stomach turning. Animal fur and waste covered everything. Empty beer bottles scattered on the coffee table. I thought I saw something dart under the couch. I didn't want to sit down in that place.

"This here's Rhonda," Jinx said, plopping down on the couch. "Everybody calls her 'Mama.'"

"Why do they call you that?" I asked Rhonda.

"'Cause they all like my kids. And I takes care of them," Rhonda answered.

"Ain't that the truth?" Jinx said, grabbing of glass bottle from the side table.

"So what's your story?" she asked, dragging on her cigarette. "Why do you need a place to stay?"

I made up stories. Somehow, I knew that I shouldn't tell them anything true about me. She listened to me. Gave me a hug after I finished talking.

"Mama's gonna take good care of you, Veronica." She handed me a glass. "Drink up, honey."

I sipped the liquid. Some kind of strong, stinging liquor slid down my throat. It burned and soured my stomach. But I didn't want them to think I was a little kid. So I kept drinking.

Within a week I drank with them every day. Not long after that I started smoking pot. I slept on the couch. Sometimes Jinx tried things with me. When I was really drunk, I didn't have the strength to push him away. He told me I owed it to him for sleeping on the couch and getting high.

"You know I love you, Veronica," he said one night, sitting on the edge of the couch.

I nodded, pulling a cigarette from his pack.

"Don't you love me?" he asked. "Even a little?"

"Yes." It was just another story.

"I got a problem, baby." He pulled me close to him, smoothed my hair. "We're out of money. We spent it all on booze last night. And if we don't pay the rent tomorrow, we'll get kicked out. We'll be on the streets."

"That's not good," I said, exhaling a lungful of smoke. Trying not to cough.

"We all got to find a way to make money."

"I can't get a job. I'm not old enough."

"I got one for you." He kissed my forehead. "Just remember that I'm the one who loves you. I'm the one who takes care of you. Right?"

"I guess."

"And sometimes we got to do things we don't want to. And we do it because we love people."

"What job is it?"

"I need you to go on dates. You know, have a good time with guys. They'll pay you and we give the money to Rhonda for the house." Jinx touched my face. "All that stuff we do, well, you gotta do that with them."

"I can't do that," I said, pulling away from him.

"You'll do it for me," he said, pinching my cheeks with his fingers. It hurt. "You'll do whatever I tell you."

"You're scaring me."

"Listen, Veronica, you're going to get used to this life. It's better than juvy."

"What do I have to do on the dates?"

"Anything they want, like I said. Might as well. You already do that stuff with me." He moved away from me, like he was disgusted. "It ain't like you're a virgin or nothin'."

I pushed my legs together, held my knees tight with my hands. Looking around the room, I realized that I'd let all of it happen. And I was stuck.

That night Rhonda had me put on a short skirt and tank top. She did my makeup and pulled my hair into pigtails.

"Don't want you looking too old," she said. "Some guys like young girls."

She took a picture of me and put it online. Within minutes I had six appointments.

"Jinx'll drive you there," Rhonda said. "He'll wait outside till you're done. Whatever you do, don't forget to use protection."

She handed me a bottle of beer. I drank it, hoping it would make me numb. I still had no idea what they expected me to do on the date.

Jinx drove me around from apartment to motel to home to office building. Each place had a man who raped me. It didn't matter how much beer I'd had, I still knew what was happening. And it hurt. I couldn't breathe. I thought I was going to die.

"You got to pull it together, babe," Jinx said. "If you don't get in there and act happy, I'm gonna have to punish you."

"I can't go in. How many more do I have to do?"

"As many as I tell you. Now get in there." He pointed to the motel.

"It just hurts so bad."

He made a fist. I flinched, covering my face.

"No!" I yelled.

I doubled over from the pain. I rubbed my side, checking to see if he'd broken any of my ribs. I glared at him out of the corner of my eye, gasping for breath. He rubbed his knuckles.

"I told you to get in there." His voice was a growl.

I obeyed him.

I sat, waiting in the dayroom for Lisa to arrive. The sun shone in the window, making a grid pattern on the floor.

There would be a day when I could look out a window that was free of bars or grids. Just glass set in a frame. And a window that could open and let in the fresh air. In my own room. Light would glow through that window and I would welcome the warmth. I looked forward to living in Lisa's house.

"Miss Cora," an orderly said. "Lisa called. She's gonna be a few minutes late."

"That's fine. Thank you for letting me know." I looked at his face. His dark brown eyes smiled at me. "Please forgive me, I can't remember your name."

"My name's Antonio."

"Thank you for reminding me, Antonio. You're doing a fine job here. You've only been here a few days and you remembered my name." I touched his arm. "I'm worried that you won't have a job when they close this place down."

"Well, I'm just doing my training here. I'll get transferred to the downtown hospital. It's closer to where I live anyway."

"I'm glad."

"Thank you. I'd better get back to work. It was nice talking to you."

"You, too, Antonio."

The sun from the window made me sleepy. I closed my eyes, promising myself that I wouldn't fall asleep. But the warmth comforted me, soothed me. I dozed off.

I dreamed of baking cookies. For some reason, no matter how hard I tried, I couldn't get the dough as smooth as I wanted it. The chocolate chips clumped together. The butter wasn't melted well enough. I dropped them on the cookie sheet anyway. Within seconds the timer buzzed and I pulled them from the oven. They weren't perfect circles. The cookies were all baked together.

"Why aren't they perfect?" I asked in my dream.

Dot and Pete came into the kitchen and ate the cookies. All of them.

"These are good cookies, Mom," Pete said.

"But they aren't perfect," I said.

"That's okay," he said. "They're still good."

"Cora, sorry to wake you up," Lisa said, touching my arm.

"Oh, that's okay." I blinked my eyes, trying to regain reality. "It was just a good moment for a catnap."

"I would have let you sleep, but I have some news for you." She took two pieces of paper from her bag. "Which do you want first?"

"I don't know. Which is the bad news?"

"Neither."

"Okay. Then give me that one." I pointed to the paper furthest from me.

"That's an email from Dot." She smiled at me. "She's coming to see you on Thursday."

Joy expanded within me. It overflowed from my full heart. I sobbed with a smile on my face.

"Are you ready for the other one?" Lisa asked.

"Yes."

"I found Marlowe." She pushed the paper toward me. "Cora, she's alive."

"Where is she?" I asked.

"Grand Rapids." She breathed deeply. "Can you believe it?"

"Barely," I answered, laughing.

"I found her email address and I sent her a message with my phone number."

"Have you heard back from her?"

"Yes. She's offering you a place to live." She smiled. "I want you to know that it's up to you. If you want to live with her, I understand."

"Is it okay if I take a few days to decide?"

"I think that's a good idea."

"Do you think Marlowe will come visit me?"

"I think she'd like to."

"Wouldn't that be the greatest?" I laughed for all the joy. "I just don't understand all this goodness."

"You know, Cora, sometimes things don't come together in the way we expect. But that doesn't mean they won't be good. God has this way of making even the ugliest things beautiful."

The words of Jesus ran through my mind.

"Peace, be still."

Gladly, Jesus. Thank you.

My life at Rhonda's house seemed to last for years. Jinx and I posted pictures of me to the Internet all day. The girl in those photos didn't look like me at all. They'd dyed my hair blond and made me pose in humiliating positions.

"Tell the men your name is Ricki," Rhonda had said. "Nobody wants to get with a girl named Veronica. Sounds too brainy."

They still didn't know my name. It was the one thing that I could keep for myself. The only thing that linked me to the good parts of my past.

After a while Jinx would beat me, even if I'd made enough money. He didn't let me sleep on the couch anymore. I had to find a spot on the floor that wasn't covered with cigarette butts or animal mess. I wasn't allowed to take a shower. They would only let me eat after all my dates were done. It was my reward. My payment.

One morning, I woke to something crawling on me. I shoved the cat off and sat up. Rubbed my eyes. I heard Jinx talking. I looked at the couch. He held another girl in his arms.

"Who's she?" I asked.

"This here's Maisy." He kissed her light brown cheek. "Ain't she pretty?"

The envy that clenched my stomach confused me.

"Rhonda says you gotta get outta here," he said to me. "Got some guy comin' over to take a look at you. You better get your stuff together."

"What if I just leave?" I asked, making my voice hard. "I don't want to go with that guy."

"Where you going to go that Rhonda can't find you?" He leered. "You in the life now, baby. Ain't no getting' out."

The doorbell buzzed. Rhonda stomped through the living room, a cigarette hanging from her lips.

"Get up, Veronica," she yelled, kicking me as she passed. "You're leaving."

She unlocked the door, opening it to a man. He stood in the doorway as they talked quietly. I couldn't hear what they said. But he wore a suit and tie. His hair cut short. Like a businessman.

"Come on," she said, stepping to the side to let him in. "She's right there."

"Rhonda, you have got to clean up this dump. It stinks in here," he said, walking into the house, kicking a pile of trash.

Rhonda approached me, grabbed me by the arm and shoved me toward him.

"Strip," he told me.

I took off all my clothes. I stood in the living room in just my underwear so he could get a good look at me.

"Why don't you feed your girls?" he asked, touching the skin of my stomach. His fingers were cool. "She's too skinny."

"Who are you? My boss?" Rhonda asked. "Men don't like fat women."

"What would you know?" he asked, turning me. "And Jinx has to stop beating them so much. Look at her back."

"She got out of line."

"Put your clothes on," he said to me. "She's okay. Does she always use protection?"

"Every time."

"She been tested?"

"For what? She uses protection."

"You have to do tests. These girls could have all kinds of stuff going on."

"She's clean. I swear."

"You ever been pregnant?" he asked me.

I shook my head, pulling up my jeans.

"Good." He took me by the arm. "Rhonda, I'll give you one-hundred-fifty for her. Next time, make sure the girl has a little more to her."

Rhonda took his cash, and he pulled me out of the house.

He let me ride in the front seat of his car. I'd never been in such an expensive vehicle. The leather seats radiated heat. It had been so long since I'd been warm.

"Hungry?" he asked, pulling into a fast-food drive-thru.

"Yes," I answered.

He ordered me a pack of chicken nuggets and french fries.

"Rhonda doesn't know she's talking about. Guys like a little cushion on their women." He handed me the food and drove away from the restaurant. "How old are you?"

"I just turned thirteen last week." I tried to keep myself from shaking.

"A lot of dates will ask you that. You just tell them it don't matter. Got that?" He stole a french fry. "You like doing this?"

"Sure," I said, my jaw tensing.

"Don't lie. You hate it. I know you do."

I nodded, chewing.

"Nobody likes this, you know. It's survival." He wiped his nose with the back of his index finger. "But nobody in the whole world likes their job. You think the guy that fried up that food for six bucks an hour likes it? Nope. But he's got to do it. He's got to survive."

The city moved so fast out my window, I couldn't be sure where he was taking me. My head ached from trying to figure it out.

"How many tricks did you turn every night for Rhonda?" he asked.

"Ten. Sometimes fifteen. I'd do any she could get."

"That's not how we do things. Here's how it works. You have to meet up with one of my guys at the motel every hour with one-hundred bucks on weeknights, two-hundred on weekends." He spoke in a professional tone. Like explaining a business transaction. "I don't care how you get it. You just got to deliver the cash every hour. On time. And whatever extra you get is yours."

I nodded.

"It's pretty simple. Problem is, if you don't have the money there are consequences." He parallel-parked the car in front of a dark, run-down motel. "And if you don't show up, one of my guys will come looking for you. And if you run away, we will find you. And then you will disappear for good. Do you understand what I'm saying?"

"Yes."

"We got eyes and ears all over this city. You believe me?"

I nodded.

"You'll get arrested. It happens a lot." He smoothed back his hair. "If they ask you who you work for, tell them you work for yourself. If you tell them about us, we'll find out. I promise you that. Fact is, some of the cops will just ask you to 'do' them and then they'll let you go. That's always the best thing to do. They don't pay for it, but you don't got to spend the night in jail. Got it?"

"Okay."

"But you get arrested by a female cop, well, you're screwed."

I nodded.

"This is where you'll stay." He pointed at the building. "It's abandoned. The cops don't know anybody lives here. Let's keep it that way. Don't bring dates here. Take care of business in their hotels or in their cars."

"Okay."

"You ever shoot up?"

"I have a couple times. Jinx gave it to me."

"You ever do meth?"

"Just once," I said. "Rhonda showed me how. Said it made things easier."

"Well, at least she's right about one thing," he said.

"Yeah."

"I can make sure you get whatever you need." He pulled a baggy out of the glove box. "It'll come out of your own money. And use a clean needle every time. I don't need you getting AIDS."

I got out of his car. He called me back.

"You got to report to Mack right here on this corner at eleven tonight. That's when the first hundred is due." He put the car in drive. "Don't be late."

"How will I know it's him?" I asked, leaning into the window.

"You can't miss him. Mack's got to be four-hundred pounds."

The man sped away, leaving me to figure out where to sleep, how to find dates, how long I'd be expected to bring money to Mack.

That night I worked so hard just to survive. Every man who used me made me sick, regardless of who they were or how they were different from the last one. Young, old, clean, dirty, educated, ignorant. I just closed my eyes, praying that they would finish fast. That they wouldn't hurt me.

From that night on I spent most of my money on what I injected into my arm. I knew it wasn't right. But I had to do what it took to survive.

The color had drained out of Paul's face. His eyes turned down and his hands clinched together into one big fist, knuckles turning white.

"This all started when you were twelve?" he asked.

"Yes."

"That's way too young." His jaw clenched.

"I know."

He rubbed his eyes with the meat of his hands.

"You must think all men are so bad," he said.

"Not all of them." I cleared my throat. "A lot of them, yes. But I think that if they knew what they were doing they'd stop."

"I don't know." He couldn't look at me. "I think they know the girls are too young. I mean, there's no way a thirteen-year-old can look old enough."

"Well, they don't exactly spend a lot of time thinking about what they're doing."

The silence between us thickened, suffocating me. I cleared my throat, sniffed a little. Just to have some kind of noise.

"I'm sorry, Dot. This is just making me really angry."

"I guess that's pretty normal."

"This shouldn't have happened to you."

"When I started working for Mack, he took me to this place. Somebody's house." I pulled up my sleeve. "He had his name tattooed on my arm."

"Why?" He covered the black ink scar with his hand.

"A lot of them brand their girls. That way everybody knows who they belong to. I'm just lucky. Mine is easy to hide."

"You aren't an animal." He closed his eyes. "Is there more?"

"Yes."

"Okay. I guess I'm ready to hear it. Are you all right?" He opened his eyes and looked at me.

"I am," I answered. "I kind of want to get this over with."

He squeezed my arm gently. "I just wish I could have protected you."

"Me, too."

I'd been walking the track for over a month. It didn't take me long to figure out where to go to meet the men who paid higher prices to use me. I learned how to look at them, what to say.

Every day, before going out, I wondered about my future. If I even had one. How long could I do the drugs before overdosing. When the date would come that got pleasure from strangling me. How long I had before Mack got tired of me and dumped me under a bridge.

No one would care about one more dead whore.

Every once in a while a girl disappeared or rumors spread about how she was murdered or moved away. Sometimes, they did it to punish the girls. Other times, they moved them or killed them because someone was poking around. Asking too many questions. Trying to rescue their daughter or friend.

I tried to mind my own business. I didn't become friends with the other girls in the motel. Early on I realized that it was important to switch up dealers and neighborhoods just to keep myself safe. Survival wasn't easy. But I knew I had to do it by myself.

One night a man pulled up and rolled down the window of his SUV.

"Hey, you want a date?" I asked, flipping my hair and swaying my hips. I wore a pouty smile.

"Get in," the man said, unlocking the doors.

"What ya want, handsome?" I asked, climbing in.

"What all do you do?" He licked his lips, ogled my body.

"Everything," I said. "Anything you want."

"Tell me." He wrinkled his nose.

I listed everything I did and how much I charged. He touched me as I spoke.

"Hey, I get paid first," I said.

"Sounds fair." He handed me a few twenty-dollar bills.

As soon as I put the money in my pocket the door opened and someone pulled me out.

"You're under arrest for solicitation," a woman in uniform said as she handcuffed me.

She stuffed me in the back of a squad car and drove me to the station. She glanced back at me every few minutes. Her eyes squinted.

At the police station they took my mug shot, fingerprinted me, and told me to sit in a small room. The officer who arrested me entered the room. She sat on the edge of the table, looking down at me.

"Can we get a bigger room?" I asked. "I'm a little claustrophobic."

"Nope," she answered, flipping through a file. "What's your name?"

"You want my real name or my street name?"

"What do you think?"

"My name's Dorothea Schmidt."

"How old are you?"

"Thirteen."

"A little young to be out selling yourself, huh?" she asked, harsh voiced. "Walking the track like a big girl, huh?"

"Yeah. I really enjoy my job," I said, rolling my eyes.

"How long have you been a prostitute?"

"I don't know. Almost a year maybe."

"What's your pimp's name?"

"I don't have a pimp."

"Really." She pointed at the tattoo on my arm. "You don't happen to work for Mack? Big fat guy?"

"I don't know what you're talking about." I paused. "Seriously, lady. Do you really think that a kid like me wakes up one day and just decides that she wants to be a hooker?"

"Oh, honey," she said, her tone patronizing. "Do you know how many times a day we hear that?"

"Then maybe you should start listening." I leaned forward. "If I stopped doing this, they would kill me. Do you even understand that?"

"Well, you don't look like you have a leash around your neck." She pointed to the track marks on my arms. The proof of my heroin habit. "And I see you aren't too good to party."

"I'm not talking to you anymore." I folded my arms across my chest. "So either lock me up or let me go."

I spent the night in jail. They released me before the sun broke the darkness of the morning. That day Mack beat me up for not bringing him enough money. He didn't care that I'd been arrested. He told me I should have been more careful.

The image in the mirror startled me. Still smelling of hair dye, my auburn locks rested on my shoulders. I saw myself in the mirror. A skinnier, older, more worn-out version of me. Even with all the baked goods Lisa had been feeding me, I was still too thin. Lines ran deep through the skin of my face that hadn't been there ten years before. All my skin sagged, hanging loosely on my bones. My neck rippled with old, funny-looking flesh that had a strange, tissue-paper-like texture.

The hair dye helped, but it couldn't reverse the aging process. It was natural. I decided to accept it.

Pulling my hair back and twisting it into a bun, I thought of the day I met Steven. I closed my eyes, trying to remember his face, his voice, his scent. The way he looked at me. He loved me. He really had.

What a journey my life had become. How I wished I could have shared more with him. Everything would have been different. We could have watched our children grow up. He could have been with me to meet my sister. I could have told him about my childhood. And I knew he would have helped me heal from it all.

But I couldn't have changed what happened to him. He was gone. Dead. And I was alive because God kept me from so many things that could have killed me. I needed to stop trying to make up for all the ugly, dark moments in my life. To stop cleaning up the messes. To let them be. And to learn from them. To find joy in the God that heals.

"I want to live for You," I prayed. "Help me to start over."

54

Winter was a tough time for girls working on the streets. The freezing wind stung my face, cut through my jacket. I pulled it closed around me. Feeling the fake leather, the torn out pocket, I stood with my back against an old, red-brick building. I waited for someone, anyone, to stop. I needed a date.

It was the week after my arrest. A blizzard blanketed the city in white and it seemed like everybody stayed home, out of the snow. But I had to work.

"You gots to make up for your night off," Mack had said after my arrest. "Two-fifty every hour."

I didn't remind him that my night off had been spent in jail.

That night, holding my jacket closed, standing against the building, I'd only earned twenty-five dollars. Nobody would stop for me. The fat lip, the black eyes just weren't attractive to the dates. I wore a stocking cap to cover up the places where Mack had ripped out my hair.

I hadn't shot up all day. I shook, nauseous from withdrawal. Every time I breathed, my heart fluttered, my gut clenched, knowing that I needed a fix. But I couldn't spend the twenty-five bucks on heroin. Mack knew all the drug dealers. They would tell him.

"Jesus, I need You," I prayed out loud into the icy air, my breath making smoke from my lips. "It doesn't matter what You do with me. But You have to make this end. I can't do it anymore. Just let me freeze to death. Please, don't let Mack kill me."

I slumped down to the sidewalk, back still resting on the building.

The pavement's chill absorbed into my legs through the tiny, denim skirt. I pulled my knees up to my chest.

A police car drove past me slowly. The officer looked at me as he went by. He parked up the road and left the engine running. Within a few minutes an old Jeep pulled up next to me. I saw a woman inside. For a split second, I thought it was my mom. I thought for sure I'd lost my mind from the withdrawals.

"Would you like to get in, young lady?" she asked through the cracked-open door.

"Well, that would be a first," I answered, standing up. I'd never had a woman pick me up before.

I climbed into the vehicle from the passenger's side. The vent blasted warm air onto my face. My teeth chattered.

"Here's the thing. There's a cop right there, so we'll have to go some place else." I looked at her. "And it's going to be two-hundred-fifty bucks for whatever you want. But we have to make it quick. I got somewhere to be in ten minutes."

"That much, huh?" she asked.

"Yeah, that much. Come on. I'm not kidding, lady. That ten minutes is serious business."

"What's your name?"

"It doesn't matter." I tucked my hands in my armpits to hide the jittering. "We can go to an ATM if you need to."

"My name is Lola."

"Nice. Listen, Lola. If you just want to talk, that's fine. But I need the cash first. And you'd better start driving. That cop's watching us."

"Do you want to stop doing this?"

"What, hooking? Yeah. I mean, who wouldn't? We all hate it. But it's survival, right?" I cleared my throat. "Even the guy flipping burgers hates his job. But we all have to find a way to survive."

"Oh, you work for Edmund."

"Who's that?" I asked, gnawing on my thumb nail.

"Right, he wouldn't have told you his name. Edmund is the head of a prostitution ring. He drives a nice car, wears expensive clothes."

"Yeah, that's him." I squinted my eyes at her. "Are you a cop?"

"No." She paused. "How old are you?"

"Are you sure you aren't a cop? I really can't get arrested again. Seriously, I'm still trying to get enough money to pay my pimp for the last time."

"I promise that I am not a police officer."

I looked at her face. Same color eyes as my mom. Same face shape. But there was something different about her. This woman's smile seemed to go from her feet to the top of her head.

"What's your deal, lady?" I tried to keep my voice tough.

"Believe it or not, I used to work these streets. Years and years ago."

"No kidding." I held the door handle of the truck with one hand. "Then you'll understand why I need to get that money right now. So if you're from some kind of charity, I'll take all the cash you can give me. But I'm not going anywhere with you."

"I do understand." She looked directly into my eyes. "But you don't have to do this anymore. You can come with me right now and get help."

"You are a cop." I cussed at her. "You lied to me."

"No, dear. I didn't. But I do have a safe place where you can live."

"I've done that before." I thought of Jinx. "I'm not doing that again. It was a trap."

"This isn't a trap. It's a place where you can heal."

"What about him?" I pointed to the police car.

"He's the one who called me. He knew I could help you."

"And you aren't taking me to jail?"

"No."

"Are you going to let me shoot up first? I'm already sick. I need something."

"You'll get sicker before you get better. That's the truth. But that poison will kill you. I can help you through the withdrawal."

"And what about my pimp? He'll come looking for me. He'll kill me."

"My neighbors don't take kindly to Edmund and his pimps. They watch out for us." Her eyes sparkled. "And I have a stronger Protector than even them. My God will watch over you. And He never sleeps. He will guard you."

"I don't know."

"No pimp has ever hurt a girl from my home."

"But what about my stuff? It's all back at the motel and Mack's there."

"Our police officer friend will be glad to get it for you."

"Will he arrest Mack?"

"If you're willing to testify against him, yes."

I looked at the clock on the dashboard. Five minutes past my meet up time. I had nothing to lose.

"Let's go," I said, buckling my seat belt and locking the door. "I don't need to get beat up again."

"You will never regret this." She put the Jeep into drive and stepped on the gas. "So will you please tell me your name?"

"My name is Dorothea Schmidt."

"What a lovely name." She smiled. "It's a pleasure to make your acquaintance, Dorothea."

It took awhile for me to stop regretting my decision. Detoxing from heroin felt like death. Eventually, though, I began to experience life again. Pain and joy and boredom. Some days, I couldn't figure out what to do with my emotions. They terrified me. But Lola stayed close to hug me and laugh with me and play a card game at the kitchen table.

A few other girls lived with Lola at the time. In my five years at the house, many girls came in and out of the program. Some graduated and moved on to have whole lives. Others ran away and went back to the life.

I stayed longer than most. Lola became my legal guardian a few weeks after I moved in. I had no family in Michigan. The idea of going to live with the Wests scared me. It would have been too hard for me to tell them what happened to me.

"So, did your pimp ever come looking for you?" Paul asked.

We sat in the living room at his parents' house. We'd talked every night since Sunday. It was Wednesday. I yawned, stretching my arms.

"Yes. Mack came around a few times," I answered. "But our neighbors made sure he knew that he wasn't welcome back."

"I just hate how they treated you like an animal."

"Me, too." I sighed, pulling the sleeve over my tattoo. "They knew I wouldn't fight back. I was too scared."

"What happened when he came looking for you?"

"He got beat up every time. Eventually, he just gave up."

"Wow." He stood up and stretched. "So is that the end of the story?"

"Yeah." I rubbed the nape of my neck. "I think I should go home now. Tomorrow is my visit with Mom."

"Right." He grabbed his keys. "I'll drive you."

"Thanks."

"Okay."

We walked to his car. He went directly to his side and climbed in. I opened the passenger's side door and sat down. He'd always opened the door for me before. I tried not to take it personally. But it made me wonder if I was cheapened to him.

"Listen, Paul, I know what I told you is some pretty heavy stuff," I said after a few minutes of him driving in silence.

"Yeah. It was a lot worse than I expected."

I thought about Lola's boyfriend. How he left her after he learned about her life.

"You know, this whole thing with us probably isn't going to work," I said.

"You don't think so?" He looked at me quickly.

"Yeah. I mean, I'm not what you deserve. You need a girl who's innocent. That's just not me."

"What are you saying?"

"I'm giving you an out. And I understand if you take it. I really do."

"An out?"

"Seriously, I don't want you to feel like you have to be around me just because of what happened to me. And don't feel like you have to be my friend out of obligation. I could always find another college."

"Stop. Just stop that, Dot." He pulled the car over, put it in park. He turned to me. "I know I'm breaking Lola's rules, but I don't care. You need to hear me."

I looked at my hands.

"I'm not mad at you." He softened his voice. "What happened to you was evil. But it didn't take away who you are. You are no less of an amazing person."

I lifted my eyes to look into his.

"Actually, you might be more amazing for surviving it," he said.

I shook my head. I didn't fight the tears that spilled over.

"Yes you are." He touched my hair. "And I'm going to make it my personal mission to show you how valuable you are."

"You are?"

"Yes. It'll be great," he whispered. "Dot, I am so glad to have you in my life. Do you believe that?"

I nodded. He used his thumb to wipe the tear that rolled down my cheek.

We drove the rest of the way to Lola's in silence. A good kind of comfortable quiet.

When we got to the house, he walked me to the door.

"I can't wait to hear how things go with your mom," he said.

"I'll call you right away."

"You are amazing, Dot."

He bent down and kissed me on the forehead.

The night before Dot's visit, Lisa brought me a bag.

"What's this?" I asked.

"Look inside," she answered.

I reached my hand in and felt soft fabric. Silky material. Pulling out one dress after another, I held them up to myself.

"You have to find the perfect one for when you see Dot," Lisa bubbled. "It's like we're picking out your prom dress."

"I never went to prom," I said. "And I'm not too upset about that."

"Trust me, it's overrated. It's more for the popular kids than anything. Just too much drama."

"I've had plenty of that without ever attending high school."

We laughed as we took the dresses to my room. She stood outside as I tried each on. I slipped on a brown one. It made me feel more like myself from my happily married days. Confident, friendly, calm. I opened the door.

Lisa inhaled quickly, putting her hands over her mouth. Tears collected in her eyes.

"I guess I don't have to ask what you think," I said, twirling in the dress. The fabric swung wide around my legs.

"Cora Schmidt, I do believe you are the loveliest creature." She hugged me. "It's like you've grown up right in front of my eyes."

"Just remember, I'm old enough to be your mother."

"Hardly," she said. "So how do you feel about tomorrow?"

"I can't wait. In fact, it might be hard to sleep."

"Do you want the nurse to give you something to help?"

"No. I want to feel every moment of this. If I don't sleep, then I don't sleep. But I don't want to miss out on this feeling of excitement."

Lisa went home after helping me pack a few of my things for the move the next day.

I decided that I would stay at her house. Temporarily, at least. I wanted to ease my way into a relationship with Marlowe. I knew that she would understand.

That evening I struggled to keep myself calm. It was like waiting for Dot to be born all over again. I couldn't wait to see her and hold her in my arms.

56

The night before I saw my mom, I hardly slept. My brain wouldn't slow down. I tried to imagine what she looked like, if her voice would sound the same as I remembered it, if she'd let me hug her.

I tried to remember the last time I'd seen her. The night I found her in the kitchen. The thought of her being like that scared me. I had to hope that she had gotten better.

My alarm screamed at me so early. Seven a.m.

"Shut that stupid thing off!" Grace yelled from her bed.

I hit the off button, proud of her for not swearing even that early in the morning.

When I got to the kitchen, I noticed that Lola wasn't home. She left a note on the kitchen counter.

"Went out for the day. I shall be home before dinner. Kristi West will be here for lunch. Have a lovely day, my dears."

I wrote a note on the bottom of the paper, "Oops, forgot to tell you all. Seeing my mom today! Love, Dorothea."

She'd made coffee before she left. I poured a cup and read my Bible at the table. But I couldn't concentrate for all the excitement. My mind kept wandering away from the words. An hour later, I stood on the porch waiting for Lisa to pick me up. I zipped up my black hooded sweatshirt, wondering if I had time to change into something nicer. I looked down at my jeans. But before I could go back inside, someone pulled up to the curb. A woman waved at me.

"Lisa?" I asked, opening the car door.

"Yup. Dot?" she asked.

"That's me."

"Just a sec." She had to move papers from the seat to make room for me. "Sorry, I'm kind of messy."

"And you're friends with my mom?" I laughed, sitting in the car. "She's the cleanest person I've ever met."

"Well, I can tell you that some things haven't changed."

"That's good to hear."

"Dot, I'm so excited about today. I've been praying for a really long time for you two to get back together."

"Me, too." I felt my hair. "I feel like I'm going to puke."

"Well, that's understandable." She sped away from the neighborhood. "Gosh, you really look like your mom."

"Thank you." I smiled.

"That smile," she said. "Just like your mom's."

I loved having little pieces of my mom. Within the next hour I'd have the whole thing.

57

I didn't sleep at all the night before seeing my daughter. At breakfast I couldn't eat. I'd never been that nervous before. It felt akin to panic. However, I realized the sweetness to that sensation. That sweetness was joy. The panic, really just anticipation. And that, I concluded, was a very healthy emotion.

The way the brown fabric of the dress danced around my legs as I walked made me feel glamorous. I dug into the small bag of makeup Lisa had brought for me. Applying the powder and eye shadow, I realized that it had been almost a decade since I'd done up my face. I hoped I didn't make myself look too much like a clown. I left my hair to sweep across my shoulders.

Walking into the dayroom, I glanced at the clock. Visitors would begin arriving soon. I sat on the old couch, refusing to look out the window. I wanted my first look at Dot to be when she walked through the door.

My heart pounded.

The door opened. I stood up so fast that I got stars in my eyes and a dizzy feeling in my head.

Wesley's wife walked into the room.

Next came Edith's parents.

I sat, feeling frail and tired and hungry.

"They'll be here," the orderly reassured me.

"Thank you, Antonio," I said.

"You remembered my name." He smiled. "You know, sometimes people are just late. I know your daughter will be here real soon."

My heart couldn't decide whether to thump out of my chest or sink into my gut.

Lisa and I arrived at the state mental hospital. It was the kind of place you would never notice if you were just passing by. A tan building with tan doors and a tan roof. Boring.

"Look in that window," Lisa said, cutting the ignition. "See that head?"

I looked and saw a small brown ball.

"I think so," I answered.

"That's your mom." Lisa smiled at me. "Hey, I should have told you this on the way here. I actually found your aunt."

"Aunt?" I asked. "My dad didn't have any siblings."

"Oh," she winced. "You didn't know that your mom has a sister?"

"No. She never mentioned that."

"Well, I guess she's really good at keeping secrets."

"Who is this aunt?"

"Her name is Marlowe."

"Oh, my gosh. My mom was screaming that name when she had her breakdown. Marlowe and Tim or Tom."

"Could it have been Titus?"

"Yeah. That's it."

"Titus was her brother."

"Was?" I asked.

"Yes. He was murdered."

"Right in front of the sister?"

"Yes." She squinted her eyes. "I thought you didn't know about this."

"Right. How did I know that?" I asked, confused. Too many thoughts bounced in my mind. "Maybe she was yelling about it that night. When she had her breakdown."

"Maybe. That would make sense. Well, anyway, I found her sister. She doesn't know it, but Marlowe's going to be here today, too."

"Holy cow, Lisa. You're going to give my mom a heart attack."

"I know." She rubbed her hands together. "I can't wait."

"And she's moving out today, too?"

She nodded, her hair bouncing around her face.

"That's a lot of change for her. Do you think she's ready?"

"I know she is. She's made huge progress the last few months."

"Okay. Listen, we'd better get in there. I'm about to die. I can't wait to see her."

We started across the parking lot. We walked in and up the steps.

"My office is downstairs," Lisa said. "Trust me, you don't want to see it right now. Everything's in boxes. You'd get lost in there."

I grabbed hold of the railing. My hand slid across the smooth, beige paint as I climbed the steps. Each movement felt heavy. At the top of the stairs, a door propped open. A black sign hung above the door frame, reading "Mental Health Ward: Check In At Nurses' Desk."

"Are you ready, Dot? Here it is," Lisa said as we neared the door.

"Yes," I answered. "I can hardly wait."

She pulled the door handle.

I sat on the couch with my eyes shut. The conversations around me made me sleepy. I heard the door open. I turned my head and slowly opened my eyes.

In walked the most beautiful girl I had ever seen. I knew right away. She was my baby.

"Dot," I said as I stood, smoothing the skirt of my dress.

She walked toward me. I wrapped my arms around her neck. She was taller than I. She'd grown so much.

"Mom," she said. Her voice was heart-mending.

"Dot." I pulled away from her, grabbing her hands. "I can't get over how absolutely gorgeous you are."

"Oh, thank you." She blushed. Her deep brown eyes held a rich warmth against the pink of her cheeks. "Sorry I didn't dress up."

"I don't care." I squeezed her hands. "I'm just glad you're here."

"It's been a really long time, hasn't it?"

"It has. I'm so sorry." I looked into her eyes. "Gosh, I didn't think I'd ever be ready to see you. What was wrong with me? Why did I wait so long?"

"Maybe it just wasn't the right time." Dot smiled at me. "But it sure feels like the right time now. Are you ready for today?"

"So ready."

The door opened again. I saw the outline of someone standing behind Lisa. I didn't pay attention. Having my girl with me was all I could think of.

"Let's go sit on the couch," I said.

"Hey," Antonio called to the stranger from across the room. "You come to check up on me?"

Dot started and looked around the room. She smiled.

"Oh my goodness. The lady I've been living with is here." She grabbed my hand and pulled me to my feet. "You'll love her. You are so much alike."

We walked toward the stranger. Antonio reached her first and held the woman in a tight hug. He spun her around. All I could see of her was a long, gray braid.

"Everything's changed thanks to you," Antonio said.

"That's fantastic, Antonio." The woman hugged him back. "But I'm not checking in on you. I'm actually here to see Cora."

"Lola, I didn't know you were going to be here," Dot said. "I didn't think you'd get the note until later."

The woman turned. I saw myself standing in front of me. A little rounder, with glasses and gray hair. For a moment I thought I was losing my mind again.

"Dorothea, what are you doing here?" The woman squinted, adjusting her glasses. She looked from Dot to me.

I closed my eyes. Grabbed hold of Dot's arm so that I wouldn't fall.

"Is everything okay, Mom?" Dot asked, covering my hand with hers.

I held my eyes shut so tight. The images came along anyway. Pouring rain. The truck. Marlowe screaming for me to get away. Her face bloodied.

When I opened my eyes, I looked over her face. Clean. Whole. Smiling. I could only manage a whisper.

"Marlowe?" I asked. "Is it you?"

"Yes." She nodded, smiling, tears falling from her eyes.

"What's going on?" Dot asked.

"I was just about to ask you," Marlowe said. "But first, let me hug Cora."

My sister drew me into an embrace. So relieved that she was whole, I wrapped my arms around her, my muscles tensing to hold her closer.

She sobbed, so quietly, so gently. After a moment we let go.

"Marlowe, I'd like you to meet my daughter, Dorothea," I said, pulling Dot toward us.

Marlowe laughed through her tears. "Oh, I knew the Spirit was trying to tell me something about this girl. My own niece."

"I'm sorry. I don't understand." I looked between them. "You know each other?"

Bewildered, I couldn't recall what Dot had said when Marlowe walked into the room. Had she told me she lived with her?

"Yes." Marlowe pulled Dot to her side. "God brought Dorothea to me."

"She saved me," Dot said.

"And you've been taking care of my daughter?" Gratitude overpowered the disorientation. I rubbed the goose bumps on my arms with my hands. "It was all I prayed for. That someone would take care of her and love her."

"God certainly moved in mysterious ways here, didn't He?" Marlowe pulled Dot and me into a hug.

Surrounded by my family, calm washed over my soul. I could have rested in that embrace for the remainder of my days.

"Hold on a second," Dot said, pulling away, looking at me. "So, Lola's real name is Marlowe. And she's your sister?"

"That is correct," I said.

"Okay. That makes Lola my aunt?"

"I suppose so," Lola answered. "Cora, do you think this would be best discussed over lunch?"

"Yes. That would be fantastic," I answered, turning my head to look at Lisa. "You come, too."

"Oh, no," Lisa said, waving her hands in front of her. "I wouldn't think of intruding on this family time."

"You are family," Dot said. "Please come."

The four of us climbed into Lisa's tiny car. From my seat in the back, I looked at my daughter's face. She turned to me and smiled.

Held my hand until we arrived at the restaurant.

We sat at a round table in a small, family-owned diner and talked for hours. Marlowe and Dot explained how they met. My heart broke to know all that Dot went through. I had to excuse myself and go to the bathroom.

I locked myself in a stall. Leaned my head over the toilet. Just the thought of my baby girl, touched and hurt and used, flipped my stomach over and over. I vomited. The old urge to tear into my flesh swept over me.

"Mom?" Dot called into the bathroom.

"I'm in here," I said from the stall, wiping my mouth. Relieved that the opportunity to cut myself was gone.

"I'm okay now, you know. God really took care of me."

"It's my fault. If I could have kept it all together those things never would have happened to you." I clenched my fists at my sides. For the first time in weeks, I didn't feel ready to be back in the world.

"You can't put that on yourself, Mom. It happened and it was bad. But it's over now. I'm happy. I want you to be happy, too."

Dot pulled on the stall door. I unlocked it, allowing her to come in. She took a step toward me, looked into my eyes.

"I failed you," I cried.

"No, Mom. You can't think like that." She cocked her head to the side. "All that bad stuff is done in my life. Let's keep our focus on the future together. Okay?"

"You are beautiful. Your heart, it's just beautiful."

She kissed me on the cheek. "Come on," she said. "You want to get back to the celebration?"

My daughter led me back to our table. I sat with the three people I loved most in the world. And those three women loved me back. The day before I'd had nothing. Suddenly, I was rich beyond measure.

The day after my mom moved out of the state hospital, we had our first snow. Just tiny flakes that wisped through the air before hitting the ground and melting. As the sun set, I retreated to the kitchen to catch the scene. With the crystal snow reflecting the light, it was sure to be a beautiful sight.

My mom and Lola sat at the table. I grabbed a cup of coffee and joined them, facing the window.

"How did you ever get away from our father that night?" my mom asked Lola. "I was sure he would kill you."

"It wasn't for lack of trying," Lola answered. "But eventually he passed out. So I ran as fast as I could. A car drove past me and stopped. It was the preacher's wife. Do you remember her, Cora?"

"Oh, yes. I could never forget Mary Wheeler."

"She took one look at my bloody face and told me to get in." Lola smiled. "She told me she was sorry for the way she'd spoken to Mother and me. I just let her believe that I was you. I assume there's a story there."

"There most certainly is. Mother called her a whitewashed tomb."

"Oh, dear," Lola cried in delight. "I can't even imagine."

"That's a story for another time."

"Well, Mary Wheeler drove me to the bus stop. The woman at the counter told me that I needed to go to Michigan. That my twin had already been through and bought a ticket for me. Mary gave me a dollar for food."

"That was generous," Mom said, rolling her eyes.

"Unfortunately, she couldn't keep her lips sealed. She told just about everyone on the mountain that she saved 'poor Cora's life by sending her to Michigan.'"

"She never could resist tooting her own horn." My mom sipped her coffee. "I shouldn't have said that. It was harsh."

"It's the truth, though," Lola said. "Anyway, when Ducky and Father found out about it, they went looking for you. They found me instead. They nearly killed me. But they wanted to get a little more profit out of me. They made me walk the streets here to get them more money."

My mom sighed. Put a hand on her chest.

"Eventually, they sold me to another pimp. I worked for him for a few months or so before I was arrested." She smiled. "It changed my life. And then God called me to this work. It's been amazing."

The three of us talked for hours past the sunset. Sharing stories, catching up. Eventually, Grace joined us. Then Mercy, Peace, and Faith. We laughed together. Cried. Then laughed some more.

"Good heavens," Lola said, looking at her watch. "Look at the time. And I haven't even thought about getting dinner around."

"I can heat up some of that leftover casserole," I said, moving toward the refrigerator. "Mom, how about you bake some cookies?"

"Oh, I don't know," my mom said.

"Please, Miss S," Grace begged. "Dorothea's been braggin' about them cookies ever since I met her."

"Okay. Just don't expect too much." My mom stood, taking an apron from the hook on the wall. "Chocolate chip okay?"

She stood at the counter, all of us surrounding her. Mixing the ingredients, she taught us all of her secrets. My mom let us sneak little bits of cookie dough, laughed when the bag of chocolate chips exploded on the floor.

After she put the cookies in the oven, she turned to me and smiled.

"Just like the old days," she said, beaming.

"Look at your apron," I said, pointing at her.

Flour and egg yolk dirtied the front of her. She looked down, her mouth open wide.

"Well, would you look at that," she said. "So that's why people wear aprons."

Laughing, she rinsed her hands off in the sink. Looked around for a towel. I tossed her one from the drawer. She wiped her hands. Then stopped. Held the towel close to her face.

"This is too rich," she whispered. "I can't believe this."

"Cora," Lola called across the room. "Is everything okay?"

"This towel." She shook her head. "It was a wedding gift to me from Steven's Great Aunt Beatrice. See?"

Lola and I joined her, looking at the towel.

"She hand monogrammed it with our initials." My mom laughed.

"I remember the man who brought these," Lola said. "He had a whole truck load of donations."

"It was like Christmas," my mom said.

"Exactly." Lola pulled her eyebrows together. "In fact, I recall saying that several times."

"That was Steven." My mom hugged the towel. "All of our wedding extras came to you."

"Oh, Lord," Lola said, laughing, eyes closed in prayer. "You are too, too funny."

"So when are them cookies gonna be done?" Grace called from across the kitchen. "I'm real popping hungry over here."

My mom and Lola looked at each other and smiled.

"God is good to us," Lola said.

My mom closed her eyes. Nodded in agreement.

I woke up in my room at the house Lisa shared with me. Wednesday. Art therapy day. Inhaling deeply, I grinned. I'd been away from the hospital for a month of Wednesdays. My art therapy had changed. No more scribbling with crayons. On that day I looked forward to transforming my old house into a safe place like Lola's home. Far more satisfying than working with markers.

From my soft bed, I looked around my room, taking my time getting up. The walls displayed the pictures of my family. Steven, Pete, Dot, Lola.

"Thank You." I whispered a prayer. In recent weeks, my prayers had become laden with gratitude.

I sat up, letting my feet touch the fringed area rug. Facing the window, I looked through the clear glass. No grid obscured my vision. No buzzing of lights or dingy walls. No plastic trees or ugly orange chairs. Just warm sunshine, unlocked doors, and open fields that spread out for miles. Freedom and joy. Family and friends. And peace.

Lisa knocked on my door.

"Good morning," she said. "Just making sure you're up."

"I am," I called back. "I'm getting myself around."

"No hurry. Did you want to stop on the way for coffee?"

"That would be lovely."

After dressing in my work clothes, I joined Lisa in the living room.

"All set?" she asked, grabbing her keys.

"Yes." I worked the buttons on my jacket. "I can't wait to get started."

The Wests had walked me through the house a week before. It was

the first time I'd been there since my breakdown so many years before. Lola walked with me, holding my hand. Allowing my tears and
sorrow. The kitchen brought out the most pungent of emotions. Guilt,
shame, anger, fear, grief. She held me, helping the calm to overtake
my upheaval.

"Are you going to be all right going back again?" Lisa asked. "We're
going to have a lot going on."

"This is what Steven and Pete would have wanted," I answered.
"What's left after our suffering is being turned into good. I don't want
to miss out on that."

"If you need to take a few breaks, that's okay. You know that, right?"
She slung her purse over her shoulder. "Let's go."

About half an hour later, we arrived, carrying trays of coffee cups
into the kitchen. The rest of the crew had already started their work.

"Oh, lovely," Lola said, looking up from scrubbing the sink. "It is
the perfect time for a short coffee break."

"I ordered you a hazelnut coffee, Marlowe," I said, catching myself.
"I'm sorry. Lola. I'm just trying to get used to calling you that."

"My dear," Lola said. "You don't need to worry about it. I don't
mind either way."

"I prefer the name Lola anyway." I handed her the coffee. "It suits
you."

"Where do you need me?" Lisa asked.

"Ah, do you mind finishing up in here?" Lola asked. "I wanted to
scrub some bedroom walls with Cora."

"Fine by me," Lisa answered, finding a washcloth.

Lola and I took the steps to the bedrooms. She carried a bucket of
clean, soapy water. I had a few sponges.

"Coffee is in the kitchen," she announced, reaching the top step.

The girls from Lola's House rushed past and down the steps. Dot
kissed my cheek before going downstairs.

"Now, where to begin?" Lola asked.

"Pete's room," I answered, stepping in front of her. "It's this one."

Entering the room, I tried to remember what it was like when Pete lived there.

"He was such a messy boy," I said, smiling. "Can you believe I never made him clean it? I'd always do it for him."

"I believe that," Lola said, placing the bucket on the floor and dipping her sponge in the water.

"You know, I thought that after all this time, I would figure out why he had to die so young." I wet my sponge. "That I'd see the good that came from his death. Will I ever understand?"

She turned to me, head to one side, sponge dripping. "I don't know."

"He was a remarkable boy," I said, wiping a wall. My heart full of grief mixed with joy. "I wish you could have met him."

"Me, too, Cora."

We worked, the sudsy water in the bucket turning a gritty brown as we rinsed our sponges.

"This room used to be painted bright green," I said after a pause. "Pete picked it out."

"And whoever thought to cover it up with this color?" Lola asked. "You know what this shade makes me think of?"

"Baby poop?" I asked, giggling.

"Exactly." She moved to the door. "And dark brown for this door?"

"It isn't appealing, is it?" I continued scrubbing.

"Not in the least." She rubbed the soapy sponge on the brown door. "Perhaps if I apply enough pressure, I'll be able to coax some of this paint off."

"I believe we need fresh water," I said, lifting the bucket and taking it to the bathroom across the hall. Dumping the water, I turned the faucet on warm, looking under the sink for cleaner.

"Cora," Lola called to me.

I turned off the water and returned to Pete's door. She kneeled, her sponge in one hand, a large, shard-like paint chip in the other. Lola smiled in triumph.

"Do we have any scrapers?" I asked.

"I believe so," she answered, standing. "I'll go find a few."

After she left, I used my fingernail to pick away some of the brittle paint. Brown, white, tan paint chips fell from the door. Collected under my nail. Stuck to my skin.

I closed my eyes, remembering paint peeling from rotting wood. The yellow flower petals to hide the decay. A cedar box full of paint chips, dumped on the floor of a bus.

"Good news," Lola said from the hallway. "Not only did I find two scrapers, I also discovered paint stripper."

Opening my eyes, I smiled. "Excellent. Let's get started."

We worked at that door for hours. A pile of color gathered on the floor around us, on our clothes, in our hair. Eventually, with sore arms, Lola and I removed the last of the paint. We stepped back. Inspecting our work. The rich wood which, for years, had hidden under all those layer of paint, took my breath away.

"Now that is a thing of beauty," I said. "Why anyone would want to cover that up is beyond me."

"Indeed." Lola put her elbow on my shoulder.

"If only I'd known about this when I lived here. I would have uncovered it years ago."

"Sometimes we just don't know what we have." She looked at me. "At some point someone looked at this door and thought it was ugly. And so they covered it up. I suppose there is just no accounting for taste."

"And look at this floor," I said. "What a mess."

"A vacuum will make short work of that," Lola said, leaving the room. "Now to remember where it traveled to."

I stood by the door, brushing the paint chips off of me. Reaching out a hand, I felt the smooth wood against my fingertips.

"Dorothea," Lola woke me, jostling my shoulder. "Wake up, dear."

"Okay," I said, opening my eyes. "I'll make breakfast."

"No, thank you. Your mom's coming to do that. I want you to come with me." She stood upright. "Quickly now. We must hurry."

"What's going on?"

"I'll tell you on the way."

I dressed as fast as I could and followed Lola out into the early winter morning. The windshield of the newly donated station wagon was covered with frost. I scraped it away as Lola started up the engine.

"Now can you tell me where we're going?" I asked from the passenger seat. "It better be real important to get me up at three in the morning."

"I received a phone call from Kristi," she said, keeping her eyes on the road. "A girl is in her care at the ICU. She's badly beaten. In and out of consciousness."

"Why did Kristi call us?"

"She's been crying for me." Lola glanced at me. "I felt the Holy Spirit nudge me to bring you."

The rest of the drive, I fidgeted, nervous about what I might see.

We arrived at the hospital and rode the elevator to the ICU. Kristi met us in the hall.

"Oh, goodness, Lola," Kristi said. "I'm so glad you got here."

"I always find a way." Lola smiled. "Do you have any idea who she is?"

"She had nothing on her. And I mean nothing." Kristi looked at us with weary eyes. "Lola, whoever did this was trying to kill her."

"I'm sure." Lola sighed. "It's common. I can't tell you how many times this happens."

The doctor walked out of the room. With Kristi in the lead, we approached him.

"Doctor," Kristi said. "This is Lola."

"Right," he said. He had a soft voice. "I'll just get right to it. She doesn't have a whole lot of time. She's been assaulted in so many ways. I'll need a nurse to do a rape kit."

"Okay. I'll do it," Kristi said, rushing off.

"What happened to her?" Lola asked.

"I normally wouldn't be able to tell you, but she's been asking for you, so I feel it's necessary." He looked at the chart he held in his hands. "She was beaten with a bat or pipe. Something that could do substantial damage. She is suffering. She's had massive head trauma."

"The prognosis?"

"Grim." He sighed. "I don't expect her to make it to the morning. We're trying to keep her comfortable."

"May we go in?"

"Go ahead."

Lola opened the heavy wooden door and entered the room. She looked over her shoulder at me.

"Start praying," she said.

"About what?" I felt like a scared child.

"Whatever you can think of."

The covers were pulled up under the girl's chin. She had an oxygen tube in her nose and a needle in her arm. A machine beeped with her heartbeat. I tried to stay calm. Attempted to keep my mind from thinking of Pete.

"Oh," Lola sighed. She looked at the girl's swollen face. "Promise."

Bandages seemed to be holding her face together. Her blond hair matted and greasy on her scalp. I remembered Grace's words. Best find a way to bless her.

"God, help Promise," I prayed.

Lola touched Promise's hair. It seemed to be the only part of her that wasn't bruised or bloody.

"Lola," Promise whispered. "I'm sorry."

"Don't talk, honey," Lola said, soothing her. "You save your strength."

Promise's eyes brimmed over with tears.

"Please don't feel badly, my dear." Lola found her hand. "We love you. We always have. We never stopped."

I moved from the foot of the bed to stand by Promise's side.

"Hey, it's Dorothea," I said.

"I was so scared," Promise said, eyes turned to me.

"It breaks my heart." I looked at her face. "You were all alone."

"No, I wasn't. Jesus held me." She blinked her eyes. "He held me until it was over."

"Did it take away your fear?" Lola asked.

Promise nodded. "He loves me, Lola."

"Yes," Lola said, smiling. "He does. So very much."

"I was trying to come home." She spoke with urgency. "But my pimp found me."

"Do you remember his name?" Lola asked.

"No. I can't remember." Promise closed her eyes. "Listen, no matter what happens, I'll be okay. I know where I'm goin'."

I looked up at Lola. She held her eyes closed.

"I love you, Promise," I said.

"I'm finally gonna have a good life," she said.

Promise slept. Lola, Kristi, and I sat in the room for hours. I held her hand, rubbing it with my thumb. The doctor came in and out. A police officer stopped by. Nurses checked her IV and monitors.

I fell asleep, holding her hand, my head on the edge of her bed. Suddenly, a rush of nurses entered the room. They pushed me gently out of the way. A long, flat noise rang out. The heartbeat monitor no longer sounded its beep.

Promise was gone.

I had a dream. I was eleven years old and wore a bright pink dress. My hair fell in sausage curls around my round, freckled face. I sobbed and smiled at the same time.

Cans full of paint sat all around me. Different colors. Green. Orange. Blue. Yellow. They filled the living room of the mountain shack. I stuck my hands in the cans and covered my hair and face and body with layers of paint. The more I spread across myself, the less recognizable I became. A glob of ugly color, misshapen and stiff.

Suddenly, Jesus walked near me. I couldn't see His face or robe. I just saw a shape that glowed. I knew it was Him, though. He used His fingers to break off the paint. Little paint chips fell away and onto the floor. Soon, discarded color mounded all around my feet.

And after all the paint chips had been pulled away, there stood the adult me. I looked like myself, but more alive, more radiant. It took Jesus breaking all the layers off to see the glory of what God created me to be.

With all that weight stripped away I began to run alongside Jesus.

One morning, a few days after Promise's funeral, as I got my coffee, I heard a knock on the door. Lola answered it. Her giggle filled the house.

"Dorothea," she called. "You will want to come out here."

I walked to the doorway. Paul stood on the curb next to our old minivan.

"I drove it all the way from Lansing," he said. "And no black smoke or anything."

"No way." I stepped out to the porch. "I'd totally forgotten about that junker."

"Not me." He smiled. "If it weren't for this van, I wouldn't have gotten you back in my life."

"That's so cheesy, Paul."

"Would you like to go for a ride?"

"I would love that."

He held the door open for me. When he started the engine it still rattled a little, but nothing like before.

"Are you hungry?" he asked.

"Yes."

"Well, good. I just happen to know a great place to go for breakfast."

He drove me to his parents' house. The dining room was set up like a fancy restaurant. A bottle of soda chilled in a bucket and candlelight flickered from the center of the table.

"This is fun," I said. "But I feel kind of underdressed."

"You're beautiful anyway."

"You're too sweet."

"Have a seat. I'm going to bring out our food."

"Did you cook?"

"No. Our moms did."

He brought two plates with steaming piles of omelets and toast.

"That looks so good."

"Your mom said this was always one of your favorites." He put a plate in front of me. "Sourdough even."

After we finished eating, our moms brought out brownies and ice cream.

"For breakfast?" I asked.

"Why not?" Paul said. "We're young, right?"

"Thanks, Mom," I said.

"It's been my great joy," she said, kissing me on the forehead.

"Now we'll leave the two of you alone for a little while," Kristi said, winking at Paul.

Once they were back in the kitchen, Paul looked at me.

"Yes?" I asked.

"Dot, are you ready?"

"For what?"

"For a relationship?"

"Well, I think I might be." I blushed. "But the question is, are you ready?"

"I am."

"So, you're my boyfriend now?"

"Yup."

"What happens now?" I asked. "I mean, when we're done with our dessert."

"Do you want to watch a movie? Or we could go cruising in the awesome van."

I laughed. "I think a movie would be nice."

"Me, too."

"How about we let our moms watch it with us?"

"That's a good idea." He smiled. "Can I hold your hand, though?"

"Probably."

The four of us watched a movie in the living room. About halfway into it, Paul's dad came home.

I sat between Paul and my mom. They both held my hands. I felt safe and loved. And I had a place to belong.

65

And so it was. A beautiful life of joy and redemption from the Father of Lights who is the giver of all good and perfect gifts. He, the Giver of my amazing family.

Sometimes, just sometimes, life does come together in a pretty bow. I believe that God enjoys a happy ending. After all, who came up with the idea of heaven?

Our lives aren't over yet. We all still have a lot of pain ahead of us. We will lose people we love. We will have our hearts broken. We will still sin. Every one of us will suffer nights of sorrow. And we may never fully understand why our lives turn out in those ways. The deaths of Steven and Pete may always leave me with questions. I may mourn them for all the nights of my life.

But joy will always come in the morning. God still has so much love and beauty to show us.

He still has a lot of paint chips to peel away so that we can see who we truly are, His dearly loved children.

ACKNOWLEDGMENTS

A novel written without the support of family, friends, and mentors is a very lonely novel, indeed. Paint Chips has been a collaborative effort. And for that, I am much blessed.

Many thanks to my family. To my mom, who taught me the value of creativity and believed in my abilities when others doubted. To my dad, who passed on the writing gene and the love of story. My siblings: Ginger, Sam, and Betsy, who not only tolerated, but believed in the big dreams of their baby sister.

God provided mentors throughout my life to encourage me to write my words. What a gift I've had. Thanks to Belinda Lund Bjarki, for expecting so much more of me than I thought possible. To Sharon Somerville, for pushing me to try new things in my writing. To George Brown, for the small notes on my papers, telling me that I had a novel in me. For the opportunities to read, write, and live in the beauty of literature. To the six beautiful women at Novel Matters: Bonnie Grove, Patti Hill, Kathleen Popa, Latayne C. Scott, Sharon K. Souza, and Debbie Fuller Thomas. Thank you for the ideas, the discussions, the encouragement, and the friendship. To Ann Byle, for believing in my writing.

To the brave few who read Paint Chips in the early stages. Brian Criner, Rob and Cheryl Meyer, Bill and Joanna Leep. Thank you for believing in it even then.

To Amelia Rhodes, for pushing me. For not accepting my excuses. Thank you for sharing the dream with me.

To Michelle Reinhold, for going word by word through a very rough draft. Your red pen is precise and kind. Thank you, friend.

To Irene Kraegal, for a psychologist's perspective on mental health. You helped me approach my characters with more sensitivity and dignity.

To my critique group, Kava Writers Collective, for making me better over cups of coffee and rum dots.

Writers need cheerleaders. And I have a peppy squad. Kristi West, Jessie Heninger, Holly Becker, Darcie Apple, Carrie Leazenby, Megan Sayer, Kathi Hanson, Jen Gusey, Karon Hawley, Liz Ferguson, Kim Cooper, Sarah Schneider, Annette Deaton, and so many more. You girls may never know how much this novel rode on the backs of your encouragement and prayers.

To Hedy Clayton for praying for a publisher. Thanks to WhiteFire Publishing for giving this novel a home. To Dina Sleiman for believing enough to become the champion of Paint Chips. Thank you, Dina, for the kind and skilled edits. David and Roseanna White, for taking a risk on my gritty novel. It means the world to me.

Love, kisses, and hugs to my three. Elise Marie, Austin Thomas, and Timothy Spence. One day you will understand why I spend so much time making books. I do it for you three. To impart a little beauty in the muck of the world. So that you can see God even when things seem so dark.

I have a great love in this life. He is the steady to my spastic. The calm to my chaos. Jeff, you are my favorite. I would never have attempted a novel without your confidence in me.

And to the One who looks, without fear, into the storms of my life. Thank You for calming every single one of them. The glory is all to You.

AUTHOR'S NOTE

The average age of a prostituted person in the United States is 13 years old. That is not a choice. It is a crime. Sex trafficking is real. It affects those from every race, gender, socio-economic demographic, and level of education. Thankfully, the character of "Lola" is not just imaginary. Men and women all over the globe have dedicated their lives to the rescue and rehabilitation of the survivors of sex trafficking. They also battle to prevent it from ever happening. They utilize their talents and resources to lend a voice and a hand to those who have been exploited.

To learn more about sex trafficking, visit The Polaris Project (www.polarisproject.org) or The Salvation Army (www.salvationarmyusa.org) websites. Also, call The National Trafficking Tip Line for more information (1-888-3737-888).

DISCUSSION QUESTIONS

1. How did Cora's relationship with God change throughout the book? What seemed to be the turning point? Have you experienced significant change in your relationship to God? How has that transformed your life?

2. Cora and Dot had very different fathers. How did this impact each of their lives?

3. How does the paint chips theme run throughout the book? What does it symbolize? What could be a symbol for the way you relate to life?

4. Steven was the foundation of the Schmidt family. Then Pete took that role. How did both of them keep their family together? What happened after each was gone? Is there someone that is the foundation of your family? How can you make sure your family doesn't crumble after they are gone?

5. Cora finds herself following a pattern of behavior learned from her mother. What does she do that her mother had done? How does she respond when she realizes it? How does she defy the pattern when she rescues Dot from her father? Do you find yourself falling into tendencies learned from a parent? Are they good or negative? How would you break the negative ones?

6. Both Cora and Dot retell their stories. They find a trusted friend with whom to share. How did the retelling help them each to heal? Who is a trusted friend with whom you share the depth of your life? How does their confidence help you to heal?

7. How did Stewart's suicide transform Cora? Did the change hap-

pen in that moment with the small voice? Has a single event ever had a dramatic influence over your life? How did you change?

8. How did Cora react to the urgency of leaving the state mental hospital? What were her concerns? Why would Lisa offer to assist her? How would you respond if in Cora's situation? Or in Lisa's?

9. How did Cora's relationship with her sister flow through the book? What did you think about the sacrificial love that Cora received from her sister? Were you surprised by the final outcome?

10. At the end Cora says, "Sometimes, just sometimes, life does come together in a pretty bow. I believe that God enjoys a happy ending. After all, who came up with the idea of heaven?" How does this make you feel? Have you had happy endings? Things that came together, just right, at the end? What about a time when the ending was less than happy? How did you overcome that?

11. The very end of the novel reads, "He still has a lot of paint chips to peel away so that we can see who we truly are, His dearly loved children." What were the paint chips that needed peeling in the lives of the characters of this story? How did that sloughing help them? Do you have paint chips that need to be removed? What are they? How would your life be different without them?

OTHER TITLES

If you enjoyed *Paint Chips*,
you may also enjoy these other titles
from WhiteFire Publishing

The Good Girl
by Christy Barritt
March 2013

What's a good girl to do when life goes bad?

Jasmine
by April McGowan
June 2013

She survived her past...but can she face it?

Sailing out of Darkness
by Normandie Fischer
August 2013

Love conquers all? Maybe for some people.

CPSIA information can be obtained at www.ICGtesting.com
Printed in the USA
BVOW030943160413

318068BV00009B/69/P